Watchdog

Sage Kafsky

DEDICATION

*For those who pursue the things that bring them joy.
May you always remember to dream.*

INTRODUCTION

I'm not really sure that I know how to tell a story like this, so I guess I should go back to the very beginning and start from there. I was almost uncomfortably excited then. That was back when the world was my oyster and all those cliches. I remember the cool air in the auditorium, the anticipatory titter from the crowd. We were all waiting for the same new beginning. I had spent years of my life waiting for this day — I guess we could technically call it a graduation day and still be politically correct, although it was really the day we would be assigned our first jobs as agents of the Institute of Protective Services.

Like I said, I'd been waiting for this day for years, training long hours to reach where I was today. Finally, I — wait a minute; I guess I never really introduced myself at all. Oops. Well, hello, random person reading my reflections on my personal life! My name is Blythe Richards, but most people know me by my middle name, Artemis. Don't judge me for it if you can help it; my parents were into mythology. I'm a second-generation agent of the IPS, and I spent my life preparing to follow in my parents' footsteps (and leave the imprints of my own).

I also hate to be underestimated, which I suppose is why I was so anxious all of those months ago, but that's not really the part of my story worth reflecting on. Not if I'm going to tell my story without boring you to tears with a questionable self-analysis. For now, I'll just focus on that moment in time when everything changed because nothing really changed at all.

CHAPTER 1

I squirmed in my seat, feeling my cheeks flush with anticipation as I scanned the crowd of other students for my two best friends, Gwen and Bonnie. We had promised to find each other and sit together during the ceremony. Despite the rigor of our program, seating at the Institute of Protective Service's Academy Assignment Day Ceremony—*what a mouthful*— was unassigned. This enabled us to sit where we chose, but it also meant that there were no guarantees of finding enough open seats for our trio. For me, these last few moments together were of paramount importance, because despite the fact that we had been inseparable during our time at the Academy, this was—in all likelihood—our goodbye. The thought of saying a permanent farewell to the girls who had become like sisters to me made me frown a bit as I strained to see over the sea of bodies. My face hardened into a glower of dislike when I recognized the swaggering stride and broad shoulders of my least favorite prospective graduate, Luke Ryder. As though he felt my eyes burning a hole in his back, Ryder turned and narrowed his eyes in return, and for a moment, we paused in recognition of our mutual hatred. I knew the expression on his face well enough; I had seen it directed at me often over the years. With any luck, I would never have to see it again. My own eyes narrowed further, and annoyance speared through my body to match, but the tide was stemmed by the sudden appearance of my raven-haired, blue-eyed friend. I tore my eyes away from Luke to smile at her.

"Bonnie! About time you showed up!" I teased. She rolled her eyes, the effect shocking against her dark hair.

"Very funny, 'Blythe,'" she air-quoted around the name before wrinkling her nose with a shake of her head. "Nope. Still sounds wrong to me. You'd better listen carefully when they call your name so you don't miss it." She shook her head again before seeming to notice the source of my earlier irritation, who was still watching our interaction with a mingled expression of annoyance and amusement. She flicked her eyes between us with a snort of amusement, but as she opened her mouth to say something, I cut across her.

"Where's Gwen?" As if my words had summoned her there, our ethereal, blonde-haired counterpart materialized near one shoulder, casting a dark expression behind her that clashed with her fairy-like appearance.

"Sorry I'm late. Some people don't know how to *move!*" She tossed the last word behind her, clearly meant for whomever had held her up. "So, what did I miss?" Bonnie cut her eyes slyly in my direction.

"Just Artemis fawning over Luke Ryder again," she crowed. I rolled my eyes.

"If by fawning, you mean he's a deer, I have a gun, and it's open season, then sure," I answered sardonically. Bonnie and Gwen tossed their heads back in twin laughter, which turned even further toward hysteria as they focused on something—or someone—

behind me. The hair on the back of my neck suddenly stood on edge, and I whipped around to see my would-be target himself standing behind me, sweeping his gaze over me with cool eyes.

"Still as abrasive as ever, Richards." I matched his frosty gaze with a glare of my own.

"When people deserve it," I tilted my head in a challenge.

"Sounds like jealousy to me. Still can't handle the fact that I outscored you in our aptitude tests, can you?" I huffed as he met the challenge. Luke had outscored me by six points. The fact that we had both beaten the previously held record didn't matter to either of us; it was enough that he had edged me out. I opened my mouth to make a retort, although what I could respond to that, I was not sure. Before I could unleash my fury to tell him off, the amplified voice of our Agent Rivers, our Program Head, crackled overhead, silencing the murmur of the crowd.

"Welcome one and all! If you will please find your seats, we will commence with our Assignment Day ceremony. As many of these assignments are time-sensitive, we thank you in advance for your swift cooperation." Her business-like voice had a lilt to it that could only be called an accent in the loosest of terms, and it was not to be ignored. Unable to make my retort now that the noise in the hall had softened, I settled myself with another fiery glare in Luke's direction before linking arms with Bonnie and Gwen and finding our seats. I soothed my temper with the fact that this was almost guaranteed to be the last day that I would ever see him. Assignment Day was exactly what it sounded like; having completed our certifications with the Institute of Protective Services— or IPS— we were now full agents, and we were professionals in need of work. To my displeasure, Luke settled into the chair just behind me, and I huffed in annoyance. *Just a few more hours, Artemis, and then you'll never see him again.* It was rare for agents to reconnect after their time in the Academy. For me, it was bittersweet; I would be sad to see Gwen and Bonnie go, but it would be pretty sweet not to deal with Luke's arrogance anymore.

I sat back in my chair, allowing the magnitude of the event to wash over me. I had come to the Academy just out of high school, when my parents had divulged with me their plans of setting me up in the family business—I use family loosely, since they, being busy agents themselves, were usually away on IPS business. It had been a conversation I had expected, and now, at twenty-two, I was ready to step fully into that world for myself. Not many people know about the IPS, which is part of its usefulness. With most of the public focused on the FBI and CIA, we were able to operate in the shadows as some sort of hybrid with a similar function; defending what our higher-ups deemed worthy. Our agents wear many hats—some investigative, some intelligence-based, and some in the field. An assignment relating to one of the latter two was where I assumed I would be placed, but the assignment process was mysterious, and there was really no way of knowing your placement until it was received. To have finally made it to the point where my career would take on a life of its own felt a bit like a dream. *Better to call it a dream realized; there's little room for dreamers here.* As I settled into my seat, I stared up at Agent Diane Rivers, elegant in her navy suit, her dark hair pulled into a business-like knot at the back of her head. Silvery streaks shone where her hair was pressed against her scalp as she turned her head to scan the crowd; the effect was close to magical, as was the speed with which they fell silent.

"Welcome, students, staff, and guests, to this year's Assignment Day Ceremony. I know that this day has been long anticipated by our students and their mentors alike. From this group in particular, I know that we can expect great things. Because of the time-sensitive nature of many of our assignments, I am going to dispense with the usual, lengthy opening remarks and begin." I felt a renewed prickle of anticipation at the words of our Program Head, and even the fact that Luke Ryder was still seated just behind me could not quell the bones-deep surge of excitement that washed over me.

"This is it," Bonnie whispered from beside me. I glanced in her direction to see her blue eyes shining with the same mix determination and excitement that I felt myself.

"Our students have already been briefed on how today's event will proceed, but for those in attendance who have not shared this occasion with us previously, I will explain our procedure. When I call a student's name, that student will approach and enter the door to either my left or my right," she gestured with her hands, and I took in the gleaming doors just behind her, wondering which would contain my future. "Within that room, they shall receive their assignments. Due to the urgent nature of many of those assignments, some students may need to begin immediately. Please do not feel slighted if some of our pupils move to exit the hall upon receiving their assignment; this is the day that they have been waiting for." There was a murmur through the crowd at this, and I wondered if the few families in attendance had taken the time to say their farewells. My own parents were somewhere in Asia on some mission, so I wasn't worried, but I knew that there were others less accustomed to sudden goodbyes.

"To my students," Agent Rivers continued, "I wish you the best of luck and surety of skill in all of your future endeavors. We all have the utmost faith in you. Let the ceremony begin." With a sweep of her hand, elegant and graceful at the end of a crisp, navy suit, the lights in the crowd dimmed, focusing instead on the stage that would mark the start of the rest of our lives as Agent Rivers was further illuminated behind her podium. I may have been about to become an agent of the IPS, but I was woman enough to admire the flash of white light cast by the diamond-and-pearl pendant around her throat. The mood grew somber as we all held our collective breath. I heard a soft snicker behind me that I felt certain was Luke, but I did not bother turning my head. I had been looking forward to this day for far too long to let him ruin it.

"The first on our list this year is Mr. Wade Harper. If memory serves, which it usually does, Mr. Harper made particularly excellent strides in track and field. No doubt, his stamina will serve him well as he begins his assignment. Congratulations, Mr. Harper," she began. As Wade, a slight, brown-haired boy I vaguely recognized from some of my fitness classes made his way through the door on Headmistress Rivers's left, there was a polite round of applause before she commenced with the next name.

As she read through the list, my excitement dimmed somewhat. Well, maybe that was just the anticipation dimming since I was still very excited. We had a large graduating class, several of us second-generation agents, and our ages ranged from pupils in their 40s to those of us in our early twenties. I jumped, startled slightly, as Agent Rivers read the next name.

"Miss Gwendolyn Evans." On one side of me, Gwen rose gracefully.

"Here goes nothing," she whispered nervously not looking at me or Bonnie as she glided up to the stage. Gwen had been a star pupil at the Academy. She was never tardy, and over the years, she had become particularly adept in disguising herself. She would go far in our field; I had no doubt of that, but the pang of loss was still the same as she slipped away.

"I wish you the best of luck, Agent Evans." Agent Rivers smiled down at Gwen as she made her way up to the right of the podium. She paused for a moment, and I saw her shoulders rise as she took a breath before opening the door. I waited patiently as Agent Rivers began reading off the next name, curious as to what Gwen's mission would be. Her stealth meant that she would be well-suited—at least in my opinion—to one of the more underground missions that never quite reached the media's ears. I wondered again what it would be, but I shook my head as I reminded myself that I would likely never know.

The seconds stretched on into minutes of silence before Gwen, a look of steely determination firming her soft features, emerged from the door. She cast a look in our direction, nodding once before she squared her shoulders and disappeared toward an exit. Although I knew that there was no way she could have seen us in the dimness of the light that fell across the crowd, I knew that it was her way of saying goodbye. *One friend down, one to go.* I glanced sideways at Bonnie, whose lips had tightened, and I knew she was feeling the same loss that hollowed in my stomach. Agent Rivers continued to call name after name; some returned from their doors, and some never came back through the hall. I knew that this meant a more immediate departure for a high-stakes mission. Still, my name was not called, and as the crowd dwindled, I felt a flutter of nervousness as I wondered if I would be assigned anywhere. My nervousness abated as a name was called that made me want to shout with glee—naturally, I didn't, since self-control was the most basic of skills in our field.

"Mr. Luke Ryder." Agent Rivers called clearly. I felt the breeze of his movements behind me, and I resisted the urge to shudder. I was unable to maintain my stoicism when I felt his breath on my ear.

"Don't miss me too much, Richards," he whispered, and then he was gone, leaving me wrinkling my nose in disgust.

"Luke Ryder…. How does one begin to describe Luke Ryder," she began, and I had to muffle a fit of giggles as Agent Rivers—quite unknown to her—quoted one of the many women who had swooned and sighed over Luke throughout the course of his training. The woman in question, I had overheard in the library just before our final exams, and Agent Rivers said it with such a similar intonation—although admittedly without the breathy sigh at the end—that I could not contain myself. Bonnie shot me a concerned look, clearly worried that I had finally lost my mind, but I simply shook my head as my shoulders quaked with now-silent laughter.

"I would like to take a moment to acknowledge Mr. Ryder as a model student at our Academy. He has achieved high marks in all aspects of his training, and his exam scores were the highest this academy has ever seen. As one who has broken records that lasted decades, we expect great things from you, Mr. Ryder." I snorted under the cover of the applause as Luke nodded to the crowd, although the smirk faded from my face when I realized that his gaze was piercing through the darkness to where Bonnie and I still sat. She nudged me as though she had noticed the same thing, but I didn't respond. Bonnie always had thought that the rivalry between us was repressed emotion, and it wasn't that he wasn't an attractive person—at least on the surface. I could admire that about him from a position of detachment, and I would have been a fool to claim otherwise when the world could plainly see it. It was his personality—insufferably arrogant, pigheaded, with an absolute superiority complex that pushed every one of my buttons every time he spoke—that was the real turn-off. Unfortunately, none of those qualities counted against him in his Academy training, but in our personal lives—what little of them we had maintained here— the thought of being with him in any sort of romantic light (or around him in any light at all, actually), made me want to vomit. So, it was disconcerting that I felt a small twinge of nostalgia as I watched his broad shoulders disappear into the door to the right of Agent Rivers. We had been butting heads for years, and now, after a handful of sentences, it was over.

"For what it's worth, I think he'll miss you too, Artemis." I looked to see Bonnie looking at me with complete seriousness. I was baffled.

"What makes you think I'll miss him?" I whispered back defensively, raising an eyebrow. She rolled her eyes in the typical Bonnie fashion, somber expression gone as she shook her head.

"You'll miss the banter if nothing else," she said unhelpfully. I opened my mouth to argue, but maturely—if I do say so myself— changed my mind and chose to sit in dignified silence instead. Out of the corner of my eyes, I saw the corner of Bonnie's mouth twitch upward, her eyes crinkling at the sides with repressed amusement. I stared hard at the door that had swallowed Luke before shrugging slightly. I probably would miss the banter; I could be generous enough to admit that it had been entertaining now that I didn't have to worry about it anymore. After all, I would likely never see him again, so it was alright for me to remember him tormenting me with *some* fondness. I didn't realize that I had been lost in thought until I felt a hard nudge at my shoulder. I looked at Bonnie, confused, until I saw her jerk her chin in the direction of the stage. Heat flooded into me as I realized what she meant.

"Blythe Richards?" The smile of Agent Rivers did not falter, but it did seem a bit frosted on as I rose. I had clearly missed her calling my name the first time. The heat continued to creep up my throat and into my cheeks as I looked once more at the door where Luke had disappeared in confusion. He had only been inside for a few seconds; surely that wasn't long enough to receive his assignment and leave. *And he hasn't come out of the room yet… Has he?*

"No, he hasn't," Bonnie hissed, seeming to read my mind, "but she called your name, so *go!*" She gave me a little shove, and I stepped past her, pausing to give her a spur-of-the-moment hug. After all, this would likely be the last time I saw my friend.

"Ah, there she is," Rivers cleared her throat. "Miss Richards is another exceptional student of the Academy. She, like Mr. Ryder before her, achieved such high scores on her aptitude exam that she too broke the previous record. She is a well-rounded student who shows promise in many areas. I expect to see excellent things from her. Congratulations, Blythe," she finished. *Artemis,* I corrected silently. It didn't matter now; all that mattered was what was still to come.

I hadn't really been conscious of my footsteps, but I had reached the podium on stage before I knew what had happened. Agent Rivers's smile remained as she inclined her head toward the door reassuringly, indicating that I should continue. *Well, here it goes.* I took a fortifying breath and then stepped inside the door to her right.

The room did not look as I had pictured it in my head, but it seemed fitting to the circumstances. There was a heavy pine desk on one side, with several big, classy-looking leather chairs spread across the large Persian rug in the center of the floor. A large bookcase stood behind the desk, full of thick volumes that simply screamed wisdom, and another large bookcase graced the wall opposite. The room was smaller than I expected, but it didn't feel crowded by any means. The only thing that didn't meet my approval was the fact that Luke was still standing in the room with his back to me. His hands supporting his weight as he leaned on the desk with his shoulders tensed. I froze; had I gone in too soon? I shook my head almost imperceptibly. *No, Rivers wouldn't have gotten it wrong.*

"Welcome, Miss Richards. I am Agent Jonah Wilkerson, the Director of Placement for the Academy. It's a pleasure to meet you," a voice said. Looking past Luke, I saw that the voice came from the wiry but tough-looking man standing behind the desk. His hair was dark, growing silver near the temples, and his eyes appraised me sharply as I stepped forward. I was surprised I hadn't noticed him before.

"I apologize if I'm interrupting, Agent Wilkerson. I thought they had wanted me to come in," I said mildly, my eyes darting toward Luke as I spoke. His face was unreadable as he straightened.

"Not at all, Miss Richards. We wouldn't have been able to finish without you," he answered. Despite his position, he had a reassuring smile. I sent him a fleeting smile in return, but it dimmed slightly when I felt Luke turn a glare upon me.

"I'm afraid I don't quite understand," I said politely, feeling uncharacteristically self-conscious. It wasn't often that I was taken off-guard, and I didn't like the feeling. Luke rounded on me, annoyance flaring in his eyes.

"Come on, Richards. Don't tell me you haven't guessed yet," he snapped. At my blank stare, he continued, "think of the worst thing you can possibly think of." His mouth twisted into a sort of humorless smile as he ran one hand through his brown hair. My sense of foreboding skyrocketed, and I rounded back to face Agent Wilkerson, who was looking on with a patient smile.

"So, what does that mean for me—us?" I ended on a question, pretending that Luke had not spoken.

"Well, Miss Richards..." He trailed off, seeming to grasp that this was a delicate situation. "As you might know, you and Mr. Ryder both have an extraordinary record here at the Institute's Academy. You are two of the finest students ever to come through the program.

So, when this job came up requesting two highly competent new agents with well-rounded abilities, the board's decision was unanimous." My jaw dropped as I lost my poise. *Okay, what?! Two agents? There is absolutely no way that this can be happening.*

"Wait, so this job—we're going to be doing this assignment *together?*" I asked incredulously. Logan snorted.

"Told you it would be the worst thing *you* could think of," Luke muttered. I didn't understand his emphasis, but I did understand his point.

"Just needed to clarify, sorry," I added lamely.

"I know that you two don't always see eye to eye," Wilkerson allowed, "but your skills complement each other, so I trust you will figure out how to work together." His tone sharpened at the end, leaving no room for argument. For all of the sharpness of his words, the corners of his mouth twitched upward before smoothing again, as though he had been trying to hide amusement.

"What will we be doing exactly? I mean," I cleared my throat, "what is the nature of this assignment?" I was proud of myself for reeling myself in. *A true professional.* I bragged to myself before my eyes flickered over to Luke, who was looking intently at the desk with a mutinous expression.

"As you might know," his mouth twisted in an amused smirk, "there is a certain leader of the free world who has two children: his son Jesse and his daughter, Sara." The agent handed each of them a folder, and I began flipping through mine at once as he spoke. "Tensions have been building with other nations, as well as within the political circles in Washington, and the president made it clear that he wants more protection for his children. He does, however, want it to be discreet. So, he had the idea of bringing in two younger agents from the Institute who were closer to his children's ages. He thought it would be less obvious if the cover story was that they were companions." I looked down at the photograph of the president's son, Jesse Boyle, that was clipped to my packet of information. His fine-boned face smiled up at me, and I looked up to see Luke examining the photograph of Sara, his green eyes clearly analyzing the girl before he flipped her picture over and began reading her file. *Companions? To the First Kids?*

"Do we have a backstory?" I asked, blinking as I took in the overwhelming surplus of information. Luke raised an eyebrow at me and raised the file folder. *Of course, we do.*

"All in the folder, Miss Richards," Wilkerson said, not unkindly. For all of Luke's facade of confidence, I saw questions swimming in his eyes before he opened his mouth to ask one.

"Agent Wilkerson, just so we're clear, what exactly *is* our assignment?" he asked, looking determinedly away from me as he did. The urge to call him out swelled up within me, but I swallowed the taunt with difficulty.

"Mr. Ryder, to be perfectly clear, your assignment should be obvious: you're going to protect the First Children of the United States… *together*."

CHAPTER 2

After a quick nod of acknowledgement in Bonnie's direction, I kept my head down as I hurried to keep up with Luke's much-longer stride. Eyes followed us, despite the fact that Agent Rivers was already introducing the next graduate. How long had we been in the room, keeping those to follow us waiting? Ten minutes? Twenty? It had felt like an eternity and a flash all at once. I was determined not to run as I struggled to keep up with Luke and give the impression of a leisurely pace, and I realized that he was purposely striding to get away from me. I guess we'll be forced to keep each other company soon enough, I thought scathingly. Still, we had some matters to discuss, and we couldn't do that if he was determined to run away until we were out of sight of the rest of our class.

I waited for the final double doors to swing shut behind us before I bolted ahead to confront him, but to my annoyance, he continued pretending as though I did not exist. I felt my face heat up again as he strutted away from me—well, I guess he didn't really strut, but it felt like that at the time—but the heat was not embarrassment this time, it was unbridled irritation.

"Where do you think you're going?" I demanded

loudly, making it impossible for him to continue pretending that I had the significance of wallpaper. He looked down at me, green eyes hot and agitated, like I was scum on the bottom of his shoe. Ah, yes, the audacity of lowly me to demand a response from the great Luke Ryder! I nearly choked on the words, but to my relief, and surprise, they stayed inside where they belonged.

"Apparently, there's been some sort of mix-up with your assignment. But until they sort that out and have you transferred, we're stuck dealing with each other, so I'm going to spend my last few moments of Artemis-free bliss packing alone. Meet me in the Dining Hall in twenty minutes. Don't be late." And like that, Luke Ryder was gone, leaving me with my jaw hanging open. Didn't even give me the chance to retort. Rude. With a huff, I flipped my hair over my shoulder and stormed off in the opposite direction. I would deal with him later. As if I would be the one needing to be transferred. As if there was a mistake.

"But what does the director of placement for the IPS know when compared to the great, infallible Luke Ryder," I said loftily to no one in particular, kicking at the floorboards in frustration.

I continued internally muttering insulting comparisons of exactly how big Luke's head was as I made my way to my dormitory and packed quickly, throwing my belongings in a bag carelessly. I'd never had much of a sentimental attachment to things, sentimental as a childhood with borderline-absentee parents was, so I didn't particularly care what came with me or in what condition it arrived. I had limited time, and I was sure I would have a chance to reorganize once I arrived at The White House. The White House, I thought. The thought was dizzying. At least, that's where I assumed we were going, since the First Family was in residence. I looked down at what I had worn for the ceremony, a deep plum dress and nude pumps, with a sort of surprise; in my haste, I had forgotten how I was dressed, and now, said dress was a bit rumpled. Not exactly travel appropriate, in any case. With a feeling of pride at my own practicality, I pulled the dress over my head and stepped out of my heels in one, fluid motion, quickly tossing them in my half-packed bags. Surely the White House has an iron… Or dry cleaning. In their place, I chose tailored, black pants and a crisp, white top. It was professional, and it was easy to move around in, as long as I could find—ah ha! With some sense of triumph, I pulled out a pair of unassumingly practical flats, which were much easier to move in than their predecessors. If Luke was going to make me work to keep up with him, practicality was paramount. I glanced at myself briefly in the mirror, running my fingers through my slightly-frizzing brown hair before I nodded, finding the look passable, before I resumed my packing.

After zipping my final bag—of three, since I didn't have much—I grabbed my luggage, two wheeling suitcases and a duffle, and left the room without a backward glance. The Academy had been my home for many years now, but I preferred not to look back since I was not headed that way, even if this new journey had an unwelcome companion. I groaned inwardly at the thought of Luke. In my haste to pack, I had almost forgotten. Now, a finger of bitterness traced its way down to my stomach, where it rose like bile in my throat. My progress had been hard-won at the Academy, and now, as a fully-fledged member of the IPS, it looked as though my competition with Luke would not end any time soon. I heaved a sigh. As I neared our chosen meeting place, a dining hall, I forced myself to smooth my furrowed brow and take a deep breath. Luke would know that I was rattled by our new partnership, but I did not want to give him the satisfaction of knowing just how much the arrangement bothered me. Part of competing with

Luke was never letting him know when he ruffled my feathers. I arranged my features into what I hoped was a reasonably neutral expression as I approached where Luke stood, leaned against one wall and looking in the opposite direction. He apparently heard my approach, as he turned his head to look down at me wearing his usual expression of disapproval.

"You're late," he said gruffly, the moment I was within reasonable earshot. I rolled my eyes and resisted the urge to snap back.

"I'm not. It's been thirteen minutes, and you said we had twenty." I waved my phone in front of his face so the clock flashed. "Maybe you should try keeping track sometime," I suggested pleasantly, smiling more genuinely at the spark of irritation that crossed his face.

"You changed," he said. And you changed the subject.

"I did. Congrats on having eyes," I replied cheerfully. Very green eyes, I added privately. They were admittedly the kind of eyes that would have been enchanting had they belonged to anyone else. They could be considered even pretty when they weren't blazing with annoyance, which they usually seemed to be around me. He opened his mouth, frowning as he did so, to respond, but before he could, another voice called out to us.

"Luke Ryder? Artemis Richards?" The owner of the voice was a tall, stocky man who looked us squarely in the face once he approached. I felt my spine stiffen automatically, and I observed that Luke's did the same. I wondered briefly how on earth he had known it was us without an introduction.

"Yes sir?" I replied. The way he had spoken had held authority, and usually, agents were escorted to their new assignments by someone of rank—higher rank than their own, that is. I noticed that Luke stayed silent, his eyes roving over the newcomer, assessing. Probably I should be doing the same, I thought, but my gut instinct was that this man wasn't a threat, and my gut instincts were usually pretty accurate.

"Agent Yates. I'm here to make an introduction," the man responded, eyeing Luke.

"To?" Luke asked promptly.

"Your new boss. Ryder, Richards, allow me to introduce you to the president of the United States." Without saying anything further, Yates stepped aside to make room for a much smaller man, flanked by two men. His face was young for his age, although upon closer inspection, I could see the crinkling lines near his eyes and creases around his mouth that told me he liked to laugh. All in all, it was an honest face—for a politician, at least. Not that it mattered to my purpose; a job had to be a job, after all. He was also shorter in person than he appeared on the news, although he was still quite a bit taller than me...not that that was saying much.

"Mr. President, I am honored to be in your service." Apparently cured of his sour attitude, Luke stepped forward to shake the extended hand of President Joseph Archibald Boyle. I caught a side-eye and an almost imperceptible smirk in my direction as he stepped forward, and my eyebrows raised. Oh, no. He did not just snub me in front of the leader of the free world. I stepped up beside him, the top of my head nearly reaching his shoulder.

"Yes sir, it is truly an honor for both of us to serve our country. I hope we do so well," I said deliberately. I flashed a smile at President Boyle, trying to maintain my grip on my professionalism as it battled with my very live temper. I would deal with Luke later. President Boyle looked between the two of us with something akin to amusement as he smiled genuinely.

"A pleasure to meet you both, truly," he said, shaking my hand as well. "I will admit that members of my advisory board were skeptical of me taking on such fresh graduates for this assignment without more out-of-program experience, but I read your files myself. I'm certain that the pair of you are more than up to the task." I felt a flicker of triumph at his reference to the pair of us, and I hoped desperately that it didn't show on my face; it was poor form to showcase workplace rivalries on your first day. Luke looked mildly put-out at the mention of being doubted, although he covered it well enough. I wasn't surprised at the sentiment though; we were young. I was used to the skepticism of my superiors, though, and I reveled in the idea of a challenge.

"Was this mission your idea, sir?" I added the "sir" as an afterthought, almost forgetting myself in my eagerness. Luke shot me a look of warning. He was my equal, as much as we both may have hated to admit, which meant that he was not my babysitter. I fought the urge to glare in return and instead kept my focus on President Boyle.

"Yes, Artemis. It was," he said simply, although not unkindly. I blinked at his use of my preferred name. He really did do his research. Yates stepped forward.

"Mr. President, I hate to rush, but—" Boyle nodded at once.

"Oh, yes. We should be off. Are you both packed and ready?" He directed the question at Luke and me, seeming suddenly rushed, although not impolite.

"Yes sir," Luke answered. "We packed before we came down to meet you." Boyle smiled as Luke answered for us both, and the smile suited him. It was only his first term, but already the stress of the job could be seen in the lines of his face and the subtle shadows under his eyes. Thinking back to his campaign, only the year prior, I realized how much the job had already aged him. Hopefully, having his children looked after would help to ease some of that burden. At the thought of our wards, I snapped back into the present; this job would not be one where I could afford to drift off into my thoughts.

"Excellent. If you two will follow me, then, someone else will see to your bags. Jesse and Sara will be pleased to meet you." I was surprised by how readily Boyle spoke with us, given that we had just met, but only slightly. After all, why shouldn't he be; he knew we were sworn to confidentiality—it was a given with our trade. Then again, these were his kids; candor would make sense, since we were the ones who would be charged with protecting them. It was refreshing to hear from his own mouth instead of him using one of his senior agents as a mouthpiece. It felt authentic, sincere. It made sense. What didn't make sense was how Luke and I would be able to work in such close proximity to one another without absolutely tearing each other to shreds, but I settled the urge with another thought about the job. After all, I thought, it's the job that matters.

It was what I had spent most of my life preparing for, and Luke Ryder was not going to interfere.

CHAPTER 3

For all that our introduction to the president had been friendly and casual, the flight toward The White House—where I had been informed that we were, in fact, going—was strained; at least, it seemed a bit strained to me. President Boyle was friendly enough; he had a natural charisma. The problem, as always, was Luke. He seemed especially anxious to respond to anything Boyle said, even when it was directed at me, and to be perfectly frank, it was pissing me off.

"So, where are you originally from?" Boyle asked, looking at me, shifting his eyes to Luke, and then returning his gaze to me. I opened my mouth to respond, but once again, I was interrupted by the ever-timely Mr. Ryder himself.

"Atlanta for me," he answered casually as he mentioned his hometown, as though he hadn't just completely hijacked my moment to respond.

"It's the far west of North Carolina for me," I answered vaguely, glaring at Luke, whose green eyes were focused on his lap. That was odd for Luke; he could have been the poster boy for eye contact and introductory professionalism back at the Academy. He wouldn't even make eye contact with our boss, and somehow, I *still* could hardly get a word in edgewise.

"I hail from South Carolina myself," President Boyle said, "so I guess we're all practically neighbors." I had known that, of course, from his campaign. His tone was more relaxed, which made Luke look up from his lap and narrow his eyes at me. *What is your problem?* I hoped the thought was broadcasted across my face. Was it that he couldn't bear the thought of me having something in common with the boss, or just that he couldn't foil me in my attempts at conversation? Either way, it wasn't my problem.

"The good ole South! In any case, the Academy—the whole Institute, really—has been like home for me for a few years now," I responded, doing my best to refrain from shooting any more dangerous expressions at Luke. *Hate to ruin the mood.*

"According to your files, you've both been very dedicated to your studies. I appreciate exceptionalism and dedication. You two meet both criteria." Luke smiled at the praise and took a deep breath before he replied in a respectful tone.

"I certainly appreciate it, sir. It's an honor to serve my country by protecting its leader's children." I had to keep myself from snorting at his formality, but I did not fully succeed. The resulting noise was unpleasant, but I hid it behind a cough. Luke glanced suspiciously in my direction, but I kept my eyes wide and innocent. Self-righteous ego maniac he might be, but even I could not deny that Luke had a way with words… even if those words were full of it. I met the president's eyes, and the lines around Boyle's eyes creased in a faint smile as though he knew exactly what I had been thinking.

"My children are very important to me. My trust is not something to be taken lightly," he replied, and the tone of warning in his voice closed the subject. Luke had tossed his file on top of mine in the seat between us, so out of curiosity, I decided to pick them up and learn a bit more about our charges as the conversation stumbled into silence. I took in the photo of Sara Boyle, a very pretty seventeen-year-old with a heart-shaped face. Her auburn hair was swept round her shoulders, cut in a way that emphasized the large, almond shape of her blue eyes. I glanced up at the president, somewhat struck by the similarity. Adopted daughter she might be, but the resemblance could have connected them by blood; they had similarities around the shape of the eyes and nose. She looked altogether too innocent to be in the type of danger her father's job placed her in, but I didn't put much stock in appearances. Upon closer inspection of the file, I learned that Saint Sara had been accused of bullying her classmates at more than one private school, most recently at a private school she had attended two years ago. One of the girls she'd allegedly bullied had withdrawn from the school altogether. *I guess Sara's not America's Angel after all?* Not that I could tell anyone. Odds were good that she'd be just like every other spoiled rich kid I'd lived my life to avoid, so I felt sure I could handle it. I sighed, scratching the side of my nose absently. Oh, well; I hadn't been looking for a friend anyway. It was a job.

Jesse Boyle's file was a lot more promising. His blond hair curled around his temples, and his own blue eyes, so much like his father's, seemed kind. They didn't have the carefully crafted innocence of Sara's photograph; the tilt of his smile seemed genuinely kind. The contents of his file appeared to match this judgment. He'd been in a scuffle or two over the years, but nothing serious, and they had all been started by comments about his father. I felt a surprising prickle of sympathy. My life, despite my parents' career, had consisted of a relatively normal social experience. I'd never been isolated and ostracized because of my parents; I had no idea what that was like. *And no right to judge Sara for her choices either?* I pushed the thought away, ignoring the guilt that rose to pair with my sympathy for Jesse.

"Mr. President, we're beginning our descent." A voice crackled over the speakers, and I noticed the almost-imperceptible tilt of the aircraft, although it was slight. A sudden flutter hit my stomach that had nothing to do with our trajectory, but it was soon replaced by a cold determination. I wasn't allowed to be nervous. I had trained for this. I glanced to the side and saw Luke's jaw had tightened in a similar expression. The thought that we may actually be on the same page about something made me smile softly until I noticed that his eyes were clenched tightly shut. I raised an eyebrow.

"Uh, Ryder?" I asked, not really sure what was going on with him, although I was beginning to get an idea. When he didn't speak, I nudged him. *Was he like this when we took off?* To be fair, I tried not to make a habit of looking at him.

"Luke?" I tried again.

"*WHAT?*" The response hissed out of him, and I had to hold back a flinch. *What on Earth is his problem? Oh, wait! Is he…?*

"Ryder, are you scared of flying?" I asked in wonder, lowering my voice so that Boyle couldn't hear. Not because I was worried about teasing him, but I didn't need to expose a weakness to our boss on the first day of a new job. It would be rude.

"Shut up, *Blythe.*" Apparently, the same courtesy did not extend to me—or he was too paralyzed by fear to come up with a better response, and I snickered, causing Boyle to glance up in our direction. I shifted my body so that he wouldn't see how much Luke was struggling with the flight—*after all, that's professional courtesy, right?* — and relaxed as he returned to his conversation with a staff member. My good deed done, I couldn't resist teasing him now.

"So, the invincible Luke Ryder is afraid of flying. Oh

my *god* this is good… Good luck with that, pal, because if we're guarding the First Children, my guess is that we're going to become well-acquainted with aircrafts." Chuckling to myself and quite sure that he was now silently cursing my name, I eased my way back into my seat, leaning against the cushion and closing my eyes serenely for the peaceful descent. There was nothing that I found quite as satisfying as the discomfort of my sworn nemesis.

The only thing that interrupted the near silence of my peaceful descent was the murmuring of President Boyle in the background, punctuated by Luke's sharp inhales and exhales from beside me. *Good Lord, you'd think we were hitting the world's biggest turbulence instead of making a steady descent.* I opened one eye and peered in his direction as we neared our intended runway, and I noticed that now his fists were clenched, and his eyes were still clamped shut. *Well, he'd certainly make a good statue.* If he hadn't been such a jerk to me for so many years, I would almost feel bad for the guy. The statuesque effect was ruined when Luke nearly jumped out of his skin as the wheels jolted against the runway and shook the plane. There was no way for me to hide that from the president, and I watched as Boyle shot him a sympathetic look before he made eye contact with me. I shrugged in response; for Luke's sake, hopefully Boyle wouldn't think this was the norm for him. Otherwise, Luke wasn't making the best impression for someone who liked to be seen as superhuman. If there was a Superman out in the world, it definitely wasn't him.

When the plane finally stuttered to a stop, it took Luke a few seconds before he opened his eyes and straightened, clenching and unclenching his hands. I opened my mouth to say something, but I shut it again at the obvious distress on his face. For once, my teasing had limits. As Boyle approached, I blocked his view of Luke once more to give him a chance to stand.

"Alright Richards, Ryder, are you ready to meet your charges?" Boyle shot a concerned glance at Luke again, and I turned slightly to follow it. Out of the corner of my eye, though, I saw that Luke looked as though he was mostly back to normal. I nodded briskly, watching as Luke did the same. He appeared more confident now that we had reached a more solid surface.

"Excellent. Let's begin." Boyle smiled.

CHAPTER 4

"There is literally no point in meeting these people. They aren't going anywhere, and I have better things to do right now," Sara whined to her brother. She knew she sounded childish, but at the moment, she didn't really care. Her brother ignored her; Jesse's head was bent low over his phone as he scrolled through social media. Sara's own social media access had been revoked after that girl—*stupid little snitch*, she thought viciously— had made up those stories about being bullied. They hadn't wanted to deal with the *scandal*. She rolled her eyes at the memory and jumped in surprise when Jesse spoke again; lately, he chose to ignore her more than he bothered to have a conversation.

"We'll have to meet them eventually. Dad said these agents would be better," Jesse said blandly. Sara narrowed her eyes and thumped him in the back of the head. Why bother responding at all if he wasn't going to say anything that mattered. To his credit—and her annoyance— Jesse did not retaliate to the assault; he continued scrolling with a roll of his eyes..

"Why, because they're supposedly closer to our age? Do you honestly think we can be *friends* with these people? Do you really think Dad would let that happen? No, they're going to be the same as the overstuffed, underpaid suits we got stuck with last time. The only difference is that they'll be in a younger package," Sara huffed, feeling heat start to rise in a flush when her brother still did not look up.

"I highly doubt that a pair of college-aged adults are going to act like 'suits.' Can you please go away? You're killing the vibe," he said with annoyance. She rolled her eyes at the slang. *At least I'm getting a response this time*, Sara thought.

"What 'vibe?' Cyber-stalking a bunch of girls you're never going to have the chance to actually meet?" she jeered. Jesse scowled.

"Do you have to try to be a bitch, or does it just come naturally now? Go away," Jesse answered deliberately before resuming his scrolling. With another huff, Sara stalked out of his room. What was the point of your dad being the leader of the free world if you yourself were never actually free? Her brother was more concerned with half-clothed girls on the internet than his own sister. Most of them weren't even that pretty anyway; he was basically American royalty, and in Sara's opinion, he could do better. *Jealous much?* The thought just made her more annoyed. She and Jesse used to be best friends as well as siblings, but now, she just felt like an annoyance.

Sara cursed under her breath as she heard the approach of voices from around the corner, and she sped up, intending to blow past whoever it was. She was still stewing, so she wasn't in the mood to talk, and she was definitely not in the mood to be patronized by any kiss-ass staff who were looking to gain favor with her father. *They wouldn't care about me at all if they didn't feel like my father could do them favors.* Sara rounded the corner, speeding up, and she squealed as her body collided with something hard. Arms immediately hooked around her, stopping her recoil in its tracks.

She looked up, feeling her face grow hot with embarrassment as she met a pair of bright green eyes. *Great.* A quick glance to her savior's left showed her a small-framed girl with big brown eyes that sparkled with amusement. Slightly behind her and now wearing his usual expression of resignation, was her father, and Sara realized that these must be the new babysitters. *I guess I know how to make a first impression.*

Taking a quick step backward, Sara straightened her clothes and forced what she hoped was a charming smile onto her face. As her father liked to say, there was no first impression quite like a winning smile.

"Hi," she greeted sweetly, "I'm Sara." Inwardly, the gears of her mind were turning and shifting as she sized up the new arrivals. "And you are?" She directed this at the one who had broken her fall.

"Luke Ryder," he answered. His green eyes were guarded, but his voice was deeper than Sara would have expected. It wasn't altogether unpleasant, and she thought she might be able to get used to hearing it. "And the young woman to my right is Blythe Richards. We're your new security detail," he added, with a sidelong glance at his companion. Sara brushed off that part of the introduction. There would be plenty of time to get to know the girl later. For now, she was far more interested in learning more about Luke. To her annoyance, the girl elbowed Luke in the side and stepped forward.

"Sorry, Ryder has this annoying habit of never introducing me correctly. I'm Artemis," she said. Sara reluctantly dragged her eyes away from Luke and turned her attention to the spunky-looking brunette standing at his side. Her brown eyes flashed with annoyance, and Sara barely resisted the urge to roll her own, knowing that her father would scold her if she was anything less than polite.

"What's with the name?" The words slipped out before Sara could help it. She might have been able to somewhat control her face, but sometimes her words had a mind of their own. Plus, something in the new girl's snark reminded Sara too much of herself. *There's barely room enough for me in this house; with two of me, it might explode.*

"It's my middle name. You know, Goddess of the Hunt? My parents were into Greek mythology." She answered with the slightest edge, shrugging before she shot Luke a glare when he elbowed her in the side. Sara narrowed her eyes at Artemis appraisingly before remembering that she had been trying to avoid this interaction in the first place. She turned to Luke and directed her next words at him.

"Right. Well, Jesse is in his room. I'll see you later," Sara said. She pushed past the newcomers and her father, pretending that she could not hear when he called after her. She was in desperate need of binge-watching a tv show and pretending that the rest of the world didn't exist. She needed to feel like she was a normal teenager, just this once.

CHAPTER 5

"Well, he certainly liked *you*, didn't he?" Luke made a face at me as soon as the president was out of earshot. *Nice, Ryder; very professional.* I shot him the most dignified expression I could muster.

"I mean, personally *I* try not to run directly into my boss's kids to get their attention, but I guess some of us have to rely on that tactic. It seemed to have worked for you," I answered slyly. *Trust Ryder to make physical contact with our only female charge before they're actually introduced,* I thought nastily. In truth, Jesse hadn't been very receptive to me at all. He'd just sat with his phone in hand, alternating between scrolling and staring blankly at me like I was some sort of alien creature. I'd tried my hardest to maintain some sense of decorum, but it was disconcerting to have him look at me as though he'd never seen a girl—in the flesh, that is; I'd caught a glimpse of his social media feed. Blank stare, raised eyebrows, the hint of a smirk. Then again, he was a First Kid; he probably just needed to get out more… or at least socialize more away from the phone screen.

"It's not my fault she ran into me," Luke snapped back. I smirked, and he rolled his eyes.

"She was clearly struck dumb by your beauty," I replied, sarcasm dripping from every word. He shot me another look, but my smirk just widened into a grin. It was so easy to get under his skin; maybe I would have missed our banter after all. The next words out of his mouth made me immediately take the thought back.

"You would know. But now that you're finished complimenting me, we should probably get settled where we're staying. We'll have to meet the whole crew and be briefed on the rest of everything tonight." The rest of what he said went in one ear and out the other. *He thought* I *had been struck dumb by his beauty?* I spluttered for a moment before coming to my senses. This was always what he did, trying to unnerve me. I should have learned by now not to let it work. *Or not to dish it out if you can't take it,* my inner voice interjected slyly. I ignored it, trying to muster the dignity I had left.

"Obviously," I sniffed, uncharacteristically letting the matter rest. A glimpse in the mirror conveniently placed across the hall displayed my reddening ears. My recognition of my own embarrassment made the color deepen further, and I brushed my hair forward to cover the evidence. I scowled as I met Luke's eyes in the mirror, where he was watching me with a lopsided grin.

"Are you finished admiring yourself and primping, or can we go?" he asked. I snorted, somewhat relieved he had ignored my obvious state of fluster.

"And you know the word 'primping' because…?" I changed the subject, and he mumbled something mostly incoherent under his breath as we turned left and arrived at the end of our hallway. As we made another turn to take some stairs, we strolled in silence, and I distracted myself from the lack of conversation by trying to memorize our surroundings. The place was a surprising maze, but I could still appreciate the stately flooring and wallpapering of the halls; it suited the setting. I felt a slight flutter of awe in my stomach as I drank in every detail. Never in a million years had I thought I would ever be standing in The White House at age twenty-two as an *employee.*

Most of us at the Institute began our careers by being outsourced to private, government-funded companies to act as their security or assist in the more clandestine operations between businesses. It was rarely, so rarely, that one of us would be taken in by such a direct government job so fresh out of training and into our careers. Maybe in a few years, the odd agent would work their way up, but most agents spent their career working behind the curtain, trying to work their way up to where our career was beginning. *And the fact that it's two of us?* I shook my head, somewhat dazed by the thought. I cast a sidelong glance at Ryder. It was a rare occasion that I could observe him without him knowing it; it was even more rare that I could do so without seeing his face twist into the semi-pained expression he usually wore for our interactions.

He was tall and broad, a walking cliche really, and he moved with the surefooted grace of an athlete, which had made most of the Academy girls either hate him on sight or fall in love with him immediately. There was rarely an in between. Naturally, I fit into the first category from the moment he opened his mouth. He had a confident stride that I knew from gossip had developed over the years as he pushed through the awkwardness of puberty, and his hair—at this moment— had that messy-but-not look that made most girls swoon. His clear green eyes were intelligent— I could grudgingly admit that— and they were currently doing the same thing that mine were. Memorizing our surroundings, that is, not analyzing me. I chuckled to myself as I realized that if he was ever placed in a work of fiction, the fangirls would probably be likewise split, either in love with the fantasy of his appearance, or ripping him apart for seeming too perfect. *Too bad the looks and personality don't match.*

Conventionally attractive he might be, but he was also viciously competitive and extremely arrogant in that competitiveness. The competitiveness was a quality that could get us into trouble in the field, since it was something we shared. *Aw, you found common ground,* my inner voice reminded me. *Shut up,* I fired back. He had a slow temper, which meant he wasn't prone to overreacting, but his sharp tongue, so like my own, would be the source of too many arguments between us, if our workplace relationship was anything like it had been in school. He had a very dominant personality, but so did I. He wanted to be the best at what he did, but so did I. His strength was that he could lie and that he could fight; those would be useful in a partnership, especially in any physical altercations. I was strong, but I was under no illusion that I would have a size advantage if it came to combat. His skills would balance out my strengths in stealth and strategy. That would, of course, mean that he would be more likely to be taken out first in any sort of combat situation, but that would hopefully give me room to use the element of surprise.

I screeched to a halt, silencing my mental appraisal, when I realized that I had taken several steps forward on my own. Glancing backward, I saw Luke eyeing me with suspicion from in front of an inconspicuous door, whose pattern matched that of the walls. In fact, had it not been for the subtlety present brass-colored hinges, I wouldn't have noticed it at all.

"Forget where we were going?" Luke asked with a raised eyebrow.

"Of course not!" I shot back in annoyance. *Alright, adding that to the list of things I need to work on. Note to self: stop getting lost in thought.*

"Okay, well I guess we're here," he said, dropping the subject to my great surprise. He gestured to the panel door and then pulled a well-concealed handle, nodding for me to enter first. The politeness surprised me as well, but I chose not to comment on it as I strode inside, trying my hardest not to make eye contact. The inside layout was essentially what I would have expected, maybe a little more spacious. The interior design, however, was not. We had stepped into a small common area that held two desks, a small couch, and a small television mounted on one wall. A radio set sat on a side table, accompanied by two earpieces that I knew would be part of our everyday uniform moving forward. A royal blue rug, which somehow didn't overpower the room, covered most of the floor, and the wallpaper had changed inside to an alternating pattern of cream and gold. Luke let out a low whistle, and I couldn't bring myself to disagree with him; this was a step up from dorm life, there was no doubt about it.

"A little much for a security detail for a couple of kids, yeah?" I asked. "Not that I'm complaining." He nodded. The television was unexpected; I knew that neither of us had time to waste on that for a few years. Everything in us had been focused on progressing through the Academy. Pathetic, I know, but it had worked. *I guess it's important to know what's going on in the world now.* We were not cloistered at a school anymore; we had made it to the real world.

"Not bad," he allowed, stepping over to inspect the couch. I left him to it and meandered over to the door at the left side of the room, glancing toward its twin that was set opposite. Leaving Luke to examine the technology, I pushed open the door and was greeted by a fairly standard double bed with a nightstand and small desk lamp. My bags sat piled in one corner of the room—I guess I had chosen the right door— where a wardrobe loomed against one wall. To my surprise, there was also a small vanity, but I did not see anywhere that led to a bathroom. Surely, they didn't expect us to—

"First dibs on the bathroom in the mornings!" Luke called from the other room. *NO!* There was absolutely no way we were sharing a bathroom. That was unacceptable, borderline inappropriate, and honestly gross. I refused to take my showers with the Institutes newest man-candy graduate on the other side of the wall.

"Absolutely not," I answered flatly as I left my room. My horror must have shown, because in the next moment, Luke smirked again.

"Oh, please. Are you going to be the first one to complain to our new boss? Typical girl," he taunted. I knew he was baiting me, but I couldn't resist a retort.

"Sexist pig," I muttered, returning to my room and shutting the door against his laughter. He was right; I couldn't complain. All in all, our accommodations were more than adequate. We were lucky to have this job, and since the agents in our field were overwhelmingly male, I knew that the odds of any of my complaints being taken seriously would be slim. *Most dudes don't care about sharing a bathroom, Artemis. Get over it.* If I was going to be a professional, I would need to act as one unbothered. I took a moment to muster what was left of my dignity by unpacking. I had traveled light. I could have everything situated in half an hour, and there was no sense in spending any longer than that. I did just that. When I had finished, I glanced in the mirror, noting the way that my hair had started to frizz, so I procrastinated a few moments more to run a brush through it until I felt presentable. Then, taking a fortifying breath, I stalked back out into the common area, where Luke sat on the couch, leaned backward with his hands clasped behind his head to support it.

"We have a briefing to attend?" I asked acidly. Luke straightened and looked at me with wide eyes, as though I had startled him, before his face settled into its familiar lines.

"After you," he said politely, gesturing to the door once more. Without another word, I swept out of the room. He wasn't going to get to me again today. He wasn't!

CHAPTER 6

Ryder held the door for me as we stumbled over the threshold and into our suite, completely drunk on our own exhaustion. It had been a long day, so long that I didn't even have it in me to harass him for being nice to me. My head was spinning with so many names, codenames, locations the kids frequented, approved contacts, assignment details, and facts about The White House, that I couldn't differentiate between Oak and Maple—which were two of the codenames, in case that part was unclear. It was a wonder we'd been able to find the room again without getting lost, and it made my head spin to think that it was only that morning that we had been graduating from the Academy. I wondered briefly if Bonnie and Gwen's first days had been as eventful as mine. That train of thought jumped the tracks as Luke flopped down hard onto the couch. I winced as it made a loud squawk of protest; there was no telling how long the furniture had been here.

"Should be a fun assignment, don't you think? An involved one, if nothing else," Luke said. I raised an eyebrow in faint surprise. Luke Ryder was making casual conversation with me, like I was an actual person instead of just the nearest bear he could poke with a stick. *He* must *be tired.* I shrugged and pulled my hair out of its hair-tie, relaxing the tension in my shoulders as it fell around them.

"I'm surprised you'd think so. I always thought you would want something with a little more action," I answered honestly, sitting on the opposite end of the couch. For all that this job was a total honor, it was, in essence, babysitting two people our own age. He sat up and tilted his head to one side curiously.

"Seriously? What makes you think that?" The intensity of the curiosity in his eyes made me a bit uncomfortable, so I looked away as casually as I could manage.

"I don't know, really. You just always seemed like you wanted to be the hero of the Institute; I would've thought you'd thrive more on adrenaline. This job seems to be pretty straightforward; you might end up missing out on all the glory," I answered, feeling so self-conscious about revealing that I knew so much about him. Sure, we'd known each other for years, but that was as mortal enemies, and this was killing the act of absolute indifference that I had spent years cultivating.

"I mean, this job will have its moments, I'm sure. We're protecting high-value targets; I'm sure there'll be plenty of action, whether we like it or not." My eyes shot up to meet his, fully prepared to see some type of challenge given his disagreement. To my surprise, there was none. "Anyway, I'd much prefer this to dodging bullets every day for some nothing cause. This is the most high-profile job in the country," he added evenly. It hit me then that this was the longest we had gone without baiting one another since… well, ever.

"I guess you're right," I ventured. He blinked in apparent astonishment that we had agreed on something. "Pretty stiff bunch we're stuck with, though. I hope they're not always that formal." The group that had met us had been comprised of three men and one woman, all roughly the same age—older than us. They hadn't so much as cracked a smile when we had been introduced.

"They've probably seen stuff that we've only heard about. You know that most of them are former military, right?" he asked, lacking his usual air of condescension. *This is almost like talking to a real human being.*

"I figured," I answered simply, wondering how he had known. They certainly hadn't divulged anything about their pasts. Then again, it was not uncommon for members of the secret service to come from a military background; in fact, it usually helped speed along the application process for them. Regardless, the certainty with which he spoke was a little unnerving. Luke stared at me for a moment, his green eyes carefully contemplative before he rose suddenly to his feet.

"Wait here," he ordered. My feet twitched as I fought the urge to get up and follow him just to prove a point, but with a sigh of resignation, I flopped back onto the couch, leaning back and kicking my feet up on the coffee table. *If we're going to be living here, we might as well get comfortable,* I reasoned. Ryder returned with an unfamiliar manilla folder in his hand, and I sat up straight.

"What's that?" I asked, feeling suddenly guarded. He looked sheepish and looked down, seeming to suddenly find the object in his hands fascinating. I narrowed my eyes, my suspicions deepening.

"Before we left the Academy, before we came here, I mean, they gave this to me. I meant to pass it on to you, but things got a little chaotic once we left, and I…" he trailed off. By "they," I assumed he meant Agent Wilkerson.

"So, what you mean to say is that you withheld information from me because you were being an ass, and now you feel bad about it, so you're going to let me see what you were hiding?" I interrupted. Luke's eyes jumped up to meet mine, and he looked alarmed before he realized that I was only half-serious.

"Something like that," he admitted sheepishly, and I resisted the urge to laugh.

"Let's see it, then." I held out my hand, and my resistance cracked, allowing a laugh to escape. The corners of his mouth twitched, but his eyes stayed fixed on mine.

"Will you ever stop being so bossy?" he asked. I snorted again.

"Not likely." I whisked the folder out of his hands and sat back down, flipping through the files that were attached inside. Inside were general profiles of each of the agents I had met, as well as diagrams detailing the layout of The White House. *No wonder he'd seemed so self-assured.* He really was more cutthroat than I had given him credit for.

"We don't have to call them by their military rank. Last names will be fine… At least, that's what Agent Wilkerson told me before we left," he offered apologetically. At my questioning glance, he tensed defensively. "I asked," he added.

"I probably would have asked too if I would have *had the information,*" I emphasized, tossing my hair over one shoulder before settling back in. Luke fell silent, apparently having no further remarks. So, we would have Bryant, Katz, Jennings, and Welsch. That would be easy enough to remember. Katz was the one who had been the most welcoming, not that it was a high bar. Jennings and Welsch were the other two men. Bryant was the woman. Simple enough, right? Two former marines, one former soldier in the army, and one navy man. *Tremendous.* Given the titles of their past assignments, it seemed as though Ryder had been on to something when he had said he thought they'd seen combat before. Their record was impressive; clearly, they had earned President Boyle's good favor. *Where does that leave us in their minds?* We were essentially two children in comparison, our experience limited to simulations and exams.

I felt my eyelids growing heavier as I read, until they felt leaden. When I glanced up, Luke was picking at one of his cuticles. A curl of satisfaction twisted in my gut at the sight of him doing something so human. My lips parted as a massive yawn leaped from my mouth into existence, and I covered it casually with the back of my hand. I closed the folder smartly with a snap and extended it to him.

"All done?" he asked, eyeing me warily. I met his cool, green eyes with an even gaze of my own.

"For now. See you in the morning." I stood, trying not to think too hard about what had turned into a very unusual evening.

"See you in the morning," Luke answered somewhat belatedly as I shut my door. I quickly stripped out of my work clothes and changed into sweats and an oversized t-shirt, half-convinced that the last hour or so had been a dream. I planned to study this new turn of events when I had the time and energy, but for now, sleep was calling.

CHAPTER 7

Beep. Beep. Beep. I yawned myself awake as my alarm blared in my ear. Six a.m. had come far, far too quickly, and I felt considerably like the living dead. I got to my feet slowly, stretching out my tired muscles, and I stumbled out of the room and made my way toward the bathroom without checking what I was sure would be my absolutely terrifying appearance in my mirror. A groan ripped out of me as I leaned my forehead against the closed bathroom door; it was too early for this. As if the universe was conspiring to strengthen my misery, Ryder's head popped out of the bathroom door, annoyance plastered across his face, and I stumbled forward at the sudden lack of support. I scowled up at Luke to see that he was one of those people who could roll out of bed looking perfectly normal, while I was pretty much convinced that I resembled a gremlin. The realization did nothing to improve my mood.

"Can I help you?" he asked, sounding just as grouchy as I felt. Apparently, his morning appearance did not extend to his mood. I glowered at him, unamused.

"Was I bothering you?" I asked, trying my hardest

not to snap. His green eyes were narrowed, and there was a crease between them, as though he was agitated by the light. *I guess there's my answer,* I thought with a sigh.

"Are you ever not?" he grumbled in response. I rolled my eyes, the movement uncomfortable in their heavy sleepiness. *Guess the truce is over.* I shouldn't have been surprised it had only lasted the night. That was more civility than we'd had in years. *In all likelihood, I dreamed it,* I said to myself. That was really the only reasonable explanation for our mutual politeness the previous night.

"Just returning the favor," I snapped back before pushing past him and entering the bathroom, shoving his back to push him out of the room and snapping the door firmly shut. I placed my hands on the sides of the sink and leaned, looking close at the dark circles under my eyes. The effects of the previous day were obvious. *Stressful day much?* I definitely needed to look more put together before my workday officially began.

The water in the shower burned hot as it ran over my tired muscles, flooding the tub around my feet and putting life into my chilled limbs. Slowly, the pounding in my head had receded to a dull throb, then to a slight pinprick behind my eyes. It was still unpleasant, but it was manageable. If I could get my hands on some coffee, the day might actually be bearable. By the time I stepped out of the tub with a towel wrapped around my body, I was feeling much more collected. The towel was soft as it wicked the water off of my skin, and the trickle of water in the sink was satisfying as I wrung out my hair. I flipped my head over to towel-dry when a pounding at the door made me jump.

"Ow!" I cursed under my breath as my head cracked against the underside of the sink. *That piece of...*

"Are you done in there yet? I need to use the shower." Luke's voice was muffled but undoubtedly annoyed. I had woken up more fully. He, apparently, had not.

"What were you doing in here before?" I asked, startled.

"Seeing what you wanted," he replied.

"You should have gotten up earlier," I called back sweetly, pressing my face to the crack of the door. The booming contact of his fist against the door made me jump away.

"Says the one who literally pushed me out of the bathroom. Maybe I was trying to be a gentleman. Hurry *up*!" he growled back. I snorted; he'd be a gentleman when Hell froze over.

I grabbed my hairdryer and make-up bag out of the cabinet and stalked out of the bathroom with the towel held tightly around me. He chuckled as I passed, and I flicked my hair out of my face, showering him with water without a backward glance. By the spluttering noise he made, at least some of the drops had hit their target.

When I emerged from my room, hair smoothed straight and blouse crisp under a stiff blazer, I felt like I was five years older than I was. A pin held the front strand of my hair back, and my make-up was simple and understated, but it covered the signs of a late night. I opened my door, feeling much more poised, and I promptly ran directly into Luke.

"Excuse you," I said smartly, without looking up. He huffed, stepping slightly to the side so I could get by.

"Why do you look thirty?" A glance backward showed that he was wearing khakis and a polo. It was a little more casual than what I was wearing, but the slight stubble that shadowed his cheeks helped him to look his age.

"Why do you look like you're pledging a frat? And why were you lurking outside my door?" I asked, looking him up and down with a smirk. He frowned.

"It pays to look professional, Ryder. Are you ready to go?"

"I was about to ask you the same question," he muttered, plainly intending to ignore my other two questions. I shrugged, grabbing the bag I had tossed on the coffee table the night before.

"I guess you have your answer, then." My low heels clicked softly against the tile as I crossed to open the door and exit into the hallway. I was conscious of Ryder lengthening his stride to catch up, and I slowed to match our steps. I was content in silence. It was a nice change for us to not have to struggle to make civil conversation or argue. Personally, I also thought it made us seem self-important, and one of the many workers of the White House even head-nodded as he passed. *See, Ryder. There really is something to looking professional.* A glance out of the side of my eye showed his hair curling slightly at his scalp as it dried. *Men have all the luck,* I thought grouchily as we rounded a corner. Apparently, every member of the male species could shower and be ready to go within minutes; it was markedly unfair. A shadow of movement caught in my peripheral vision, and I spun, immediately defensive. A door shut behind one of the men from last night as he exited and met my gaze, and I relaxed.

"Agent Ryder. Miss Richards. I presume you looked over the agenda we gave you last night." I rankled at the blatant difference in title as my mind searched furiously for his name. He was a tall, wiry sort of man with a receding hairline of reddish-brown. His eyes seemed to bore into me as I fought to remember which one he was. Apparently, Ryder sensed me struggling beside him because he responded for the both of us.

"Thank you, Agent Jennings," he answered smoothly. I breathed a sigh of relief, thankful for Luke Ryder for what might have been the first time in my life. "We did. We'll be glad to accompany the family to the museum this morning." I may have looked the part, but I was at a loss this morning— not that Luke or our superiors needed to know that.

"You two will meet Oak and Poplar over by the East Wing. I will meet you four later with Birch and Maple. You'll have to occupy yourselves until we get over there. Think you two can manage that?" I bristled at the implication in his tone, but Luke's voice was steady as he replied.

"I think we'll manage," he answered dryly. I forced myself to swallow the words I wanted to throw back in Jennings's face. It was only our second day; it was too soon to be bickering with our coworkers. *Plus, it's not as though you've done anything to inspire their confidence in the field yet.* A smirk twitched on Jennings's thin lips before he simply inclined his head and moved away. Luke didn't hesitate before turning back and continuing down our path. I turned to follow him and had a moment to wonder why being around me seemed to instigate more conflict with him than someone outright doubting his abilities as an agent before a hand caught my arm and spun me back around. I was startled as I turned to face Jennings, who looked down upon me with hard, blue eyes. I tried to yank my arm away, but his grip was like iron.

"I hope you understand that this isn't some game. Their lives are worth twelve of yours." Jennings's voice had lowered, but it didn't take away from the menacing nature of tone. If anything, it added to it.

"Excuse me?" I asked haughtily. His eyes hardened even more, a dangerous warning light flashing in them now.

"I hope you know what you signed up for." He slung my arm away before spinning around and stalking away before I could remind him that we had been hand-picked by President Boyle himself. I cast a look at his retreating form, his shoulders tight and proud, before wheeling around and hurrying to where Luke stood waiting. His jaw was tight as he stared at the place where Jennings had disappeared into another hallway.

"What did he say to you?" he asked. I glanced cautiously up at him, but aside from the muscle ticking slightly in his jaw, his face gave away nothing.

"Nothing important. Just wishing us luck on our first day." I managed to keep my voice from shaking, and I resisted the urge to rub the spot where my arm was still struggling in its return to normal circulation. We would need all the luck we could get if everyone was that welcoming. It was only my second day, and I already had a new enemy. *Welcome to Washington, the land where friends and foes usually wind up playing for the same team.*

CHAPTER 8

It was not entirely unrelated to the doubts of the older agents that I was tapping my foot anxiously as I checked my watch. We were positioned, waiting exactly where we were supposed to be, and the ever-responsible First Kids were late. We'd never been given a specific time—at least, I had not. There was no telling what had been told to Luke and then not communicated to me, so maybe he knew more; that seemed to be the running theme. I stole a glance in his direction, but he was leaning passively against the wall, looking infuriatingly unbothered.

"Are you *sure* we're in the right place?" I asked for what was probably the fourth or fifth time. Luke heaved a sigh and peeled himself from the wall.

"Yes, Blythe. For the sixth time, we are in the right place," he replied exasperatedly. I screwed up my nose at the sound of the first name. He had known me since our first day at the Academy, and yet he continued to call me Blythe whenever he felt like it. *No better way to kill time than to try and figure out why.*

"Why do you keep calling me that?" I asked curiously, thankful for the opportunity to take my mind off of my present anxiety. He looked a bit taken aback, but that was quickly erased by a smirk as he lifted his shoulders in a shrug.

"I mean, it's your name, so…" he trailed off, raising an eyebrow before looking away from me and out into the museum crowd. Probably to his dismay, I did not let the issue rest.

"I mean, not really. I've gone by 'Artemis' since I was six. You've known that for years, so what gives?" I crossed my arms and leaned against the wall beside him. He leaned closer to me, and I could almost feel his breath on my face. I stiffened, not quite sure what to expect from him next.

"Maybe that's your problem," he murmured. Now it was my turn to raise an eyebrow.

"What, your morning breath?" I asked in a determinedly normal volume.

"That you let a six-year-old-choose your name." He yelped as I swatted him with the back of my hand. *Rude*, I thought as I narrowed my eyes at him, turning pointedly away. *I don't know why I bothered.* Still, the comment stung a little bit. I liked my name; I felt like it suited me. It was different, sure, or original—as I liked to think of it. *Perhaps a little bit too dramatic?* I snorted at the thought, making Luke jump at the sound. I ignored his wary look. Honestly, I couldn't pinpoint a reason why I hated my first name so much; I simply liked my middle name better. There was no harm in that, and I wasn't sure why it was always such a big deal. Plenty of people went by their middle names.

"Could be worse, I guess. I could have a boring personality *and* a boring name. But I guess you've got that handled." My retort was muttered and very late, and I guess it was not much of a comeback, but I was determined to have the last word all the same. I pretended not to notice as I heard Luke let out a laugh.

"You seem entertained enough," he fired back. I ignored that.

I was almost relieved when I heard footsteps

approaching. *Thank God.* The last thing we needed was to run late because the Boyle kids couldn't stop staring at themselves in the mirror. Sara's auburn hair was curled neatly around her face, emphasizing the misleading sweetness in her cheeks and framing the spark of life that flickered in her bright, blue eyes. I quickly took in her outfit to assess what we would be working with if some sort of threat presented itself. *Ah, classic,* I thought scathingly, taking in the icepick heels, which were just high enough to raise a few eyebrows regarding their appropriateness. Her simple blue dress, however, was the picture of patriotic modesty, right down to the American flag she'd thought to pin on the lapel of her black blazer. *The campaign knows no rest.* Her eyes rested on Luke, but I didn't turn to see his reaction, as I shifted my gaze to size up Jesse's attire.

He had cleaned up nicely too; his blond hair laid flat against his forehead, much different from the dancing strands that had seemed to have a life of their own when we'd met him. His suit was well-tailored and slim-fit, and his shoes were undoubtedly made of some kind of expensive, foreign leather, as befitted the son of a politician. *And I'm sure the soles are just as slippery.* At least he seemed as though he would be in a better position to flee if any situations arose. *That's more than his sister can say.*

"I'm glad you decided to join us." Luke's gruff tone of voice surprised me, and as I glanced curiously at him, it was all I could do to mask it. Sara blinked several times, clearly taken aback, if the wounded expression on her face was anything to judge by. I pressed my lips together to hide my smile; she'd met him *once*; surely, she couldn't be that affected by his tone—unless her "charms" had never gone so unrecognized before. *Good luck with that. The only charm Ryder cares about is his own.*

"Sorry, we got held up," Jesse answered mildly. I

kept my mouth shut, and I hoped that Luke was wise enough to do the same. We were already late, and I knew that Jennings would be watching our every move, waiting to criticize us—well, me.

"We have a car waiting." The president and first lady were meeting us at the museum.

"I'm sure we won't be too late; we'll just have to move quickly," I added, eyeing Sara's heels skeptically. I chose not to make a more specific comment on that, mentally patting myself on the back for my self-control.

"They'll wait for us," Sara said haughtily. I personally thought her line of thinking was a bit entitled, since the only attendants who *really* mattered were her parents. From the tight look of Luke's jaw, I had a hunch that his thoughts on the subject were similar.

"Let's hope." Privately hoping the rest of the walk would be silent, I led the way. We had a job to do, and we could not afford any more delays.

CHAPTER 9

It was a struggle to maintain the appearance of attentiveness through the entire ceremony at the museum. I wasn't even sure why the First Family was there, other than that President Boyle was recognizing some sort of something. I had always been a closet fan of history, but whoever thought it was a good idea to invite the windbag currently recounting the history of every single stone in the establishment needed a stern talking-to before their next event. Fortunately, it wasn't my job to pay attention to the introductory remarks. My eyes scanned the crowd of people, watching for any sign of suspicious movement. There was none to be found.

"It is with perseverance that we press onward, toward the preservation of history. Knowledge is the one thing that can escape the ravages of time, and it is our solemn duty to maintain these artifacts to cultivate this knowledge for future generations," the speaker continued, and I studied the way that his white hair fell in thin wisps across his forehead, giving him the appearance of a windblown dandelion. President Boyle's permafrost smile was perfectly white as he maintained his politely attentive expression, and I wondered at the fact that he seemed to be hanging on to every word of this long-winded introduction. From behind him, Sara was staring out at the crowd, and Jesse was fidgeting—presumably because he was spending longer than five minutes without looking at his phone. Mrs. Boyle seemed as attentive as her husband, drinking in every word. Sara shifted from foot-to-foot tentatively, and I figured she must be regretting her shoe choice. I had been surprised that they hadn't offered the family chairs, but who was I to question how they chose to coordinate events. I reached behind my head to tighten my ponytail, suddenly grateful that my job allowed me the luxury of comfort in these types of situations.

"The pains and sufferings of the past must never be forgotten…" the man droned on. I glanced at Luke, who stood opposite me and was surveying the crowd with a stern expression on his face. He looked as though he was daring anyone from the crowd to try something, and even I had to admit that he cut an intimidating figure. Maybe not as intimidating as others on our team, but enough. My eyes flicked across the crowd again toward the exit on our left, stopping suddenly as a quick flash of movement caught my eye. I relaxed when I saw that it was just a member of the audience stifling a sneeze. *I guess I should be thankful that nothing exciting is happening. First real day on the job and all*, I thought. Not to mention the fact that my job had a very human element to it. Still, I felt unsettled, despite the numerous levels of security on site. Every member of the audience had been subject to some degree of security check. I couldn't put my finger on what was troubling me, but something felt wrong.

"…now my great pleasure to relinquish the stage and welcome our very own President Joseph A. Boyle," the old man finished. *Finally*. There was a smattering of polite applause as the president moved from his position with his family toward the available microphone. I tensed as I zeroed in on a member of the audience who stood up quickly, but I relaxed slightly as I realized that he was just giving an enthusiastic standing ovation. *Mid-twenties, brown hair, wire-rimmed specs, overly enthusiastic, and definitely wearing—* I squinted—*eyeliner?* I took note of the white press pass clipped to his lapel. *Fanboy reporter,* I recognized. I glanced at Boyle as he waited for the applause to die down. Apparently in this setting, he was among supporters and friends. Still, something felt off, and I still could not quite figure out what it was. *First day jitters?* Maybe, but it felt like more.

"Remembering our history plays a crucial role in preserving the ideals of any republic. As such, it is my true honor to be with all of you as we celebrate the preservation of our very own history today." I tilted my head to see Luke watching the president with admiration in his eyes. *Careful, Ryder; we wouldn't want to get distracted on the job.*

Apparently, I still needed to work on my skills of telepathy, because Luke rudely ignored my silent taunt. It didn't matter; I could—and would—poke fun at him later. I refocused on the kid reporter, who was taking notes furiously. *Nothing out of the ordinary there.* And there wasn't, until I realized that his eyes were flicking between me and Luke before he returned to scribbling. *Odd.* I had thought we were far enough away to have to significance of a decorative plant, but plainly this guy was taking notice. *Perhaps not, then.* The man behind him leaned up slowly and whispered something in Boy Wonder's ear, and I stole another quick glance at Luke, who still seemed entranced by Boyle's speech. I stared hard at him for a few heartbeats, willing him with every fiber of my being to meet my eyes. It could be nothing, but then again, maybe not. To my relief, he seemed to feel my eyes burning holes in his flesh, because his own eyes jumped to meet mine, wide and startled. I tilted my head subtlety in the direction of the reporter and his *friend*, but the other man had already returned to the appearance of intent listening. Luke's eyes met mine again, and I could read the question in them. I glanced back to see that the reporter had a far less convincing poker face than his companion. Moisture glistened on his forehead, giving it enough of a shine that I could see it clearly even from my distance away. I turned back to face Luke, who had followed my gaze. *Keep an eye on them,* I mouthed silently, and he nodded, returning his attention to the crowd. I stole a glance back toward Jesse and Sara, who were watching their father with identical expressions of respectful interest, and I calculated how long it would take for us to reach them and then make for an exit if my suspicions were correct. Our odds weren't my favorite, since we were separated, but they were not as poor as they could have been. There were other members of our little band closer to the family, but their primary objective in the event of an attack was to protect the president. Only one was assigned to his wife, leaving Luke and I to look after Sara and Jesse. *Definitely not the best odds.*

My eyes snapped back toward the reporter in time to see the man behind him rise and slip through the crowd like a serpent in water. He passed through without creating more than the slightest ripple, and he exited through one of the side doors, rather than the main one. Boyle was wrapping up his speech; there was no reason that the man couldn't have stayed until the end. *Maybe he had something personal going on. Life does happen to normal humans, you know. Not everything is a conspiracy,* I scolded myself. Somehow, I still had a sneaking suspicion that this was, although that suspicion made me nervous; being paranoid was a good way to make Luke and I both look foolish.

The wide, gold ribbon stretching across the stage behind where the president had spoken was snipped with a large, ornamental pair of scissors, and I stood on edge as the camera bulbs flashed closer and brighter. *That's right; it's a reopening.* I was grateful for the fact that Jennings was enforcing the distance they were required to maintain, but the media members were, as usual, pushing their luck and pushing closer as they did. It was almost a relief when I saw Katz approach the children and slip away, toward where I stood. I glanced over to where Luke had been stationed, and I strained my eyes to see that he had disappeared. I forced myself not to jump as I saw him materialize beside me. *He's quick.* It did not take very long for Katz to join us with Jesse and Sara in tow.

"The first lady has elected to remain with the president until publicity photos are taken. She asked that you two escort Jesse and Sara back home." His voice was low, despite the fact that there was no one else within earshot.

"The car?" Luke asked.

"Will be waiting for you out one of the side doors," he gestured to one, thankfully not the one through which the suspicious man had disappeared. "Keep an eye out when you go. We had several audience members leave early, and I don't want the kids to be harassed or have any surprises. Got it?" Katz asked briskly.

"Affirmative. We'll be careful," I answered, matching his brisk tone of voice.

"We'll have decoy vehicles idling outside of the other doors, but to leave any vehicle idling for too long goes against protocol. It looks suspicious. Anyone who's done their research—or quite frankly, who has common sense— will know that, so don't look rushed, but be quick about it."

"Yes, sir," Luke answered.

I had always trained for scenarios in which the number on the security team would outnumber the protected. That's not to say that I did not prepare for scenarios in which that was not the case, but it did mean that I would have to adapt. We would, I mean.

"I'll take point," Luke and I said together, drawing an amused look from Jesse and an eyeroll from Sara.

"I'm stronger than you. If you're on point and get knocked out, I'll be short of backup," he said stubbornly. I rolled my eyes. "Plus, I'm bigger; I can help obstruct their view of the—" The last was a feeble attempt, and he had to know it.

"Nice try, Ryder, but it'll be easier for you to fight off an attack from behind. Plus, if they're occupied knocking me out, that'll give you time to try to do something useful. I'm taking point." Luke opened and shut his mouth, but no words came out. I waited a beat to see if there was an argument, eyebrows raised expectantly, and when he did not respond, I started off in the direction of the side door, setting a kind of mantra as I went.

Confident. Purposeful. Confident. Purposeful. I willed my steps to match the words. The words beat a pattern through my brain as we made our way down the hallway together. I took note of possible surprise points of entry—windows and closed doors. Threats could come from anywhere. As the thought hit me, so did the door to my left, and I narrowly avoided being knocked to the ground as I came face-to-face with a startled employee, who seemed very irritated at the interruption.

What are you doing?" he demanded, looking down on me, "Get out of the way, you're not supposed to be—" His face paled as he took in the two kids. Luke shifted in front of them and crossed his arms, and the man took several steps backward at the sight of his menacing expression.

"Oh. So sorry," he squeaked. The now nervous-looking man ducked back inside, and we resumed our walk at a faster temp. I increased the pace further, still feeling edgy. *The sooner we reach the car, the sooner I'll be—*

The thought was cut off as we rounded another corner. Strong hands grabbed me and yanked me through a door, and I felt my assailant's arms snake their way around my chest as their hands wound upward toward my throat. *Great. Now what?*

CHAPTER 10

"Oh. So sorry." The slight, balding man in the museum uniform slipped back into the door he'd come out of, and Luke let his hardened expression relax. *Richards has been so edgy today. It must be getting to me.* Determined to stop feeding off of her energy, Luke watched the closed door for a moment more before swiveling his eyes back to the front of their group. He was just in time to see Artemis disappear around the corner. *Shit.* He grabbed Jesse and Sara by the shoulders and forced them against the wall.

"Stay," Luke ordered roughly, drawing an appalled look from Sara as he shook their shoulders for emphasis.

"But—" she stuttered, but Luke silenced her with a hard look.

"Stay," he repeated, thinking quickly. *No guns unless you have to; they draw too much attention.* He withdrew a knife from the pocket of his pants and started forward before pausing. *Finish the mission at all costs.* The words of one of his mentors came unbidden to his mind, and Luke hesitated. That was the point of working in teams, so the mission would be complete. Luke stood still for a moment of contemplation before he shook it off. Whoever Blythe's— *damn it, ARTEMIS'S*— attacker was would be in his way anyway, and Luke had no way of knowing if there were more. She was his partner, and she needed help.

* * *

I felt the thickly muscled arms snake their way upward toward my neck, and I tucked my chin down, pressing it as far into my chest as I could manage. *Amateur*, I thought smugly, twisting violently to extricate an arm before I saw that one of the hands had a handkerchief in it and was moving steadily toward my face. *Okay, maybe not so much.*

More frantic now, but trying hard not to act like it, I took a deep breath and jerked hard to the left in one swift motion, praying that my guess as to my attacker's weak side had been correct. His hold on me loosened as he fought for balance, and I dropped into a crouch, taking him to the ground with me as I hunched to absorb the impact of his weight. I dodged at the last minute as he collapsed, enjoying the heavy thud that was his head slamming into the trim lining one wall. I spun, ripping one ankle away from his grasping reach as Luke exploded into the room, knife drawn. *Idiot. We have guns for a reason.* Firearms weren't technically allowed on the premises, but like with most things, there were loopholes where the government was involved, especially when it came to jobs like ours.

"About time you showed up," I managed, chest heaving as I fought to catch my breath. "Scratch that, what are you doing here? Where are the kids?" The irony of calling our wards kids when they were nearly our age was not lost on me in the moment; in fact, it seemed especially funny with the added boost of adrenaline. I crept up to the open door and looked up and down the hallway. There were no doors between us and our planned exit. We would need to hurry before whomever else was behind this figured out that their first attempt at whatever this was had been woefully unsuccessful.

"Are you okay?" Luke probed, and I shook him off, shouldering past him to survey my attacker, who was looking up at us with dazed eyes. *Black hair, thinner on top. Wide blue eyes. Gaged ears.* I had a sudden burst of ferocity in which I fantasized about grasping each of the holes and tearing through them to further incapacitate him, but I pushed away the urge. This was neither the time nor the place for revenge fantasies. I settled for rendering him unconscious, putting just the right pressure at just the right angle on just the right artery, and—

"Oh my god." Sara's voice made me turn my head. She and Jesse were staring down at where I held the man with horror. I breathed a sigh of relief as I felt him slump, and I stood, rolling him away from me as I dusted off my hands. To my further relief, there was no recognition on either of their faces. That meant that it wasn't an inside job... *that we know of.*

"I take it you don't know who this is?" I asked. They shook their heads in unison. Sara looked as though tears might spill onto her cheeks at any moment, and Jesse looked to be caught somewhere between nausea and respect. "Grand. We can leave this mess for the rest of the force to handle. Right now, we need to get you both out of here before any friends he may have had figure out what's happened."

"We are *not* splitting up to let them know what happened, and we can't chance walking back," Luke countered argumentatively, and I stared at him. *Has he lost his mind?*

"Radios. Ryder, did you forget we have radios?" he stared dumbly at me for a couple of heartbeats, confusion swimming across his face before awareness dawned on him. He reached into his pocket, gesturing for Jesse and Sara to move in closer and away from their exposed position near the door.

"Katz, Jennings? We had a situation in transit.... Yes, it's been handled, but we can't manage clean-up.... No, not a huge mess, but too much for us to deal with. Should we wait with the subject...? Yes, he's conscious—err he was." Luke finished, and I rolled my eyes. Ignoring his attempts to get my attention, I stepped over to where the handkerchief had fluttered to a rest on the floor. I picked it up and gave it a whiff from afar. I wrinkled my nose, holding it out from me like it was contaminated, which—naturally— it was. *Chloroform*. Rage, white-hot, shot through me, and I approached the man, seized with the desperate urge to stuff the rag down his throat. I shot a quick glance at Sara's glistening eyes and figured such ruthlessness was better suited for a different audience, so I let it flutter to the door instead.

"Alright, we'll continue transport and debrief later. Uh-huh. Ten-four." I reached my hands into the man's pockets, not stepping back as Luke replaced the radio in his pocket.

"We should go," Sara's voice was small, and it shook, but somehow, she maintained her imperious tone. *Masking fear, overcompensation. Classic coping mechanism.* I didn't blame her really, given the circumstances, but that did not mean that I was going to listen. She huffed after several seconds of my non responsiveness, and I wrinkled my nose as I tried to roll the guy over to search his pants pockets. Unfortunately, he weighed a bit more than I had anticipated.

"A little help?" I grunted to Luke, who was watching me silently. At my words, he jumped and crouched, and the effect was nearly instantaneous.

"What are you doing?" Jesse asked incredulously.

"Searching for ID in case he wakes up and disappears," I answered casually, tightening my lips with a sort of grim satisfaction as I pulled out a wallet.

Definitely an amateur. Carrying identification was a good way to get your known associates caught, and yourself, of course. Anyone with any sort of experience in this world would know that.

"Just take it with you; we need to go." I knew that Luke was growing impatient, but I ignored him. I flipped open the wallet and slid out a license, examining the edges and tilting it at different angles in the light to check for imperfections to make sure it was real. *Bingo.*

"Donald Baker. Hmm." I whipped out my cell phone and snapped a picture of the license. *Could be an alias, but it's worth having just in case*, I thought before replacing the wallet and rolling good ole Donny-boy back into his original position. *There, now he'll never know he was searched.* I stood, grimacing as one of my knees popped. *I'm too young to feel this old.*

"Can we go now?" Sara's voice caught, and I knew that she was genuinely on the verge of panic now. I replaced my phone and nodded.

"Probably for the best," I replied shortly, returning to my position at the head of the group. Luke's face twitched, and I could tell that he disagreed with me taking point again, but that would be a discussion for another time. For now, we were out of time and needed to move; we had wasted enough precious minutes already.

I was still on edge as we continued down the hallway, and my heartbeat beat a staccato echo in my ears. Our footsteps seemed to reach new decibels in the relative silence, but I forced the tension from my shoulders as we reached the door. I brushed my fingertips lightly against the gun strapped hidden in its holster, and I resisted the urge to pull it out and have it at the ready. Instead, I carefully pushed open the door and surveyed our exit point before waving Luke, Jesse, and Sara through. A slick black car was waiting for us, and I nearly jumped into the offensive as the passenger side window rolled down. Before I could do too much damage, however, I recognized the face of the driver as the one who had brought us to the museum. This was no fake; this was our ride. I started forward again, but Jesse and Sara nearly collided with my back as I stopped short as I realized that Luke had not followed, and he was—in fact—still staring back the way we had come.

"Ryder," I barked sternly. He jumped and turned to face me.

"A couple of guys headed down the hall," he said, nodding. My hand twitched toward my gun, and my heart froze for a beat before it thudded to life again.

"Fortunately, we have a car literally twenty feet from us, so if you'll kindly *move*, we can be out of this mess. Eyes on the mission, Ryder. They are not our problem." He seemed to debate with himself for half a beat before he stepped away from the door and followed. *How much further have they gotten since we wasted time?* I withdrew the gun from its holster now, holding it low as we approached the car. The area around it was almost suspiciously free of any unwelcome company, which made sense if the unwelcome company was still at our back. I did not question it further as I blocked the view of Jesse and Sara while they slid into the back seat. *Guess they couldn't cover all of the exits? Or they had too much confidence in their man.* Which meant either that it wasn't a large operation or that they received faulty intel and were too confident to calculate a backup plan. *Either way, I'm not complaining.*

I ducked into the back seat and let Luke take shotgun.

"Drive. *Quickly,*" Luke ordered. I glanced out the window to see two men rush through the door and look around wildly before zeroing in on our car. *Tall. One lanky, one muscular. Dark hair, pale skin. Arm tattoo.* The tires screeched dramatically as we sped away from the museum building, and I watched the scenery blur around us as we merged onto a main road and blended into traffic. I wondered briefly whether our excitement meant that President Boyle's day would have been cut short. *Definitely.* I reached up to brush a strand of my hair out of my face, glancing down as a flicker of purple caught my eye. Focusing in, I saw the bloom of fresh bruises on my wrist, contrasting with the white of my skin. Self-conscious, I glanced over at Sara and Jesse before nonchalantly pulling down the sleeves of my blazer, aware of the throbbing sensation beneath the bruises as my knuckles brushed over them. *Ow.* I would be sore tomorrow. *Still less painful than the meetings we're about to have will be.* I groaned inwardly as we wound our way back toward Pennsylvania Avenue. It was going to be another long night.

CHAPTER 11

We exited the car silently, all of us on edge as we moved toward the door. We were silent aside from the clicking of Sara's heels, which she seemed to be regretting if the way she kept pausing to tug on the strap was anything to judge by. She also seemed to be struggling to maintain her composure; she was still visibly shaking, and she pressed close to Luke, casting nervous glances around her as they went. Jesse was more casual, but I could see the wariness in his eyes as he swept his eyes back and forth across the entrance, looking a bit like a cornered cat. I wondered briefly if this was the first time that they had ever faced a direct threat. *There are snipers on the roof; no one will be able to get within more than a hundred feet of you.* I still felt blissfully numb as we escorted the kids inside and then through the halls toward Jesse's room. *You have* got *to stop thinking of them as kids. Charges, sure, or wards, but they're not that much younger than you.* Admittedly, Sara's wide-eyed stare up at Ryder made her look younger than she was. Luke's stiffened shoulders showed that he was still on edge, which was likely not doing much to reassure Sara that all was well now that we were safely inside.

We arrived in front of Jesse's door, and Sara turned again to face Luke with hero-worship in her eyes. I resisted the urge to roll my eyes. After all, it wasn't as though *he* had been yanked into a room and nearly rendered unconscious. I immediately felt guilty as I remembered the way that he had been willing to rush into my aid. *Not bad for a sworn enemy.* Apparently, Luke's loyalty to our team had beaten out his vehement dislike of me, if only for a moment.

"You aren't leaving, are you?" The plea in Sara's voice was obvious, but the surprise on Luke's face was—if possible—more so. I was also a bit taken aback by the open desperation in her tone; it didn't seem like something that would be her style. Then again, she *had* just had a big scare. Luke turned his head and glanced at me thoughtfully.

"No," he said decidedly, "we should probably stay until someone can take over for us. At least until we have more of an understanding of what happened," he added as an afterthought. Sara's shoulders relaxed for a moment before she straightened up again.

"Should we split up? That way, if someone gets in, they can't get to both of us at once," she suggested, looking hopeful. *Don't push it, princess,* I thought, annoyed at being told how I should do my job. To my further annoyance, Luke tilted his head in consideration.

"Absolutely not. *If* someone does get in here, which is unlikely, we're better off together. Four instead of two," I replied. Sara rounded on me with a frosty look.

"I'm sorry, are you assuming *we'd* be fighting? I thought that's what you were trained for. That's why there's one of you for each of us, right?" she asked condescendingly. My annoyance surged into irritation, and I fought to stay calm, reminding myself that we had all had a trying day.

"I would hope that if you were targeted, you would

care enough about your own life to fight back, but you're right about the rest," I answered. I brushed past her to open Jesse's door and step inside. These weren't the kinds of conversations that should be had out in the hallway for all ears to hear. To my relief, Jesse followed me, chuckling as he passed his sister. *At least it's not just me that thinks she's ridiculous.* Sara's voice set my teeth on edge as she refused to let the matter rest.

"Then why should we just sit here and wait for them to find us? It makes more sense to split up." I further resisted the urge to make a biting retort. "Don't you think so, Luke?" I gritted my teeth, silently daring him to disagree.

"In theory, yes, but—" Luke began.

"See? Luke thinks so!" Sara cut across him triumphantly. I inhaled and exhaled slowly before turning around.

"I'm pretty sure I heard a 'but' in there," I replied.

"But *Luke* said—"

"Sara, would you shut up?" Jesse interjected. "Two people trained in this sort of thing stand a better chance than just one." The annoyance was ripe in his voice.

"Don't start pretending you understand everything, Jesse," she snapped, rounding on her brother. I shot Luke a helpless look, and he ushered Sara inside before shutting the door behind him. Sara seemed not to notice the change of scenery.

"I understand basic math, which you flunked last year," he shot back. I shouldered my way between them as Sara took a step at her brother.

"You both need to calm down," I warned.

"Like you know anything," Sara snipped. I pursed my lips and blinked at the complete lack of logic in her statement, but she had already turned back toward her brother. "Some of us have better things to focus on. Like, some of us have people who actually want to spend time with us; not all of us have to rely on the internet for friends," she snapped at him, the fire building in her eyes.

"It's no secret how *you* spend your time," Jesse answered coldly. "Some of us just have standards." Sara moved to stand nose-to-nose with her brother, and I wedged my way further between them, looking helplessly at Luke.

"*Enough!*" Luke's voice rose over the squabble, and the words trying to force their way out of my throat died. Sara's eyes filled as she turned to face him, and I stared at her, completely out of my depth. *Seriously?*

"I'm sorry. It was just *scary*, you know? They could have killed us or taken us or done who knows what." Jesse was staring at the ground now, and it was obvious that he was still rattled too. It probably shouldn't have startled me when Sara burst into tears, but I still jumped in alarm. Sobbing, she collapsed into Luke, and it was his turn to look helpless. I held up my hands and backed away, and he awkwardly patted her on the back as he realized that he was on his own with that one.

"It's okay, you're safe," he soothed. Despite clearly feeling out of his depth, Luke's voice was a reassuring tone that I had never heard from him before. He let her sob into his chest for several moments, and I stared. *When did Luke become such a compassionate person?* I glanced at Jesse, whose face was colored with second-hand embarrassment.

"Should we...?" He gestured vaguely to the still-open door.

"Probably," I agreed and moved to shut it. Luke was still comforting Sara when I returned my focus to that train-wreck of a situation.

"That's why we're going to stick together, okay? They won't hurt you," Luke murmured to Sara, and in the next moment, she raised her head. Somehow, she was one of those people who managed to look perfect even with mascara streaking down her face. *Because of course she is,* I thought with resignation.

"Okay… I trust you. I'm sorry I'm such a mess," she chuckled in a watery sort of way. I pursed my lips. *Heaven help us.*

"You look fine," I offered helpfully, trying to mend the rift and rise above my earlier annoyance. My heart rate had returned to normal, but I still felt jumpy, and that was dangerous. Post-incident adrenaline rushes always left me feeling shaky, and it was a problem. It would be better to keep us all calm—or as calm as possible—moving forward. Sara gave me a small smile, which I returned.

"Thanks. I guess it was pretty badass the way you guys took down that guy." My pride warred with my commitment to calm for a moment before I released it.

I replied with only a small sigh. Luke looked at me in surprise, but I ignored it. He owed me one, but setting the record straight would just cause more problems. Not wanting to dwell on it, I changed the subject.

"Now, why don't we spend some time getting to know each other. We're going to be spending a lot of time together, so it makes sense that we…"

Nearly two hours passed before we finally heard a knock at the door. Luke and I exchanged a wordless glance, rising at the same time. I nodded at him, gesturing for Jesse and Sara to step out of the line of sight of the door as Luke approached it and opened it cautiously. He exchanged a few words with the rumbling voice of another man outside before stepping away to let them in. It was Welsch, accompanied by Bryant. The woman glanced between our charges, her tightly coiled, black curls bouncing as she gave the kids—sorry, Jesse and Sara— a quick once over before approaching me. Welsch stayed several steps behind, eyes flicking over us warily as he ran a hand through his hair.

"We're here to relieve you two. You're to go meet Katz and Jennings and explain what happened in more detail," she explained. She was matter-of fact as she crossed her arms, and I appreciated the no-nonsense tone after several hours with the First Kids.

"Did you get the guy?" I asked. She snorted, one of her deep brown cheeks dimpling with a small smile.

"It was too easy. He was still groggy when we got there." I felt a rush of relief and nodded before going to stand near Luke. Welsch was giving him instructions, and I had missed out on enough information in this job without missing out on more. Welsch gave me a nod of acknowledgement as I approached, without breaking his monologue, but I saw something like respect in the gesture.

"You guys good?" he asked once he had finished his instructions. Luke looked to me, and I inclined my head. "Excellent. Go debrief, and then go get some rest. You both have earned it."

* * *

"Are you okay?" Luke asked once we had returned to our suite. We were flopped on the couch, completely spent after hours of telling and retelling (and re-retelling) the sequence of events from the day.

"I'll live," I shrugged, shuddering slightly as a memory of the man's hands snaking toward my throat flashed in my mind.

"You did well today," he said awkwardly, not meeting my eyes. *A compliment? From Luke Ryder?* I sat up straight for a moment before leaning toward him suspiciously.

"What's wrong?" I normally wouldn't care to ask, but seeing as how we were supposed to be a team and all now, I guess I had to care. He still did not meet my eyes, and he seemed to wrestle with himself briefly before he answered.

"I should have taken point," he said finally. He looked up, and there was a line of worry creasing the space between his eyes. Is that…guilt? A sense of responsibility and consideration toward me? From Luke?!

"Careful, Ryder; I'll think you were worried about me," I teased, trying to lighten the mood. He did not take the bait.

"It was an error in tactical judgment," he said a bit stiffly, looking away again. I immediately dropped the front and scooted closer to look into his face once more, and his eyes met mine.

"Seriously, it's fine. I had it handled, and it made the most sense. It was better for the mission at hand. Things happen in this line of work, Luke; that doesn't mean we made a mistake," I said in what I hoped was a reassuring tone. At the mention of the mission, he looked away again.

"I guess." I thought about asking him again why he had come after me instead of staying with Sara and Jesse, but I didn't want to come anywhere near that can of worms when we were so tired. He already feels like he made a bad judgment call. That'll just make it worse. I also wasn't in the mood—probably for the first time with Luke—to argue. I hesitated, searching for the right thing to say as I laid a hand on his forearm to reclaim his attention. He glanced up on me in surprise, but I didn't remove it.

"It's seriously fine, Ryder. You don't have to worry about me or what happened because we handled it. I'm all in one piece, the Boyle kids are safe… You did everything perfectly," I said. Except leave the kids to come after me, I finished silently. The corners of his mouth quirked upward in an almost-smile.

"Good. As long as you can admit that I'm perfect," he teased, and I dropped my hand with a roll of my eyes, slumping back into the couch. "Seriously, though. I can't have my teammate bailing on me. We're a team whether you like it or not." His eyes were serious again.

"I like it," I admitted through a yawn. I could feel his surprised stare, but I was too tired to care. Get up and go to your room, I ordered my limbs, go to sleep. My arms and legs chose not to listen. I felt my heavy eyes begin to close, and I heard the couch creak as he shifted slightly. I could have been imagining it when I finally heard his reply.

"Me too."

CHAPTER 12

So warm… The peaceful thought drifted through my head as I snuggled closer, face pressed up against something firm and emanating warmth. I felt a bit like a cat napping in the sun, although instead of just hitting me on one side, this type of warmth was wrapped around me like a blanket of light, and I felt as though I was still dreaming. My lips curved into a smile; sleepless nights were all-too common for me, and true relaxation was as rare for me as vacation time. In other words, it was essentially nonexistent.

But I shouldn't have been this warm. I shouldn't have been this comfortable; it was too good to be true. Distress creased a line across my brow as my eyes flew open, and I groaned at the strain of adjusting to the light. All I wanted to do was sleep for a month in the safe coziness of this shelter from the outside world. As my eyes swam into focus, I fought the urge to close them against the lights that I must have left on.

Weird; it's been a while since I did that. I was diligent about closing everything down for the night before bed. I had my routine down to a science. Call it discipline or a compulsion or whatever you liked, but I wasn't in the habit of leaving the lights on. I sighed, knowing that I needed to get up, but also knowing that the painful adjustment to bright light was inevitable.

And so, I blinked the last of the sleep out of them, startled with what appeared before my eyes.

Luke's face was inches from mine, lines of tension from the night before now smoothed in blissful slumber. His eyes were closed, and the lashes rested gently against cheeks that were lightly freckled. I had never been close enough to see them before, and I was surprised. Of course, he had a reputation at the Academy for being a looker, but here in this state of total vulnerability, he was almost beautiful. My eyes traced the unlined smoothness of the skin around his eyes and on his cheeks. He was a picture of tranquility, and for a moment, I understood why he had so much appeal. If he showed this side of himself to his conquests, it was no wonder that they all fell for him.

The thought was unpleasant, and I jumped a little as I realized what I was thinking. *Ew. No. Time to get up.* I wrinkled my nose in disgust as I contorted my limbs so that I could push off without disturbing him, and I very slowly lifted myself off the couch. A tiny squeak shot out from behind my teeth as strong arms encircled me and pinned me back to the couch. *What is happening?*

"Ryder," I groaned, squirming slightly to get away. My arms were pinned, so I couldn't use them to push off.

"Mmmm," came the sleepy response. Who knew Luke was a cuddler? Something in my chest tensed for a moment, and I almost thought that my heart might be giving out from the shock of it all before I realized that he was squeezing the air out of my lungs.

"Luke," I gasped, trying to use my legs as a counterweight, "can't...breathe..."

"Maybe you'll finally shut up," he grumbled, but the pressure loosened. I inhaled in great, gasping breaths as the oxygen flowed back into my lungs, and the light, already disorienting, was dazzling from my lack of airflow. Before I could fully extricate myself to stand, he had grabbed me again.

"Ryder," I groaned again, but this time his hold was gentler. Just as firm, but definitely not squeezing the life out of me. A part of my heart warmed. *Aww, he's being considerate—* I rolled my eyes as I remembered who I was talking about— *for once in his damned life.*

"Get... your lazy ass *up*." I pushed my arms free and shook him by the shoulders. He cracked open one sleepy eye staring without seeing, the emerald color bright against his freckled skin, and he shut it again.

"Shhh," he answered, and I rolled my eyes.

"If you make us late because you've suddenly decided to be inappropriately friendly, I swear to—" I broke off as he shoved me away from him and my butt collided to the floor. I fought back a laugh at his horrified expression as I skidded to a stop.

"What the...?" he was sitting up straight, hair tousled and eyes still sleepy but alight with shock. My lips tightened with what dignity I could muster as I stared up at him.

"Welcome to the waking world." I stood, straightening my now-wrinkled clothes from yesterday. He looked at me like he'd never seen me before. "Cat got your tongue?"

"Hmph." He glanced away uncertainly, and I felt the corners of my mouth curl upward slyly.

"No need to be embarrassed, Ryder. I won't tell anyone else that you talk in your sleep." Renewed horror bloomed on his face, and I resisted the urge to laugh. *Bingo.* I finally had one up on Luke Ryder. As quickly as the expression had reached his face, it was gone, replaced by a dignified sternness that did not quite reach the unsteadiness in his eyes.

"Didn't you just say we would be late?" he asked stiffly, and I sighed, rolling my eyes.

"Mostly to get you *off* of me. Check your tone though. I don't have caffeine in my system yet, so I'm not ready to deal with your attitude." A sullen silence met my words, and I sighed again. *He's cuter when he's asleep.*

"We have things to do, *Blythe*. Go get ready," he ordered. I flipped my hair over one shoulder, pushing back the irritation that shot up into my chest.

"Gee. Thanks, for the reminder." I tried my best not to stomp over to my room, smirking slightly at the scoff that he let out. *Still got the upper hand.*

I changed quickly, conscious of the time. For all that we were not *really* running late for now, I didn't want that to change. I tried hard not to think about Luke's apparent mortification at waking fully and realizing that he had been cuddled up to me. *Who'd he think it was? I know I'm not his usual type, and Lord knows he's nowhere close to mine, but...* I pushed away the embarrassment quickly. It wasn't like it had been my fault we'd ended up in the situation. It hadn't really been his either. Stuff happened. *He was probably just surprised that he woke up with all of his limbs intact, given the circumstances.* I snorted—we could just chalk the whole thing up to exhaustion. I needed to let it go; I had a job to do.

I ran a brush through my hair, flinching as it snagged one particularly stubborn snarl. I worked it through the best I could before giving it up and throwing my hair in a ponytail. There was no point in wasting more time on my hair when it was going to inevitably get pulled up anyway. One day, maybe I would care more about my appearance, but today was not that day. *Functionality first.*

When I left the room, Ryder was waiting for me, leaning expectantly on the back of the sofa that hadn't been straightened. His face was set in lines of wariness, and I felt my shoulders begin to tense in response. The constant back-and-forth had been going on for years; maybe one day we would have a truce that lasted longer than an evening.

"Ready?" I asked unnecessarily, wanting to smack

myself for asking such an obvious question as he stood there, fully dressed.

"Waiting on you," he answered without meeting my eyes.

"Right…" I trailed off, and a line furrowed its way in between his eyebrows. *Right, then. Moving on.*

"Better go and see how we have to save the world today," I offered, and he shrugged.

"I guess." He led the way out of the suite, politely holding the door for me on the way out. The silence as we walked was agonizingly awkward, and I cast my mind about for something, anything to say that wouldn't make my skin crawl more. Finding nothing, I was actually relieved when we arrived at our briefing room. Without looking at Luke, I pulled the door open and returned his earlier favor, as I held it open for him. I caught a funny look as he passed by, but to my relief, he didn't say anything about it.

As had become routine, the older agents were seated around a table, identical expressions of seriousness on their faces. I glanced over at Katz, and a frown slashed across where his neutral, tight-lipped mouth usually sat.

"Good morning," he greeted somberly, and I could tell that this wasn't going to be a fun meeting.

"Good morning." I nodded in response. Luke muttered a similar sentiment from behind me, and I stepped to the side to give him room to move beside me. *I wonder how it feels for him to be the one boxed out of conversations,* I wondered briefly, and then I banished the thought.

"We have much to discuss," Katz said in a grave tone, and I felt a thudding sensation as my heart began to pound. *Have we already messed something up?* I couldn't think of anything.

"Do we have any more information about the parties associated with the attacks yesterday?" Luke asked from behind me. I pulled my ponytail over one shoulder to get it off the back of my neck.

"Nothing like that. We *are* tracking one source we believe was associated with the man Miss Richards so helpfully incapacitated, but we don't have anything definitive on that matter yet." *Agent,* I corrected him silently. "After this attempt on Jesse and Sara, we don't feel that it is in the best interest of any member of the First Family for them to be in such close proximity right now. They are a point of vulnerability for the president, and until we have a clearer idea of what the motive for this attack was or who was behind it, we'll be separating you." Katz moved back to his seat at the table and slid a file in our direction, motioning for us to sit. I exchanged an uneasy glance with Luke. We just figured out how to work together, and it's been two days. This had to be a joke. *At least now you won't have to talk about what happened last night!* My inner voice interjected helpfully.

"So the children will be separated from each other? Is that wise?" Luke asked, flipping open the file and sliding it so I could see as well. When he didn't answer, I glanced up at Katz to see him staring at us with an expression of mild surprise.

"Of course not. They will remain together, as will the two of you. We'll be sending along agents to help you at public events, but for the most part, it'll be the two of you on call at all times. You're too untested in the field to be alone, but you've shown your ability to work as a team. That's what we need right now: a team." From beside Katz, Jennings made a noise, but the older man ignored him. *I guess the whole "Designated Survivor" thing only works for elected officials.* The children weren't disposable; I respected that. *Phew, on-call 24/7 though… Maybe we should unionize.* I laughed to myself at the thought until I caught sight of Bryant scrutinizing me, her brows pressing together over her dark eyes. I hid my smile and returned my attention to the subject at hand.

"This is all on the president's orders of course." Bryant returned her attention to the matter at hand as she spoke up for the first time that morning. I nodded, glancing at the details of our new accommodations.

"This has us leaving D.C.?" I inquired. Jennings snorted as I stated the obvious, but Katz simply nodded, shooting him a warning look.

"We'll be keeping you just outside the city limits until things settle down. You can commute in for events, and you'll have full access to transportation for outsourced things. Since Jesse and Sara are taking classes online, you won't have to worry about school, but they'll need to be able to reach their tutors as needed from the safe house." There was a pause as I processed the fact that we would be leaving so soon after our arrival, and I exchanged another look with Luke, who didn't seem as surprised. *And to think that our suite was starting to feel so homey.*

"When do we leave?" Luke asked.

"Tomorrow. I'll let you two break the news. You're dismissed." Katz stood as we rose like a well-oiled machine and turned to exit. *Well, this'll be fun.*

CHAPTER 13

I watched the siblings carefully for any signs of anger or resentment as they absorbed the news, especially from Sara, who I had noticed had a bit of an attitude whenever things didn't go her way. But the skin of her forehead and brow was unlined, and her face was an undiscerning mask. *Dang*. Why we had been designated as the ones who had to break the news was beyond me, as they hardly had gotten the chance to see us as some sort of figures of authority, but to my intense relief, they both seemed to be taking it well.

"You mean, we'll be staying somewhere else? Out of sight of everyone?" Sara's inquiry was carefully neutral, and I blinked several times, glancing over at Luke with some confusion before taking a deep breath and responding.

"Yes, that's the plan as far as we know." I did not miss the anticipatory glow that flashed quickly across her eyes before it winked out. Was it just me, or did she seem almost… excited?

"After the attempt on your lives, the Head of Security for your family has decided that it would be in your best interests to remain separate from your parents until we've uncovered the source of the threat.

You two will, of course, remain together, and we will be with you every step of the way. There's a safe house just outside the city, and that's where we'll be. They'll provide transportation to any necessary events, but we'll need to keep this very discreet." Luke explained in an even tone that I respected. *It's all business, and they don't need to be any more alarmed at the weight of the threat.*

"This is going to blow over sooner than you think, and you'll be reunited with your parents soon. Just know that everything we do is for your safety. We're asking you to trust us with a lot, but I promise that we'll do our best to keep you safe," I added. Out of the corner of my eye, I noticed a sharp nod of approval from Luke, and I felt a lightness flutter in my chest. *If I have the approval of the great Luke Ryder, I must be doing something right.* I snorted at my own sarcasm and returned my attention to Sara and Jesse.

"I trust you, Luke." Sara's eyes were wide and bright, and I resisted the urge to role my own. I studied her carefully, but before I could open my mouth to make sure she understood the gravity of the situation, Jesse spoke.

"What's the friend situation gonna be like? Do we get to keep our phones this time?" he asked, and Luke and I glanced at each other again. *That's why he's so calm; he's done this before.* I should have guessed. The First Family was under threat at all times... hence my presence and Luke's.

"At this time, we have no orders to confiscate or intercept your communication," Luke answered carefully. *Ever the diplomat.* I took a step forward, looking severely between the two and feeling a bit parental.

"That being said, be smart. Don't go giving out our location to everyone. Actually, scratch that: let's not give it out to anyone. Where we're moving is technically a safe house, and this plan hinges on your discretion and ours. Don't make us take the extra step and confiscate your phones. Let's make this as painless as possible." I looked both of them pointedly in the eye to make sure that I had gotten my point across before addressing Luke. "I'd say we should let these two get packed. We're expected to leave as soon as possible." I waited another beat in case they had any questions, but they simply looked at me before turning and heading toward their respective rooms. *Huh.* I turned on my heel and strode back toward the door, conscious of Luke following close behind. We had our own preparations to make, and we could not afford to waist any more time.

"That went well." Luke's long legs kept up with me easily, and I nodded, running through a list of what we needed to do before we left. They were trusting us on our own, and we could not afford to mess it up. I was going to be the best watchdog they could ever have hoped to hire.

CHAPTER 14

The ride to the safe house was a quiet one, with all of us staring out of our respective windows—with the exception of Jesse, who was fixated on his phone— and none of us quite knowing what to expect. I knew roughly where we were headed from our earlier meeting, but I still was not sure how things would go with the four of us trapped in one house indefinitely. Luke appeared to be similarly lost in thought. Aside from events that would require Sara's or Jesse's attendance, I knew that our stay in the safe house would be relatively uneventful in the day to day. Granted, there was sometimes peace in the mundane, but it still made me wonder how we would fill our time. *Maybe they like chess,* I thought with a chuckle to myself. Somehow, I couldn't see the First Kids sitting down to any type of board game. Then again, I had been surprised before; there was nothing to say I could not be again.

The drive was taking longer than I had anticipated. I had expected us to take some detours—and of course we had to account for traffic— but the commute seemed to last an eternity. This was not helped by the heavy silence hanging over all of us, as the middle-aged driver wasn't particularly talkative. *Probably doesn't know what he would say to four people our age, honestly.* It was an interesting position for Luke and me to be in, now that I really thought about it. We were somewhat of an authority here, and we had the responsibilities of any adult—arguably more, given our profession—but the fact remained that we had barely crossed that threshold. Most adults could not understand the position we were in—obviously most other people our age would not be able to either—so we were just slightly out of step no matter how we were to look at it. It was ironic that the only people able to fully understand what we were going through were each other. *I wouldn't have put money on me understanding Luke, and I especially would not have bet on Luke understanding me last week.* We were three days in now, and our world had changed. We had jumped headfirst into the expectations of our new position, and life before felt like a distant dream. *Life comes at you fast.*

After what felt like an eon of waiting, we pulled in front of a house that stood some distance behind a high-walled fence. *Oh, yeah. Totally doesn't look like there's anything to hide in there,* I thought sarcastically. Then again, Jesse and Sara were pretty recognizable figures, especially in the areas around Washington D.C., so at least the fencing meant that they wouldn't be trapped inside indefinitely. Sunshine was good for the soul, and hopefully, it would be good for morale if there was a yard available. We approached the iron-wrought gate, and the driver fiddled with something that I realized was a remote. At what must have been the press of a button, the gate slid apart, and we approached the house.

It was a cute place, I had to admit, although it felt weird referring to any building hidden behind an iron gate as 'cute.' A southern-style veranda wrapped around the front of the house, and it appeared to continue around the back, complimenting the graceful ivory of the brick that was a defining feature of the outside. I could smell roses as we stepped out of the car. *I guess they have landscapers.* I wondered briefly if we would need to take over the gardening while we were in residence, and then I laughed at the ridiculousness of the fact that I was thinking about the flowers. *You may wear a lot of hats, but you can't wear all of them,* I reasoned.

My mind was still reeling as we left the car, grabbed our luggage, and prepared to enter the house. Luke shared words with the driver before he turned around and pulled back onto the street, but I was too far away to make them out. Then it came crashing down on me that the four of us were alone. The weight of the responsibility felt suffocating for a moment, and I felt a bit like I was dragging a ball and chain as I made my way up the stairs with my bags and inside the house. After getting the lay of the land inside, however, the feeling passed—or maybe I was just really distracted.

"Could be worse," I said softly, looking around what was, quite frankly, a beautifully decorated interior.

"It's not a bad place," Jesse agreed, "we don't really mind it here." I blinked at him in twofold surprise. I hadn't realized that he had been close enough to hear me, and I also had not realized that they had stayed here before.

"You two have been here before?" I asked, inviting him to explain. He shrugged noncommittally.

"Once or twice. This isn't our first rodeo." Without a further explanation, he hefted one of his bags onto his shoulder and disappeared up the graceful flight of stairs that took up a lot of the entryway, heaving his other suitcase with him as he went.

"What do you reckon happened for them to be moved here before?" I asked Luke once Sara had followed her brother. His eyes followed her until she disappeared around a corner on the next floor.

"I don't know, but whatever it is couldn't have been good," he answered.

"Their dad's only been in office for a little over a year. That's a lot happening in not a very long amount of time," I observed. He looked at me with a raised eyebrow as I stated the obvious. "I mean," I began defensively, "it's possible that it's the same group or person behind it all, right? Since they still haven't figured out who was behind this last attack?" Luke considered this for a moment, nodding slowly as he contemplated.

"I guess that's possible," he allowed. "That would explain why they were so quick to send us here, if something similar had happened before." Bile rose in my throat, and I swallowed hard at the thought that rose along with it. *Maybe our assailants weren't so inexperienced at this after all, if they've escaped notice for that long.*

"Well, maybe it won't be for long, then," I said hopefully. The withering look that he shot me told me he did not hold out much hope, but to my surprise, he didn't argue.

"Maybe," he answered, but of course, it was obvious that he didn't believe the words. "I guess time will tell." *It always does.*, I agreed.

CHAPTER 15

A bloodcurdling scream jolted me out of my sleep, and I leapt to my feet, nerves tingling as I bolted from the room and toward the source of the noise. I almost ran headlong into Luke, who was coming from across the hall. Without acknowledging each other, we turned at the same time and resumed sprinting up the hall, his steps overtaking mine as my shorter legs fought to keep up.

The screams were coming from Sara's room, and as I darted in behind Luke, I actually did run into him as he stopped short. Rather than a would-be kidnapper or assailant, as I had been imagining, Sara was thrashing in her bed, completely alone and unencumbered by any sort of attacker. *A nightmare?* I asked in disbelief as I fought to slow my breathing and ease my adrenaline. It spiked again as she let out another unworldly shriek. With a hesitant glance at me, Luke approached the girl, who was glistening with a sheen of sweat, and put his hands on her shoulders, applying a careful pressure to still her. A sob choked out of her still-sleeping form, and I opened my mouth to remind him that it was a bad idea to wake someone having a nightmare—kind of like waking a sleepwalker; you just didn't do it.

Before I could get the words out, she opened her eyes and stared up at Luke in surprise before letting out a squeal of astonishment.

"What are *you* doing in here?" she demanded accusingly, pushing her wild strands of hair from her eyes and forehead, where they had plastered to her skin.

"You were having a nightmare," I answered helpfully, and Sara swiveled her head around to glare at me.

"Get out, both of you. Get out! Get *out!*" Her voice rose again, and Luke lifted his hands in a form of surrender, backing away slowly.

"Is there anything we can—" he began carefully.

"Leave me *alone!*" she almost sobbed, and at the order, Luke turned tail and fled. I, however, stayed put.

"Sara, I—" I began tentatively.

"Are you deaf or just stupid? I said leave!" she snarled. I crossed my arms and stared at her as she clawed at her hair once again, chest heaving with a bubble of barely concealed hysteria.

"You were having a nightmare," I repeated.

"So? Everyone has bad dreams," she snapped, apparently giving up on banishing me from the room.

"Want to share what it was about?" I asked. "You were screaming," I added at her blazing look.

"Why do you care?" she asked. *I don't really*, I thought, but I didn't think my candor would be very helpful in this situation.

"Sometimes it helps to talk about it," I replied, dodging the question.

"Not to *you*," she retorted hotly, not meeting my eyes.

"If you're dreaming about the reason we're here, I already figured that you've been in danger before," I prompted, "since this isn't the first time you've been here." She took a deep breath.

"No," she said, "it's not." Then she looked up at me, eyes guarded. "If you think I'm going to share my deepest, darkest fears with someone I just met though, you're stupider than I thought." It took all of my willpower to let the insults continue to roll off of my back, but I was determined not to give her the reaction she was so plainly looking for. *If only I could apply this level of self-control to my conversations with Luke,* I thought with some amusement.

"I'm not asking for girl-talk, Sara. It could just be that you're remembering something that could be helpful," I replied wearily.

"I don't. I mean, nothing other than what I already mentioned to everyone before," she said. She dropped her eyes, though, and I had a sneaking suspicion that there was something she wasn't telling me. If she was determined not to share it, though, there was nothing that I could do to force her, especially not at—I did a mental calculation— 3:00? 4:00? Whatever time it was, it wasn't time to push.

"You'll let us know if that changes." It wasn't a request.

"Sure," she answered, still not meeting my eyes.

"I'll leave you to it, then." Without looking back at her, I left the room, closing the door firmly behind me.

"Get anything out of her?" As Luke's voice jumped out at me from the shadows, I leapt about a foot in the air, clutching at my chest.

"Geez. Don't *do* that!" I hissed. He let out a little laugh, and I was able to pinpoint where he stood in the shadows.

"Ow!" he complained as my smack made contact with his arm. "It's not my fault you weren't prepared. What if there *had* been someone lurking out here?" The thought made my blood run cold; I knew that he was right. I *had* let my guard down.

"Then I guess I would have gotten jumped," I answered in a harsh tone.

"Which would have been especially helpful to Jesse and Sara, I'm sure," he replied dryly.

"Would have probably made *your* stay much more pleasant though," I muttered. He averted his eyes. *That's what I thought.*

"Did she say anything? She was screaming like she was being murdered," he said.

"No," I answered dully. "I can't say I blame her though. We're not exactly besties; I've only known the girl three days, and she was in a vulnerable position. You'd probably have better luck," I finished bluntly. I practically felt him bristle.

"What's that supposed to mean?" he demanded.

"That she looks at you like you hung the moon? Don't tell me you haven't noticed." I wasn't sure what was worse, him basking in female attention or him not knowing he was receiving it in the first place.

"What are you talking about? I barely know her," he seemed genuinely startled, but that didn't exactly endear me to him at that particular moment.

"Which is probably why she thinks that in the first place," I retorted rudely. He stiffened.

"You sound jealous." His voice was just as sharp, and my annoyance grew even more pronounced when I realized that he was right. I did sound jealous.

"I'm too tired for this. I'm going back to bed; we can try talking to her again in the morning," I said, turning sharply and stalking back up the hallway toward my room.

"You didn't deny it!" he called after me with a light laugh, and I felt a surge of irritation as I realized that he was right. I slammed my door on the evening, Luke's mocking laugh still floating up the hallway.

When I finally committed to starting my day and made my way down to the kitchen, my eyes were still heavy from the late-night adventures from the wee hours of the morning. I was annoyed to find Luke sitting in the room with a smug expression on his face.

To my relief, he had at least brewed some coffee, and I felt some of the tiredness in my bones release at the embrace of the familiar aroma. Still, our conversation from hours earlier had rubbed me the wrong way, and I had tossed and turned for most of the rest of the time I could have been sleeping, replaying the situation over and over again. It was not just our conversation, either; the whole situation with Sara had me unnerved, and there was clearly something that had happened that she wasn't telling us. It was harder to do our jobs without access to all of the information. I had spent the night wracking my brain for ways to earn her trust and convince her it was safe to tell me. By the smug expression on Luke's face, though, my late-night efforts had been in vain, and that did nothing to reduce my state of heightened annoyance.

"Good morning!" He was chipper. In that moment, it was the combination of that and his apparently well-rested features that made me hate him more than ever.

"It's a morning," I grumbled in reply. He smirked.

"There's coffee, sleeping beauty," he said, gesturing with one hand. I lacked the energy to be even remotely surprised at the gesture, so I grunted noncommittally, fished a mug out of the cabinet, and filled it to the brim with the steaming liquid. I found one of the seats at the island and took a sip, reveling in the bitter taste; he had made it strong. Preparing myself for the worst of his good mood, I wrapped my hands around the warm mug, sitting in front of him and holding the cup to my face, inhaling deeply. *Sweet, sweet bean water.*

"You know, they say that the coffee works better if you actually drink it," he offered with a small smile. The look I gave him was unamused. "Just saying." *Is this his idea of a ceasefire?* It would take more than a cup of coffee to get us there.

"Thank you for that helpful insight." Just to be contrary, I sat the mug down, feeling like I was punishing myself as I did. "Why are you in such a good mood?" I asked.

"Because you were right; Sara trusts me," he gloated. I rolled my eyes.

"I don't know that 'trusts' is the word, but it rhymes with the one I had in mind." I rose to the bait, and he made a face. I thought privately that it didn't really matter, as trust and lust could often yield similar results when fishing for information. That wasn't anything *I* was interested in trying any time soon though. "Go on, then. What'd you find out?" He muttered something under his breath that I could have sworn was 'jealous,' but I elected to ignore it, sipping my coffee with a stiff sort of dignity as I waited for him to share.

"This all *has* happened before, with the last agents," he crowed, looking smugly as though he waited for me to congratulate him at his tremendous insight. I blinked at him.

"Well…yes? We knew that this has happened before. Jesse said they'd used the safe house in the past, remember?" I asked, having the distinct sensation that I was missing something big. Had I been the only one who had heard that? Was I slowly losing my mind? *Working with Ryder? Probably.*

"No, I mean this has happened before with the last *agents,*" he clarified, actually clarifying nothing.

"Am I missing something? We knew that this happened before we were hired on. Of course it happened with the last agents," I replied. His eyes darkened, but I was not intentionally misunderstanding him; I was fully missing why he thought this was brand new information.

"But we didn't know that the last agents were *involved* in what had happened. They weren't vetted properly. They helped kickstart this whole mess, getting to the kids to get to the president. It's a whole conspiracy," he explained earnestly. I looked hard at him.

"*That* was what she didn't want to tell me last night? I thought it was some deeply personal trauma or something. That's why I didn't push," I said, irritated once more.

"I mean, it kind of was. She trusted them, they betrayed her. Sounds traumatic enough to me," he said. *For an average citizen maybe.* I dismissed the thought with a wave of my hand.

"Why weren't we told about this?" I asked. It was strange that we had not been filled in.

"Maybe they didn't want to give *us* any ideas?" he said with a twisted sort of sarcasm. "I don't have all the answers, Blythe, I just know what Sara told me this morning." *Makes sense. I guess she wouldn't know all of the ins and outs,* I allowed.

"Where *is* Sara?" I asked, changing the subject and ignoring his misuse of my name.

"Asleep," he said nonchalantly. I blinked at him in confusion.

"How long was she up?" I asked.

"She told me everything she knew after you went to bed. I went back in to talk to her," he said with raised eyebrows, as though it should have been obvious to me. *Because of course he did.*

"Oh, so you just needed me to calm her down so you could swoop in, and—" I began hotly.

"First of all, I didn't *need* you to do anything, and as for swooping..." he trailed off, as though he was treading carefully with what he would say next. "There was no swooping," he finished lamely. I rolled my eyes.

"I'm sure she was just dying to spill her deepest darkest secrets to you," I said dryly.

"She trusts me," he repeated.

"Yes, I'm sure *that's* why you're so chipper," I muttered. He blinked at me in apparent confusion.

"What?" he asked. *Such an eloquent man.*

"Never mind. What is there to cook for breakfast in

here? I'm starving," I changed the subject. He shrugged awkwardly his face creased in uncertain lines. As I stood and walked over to the fridge to check for myself, it occurred to me that I had never thanked Luke for the coffee. I turned to do just that, but as I looked openmouthed at the spot that he had occupied just moments before; he was gone. I listened for footsteps, and hearing none, I turned back to the fridge, pulling out my chosen ingredients. Eggs it was.

CHAPTER 16

I don't know why I had expected something explosive to happen at the revelation that one of our own had betrayed the Boyles, but it unnerved me that the next few days passed uneventfully. Each day felt like a repetition of the one before, and I felt a bit like one of the horses on a carousel: fixed in place and silently screaming. You wouldn't think it would be hard doing nothing all day in a nice house, but when you're on lockdown with people you have nothing in common with, it becomes the most inhumane form of slow torture. I wasn't suited for idleness, and that's probably why I had a reason to feel grateful to Luke when he brought the news that we had an event to attend.

"I just got the call. This afternoon, they want us to attend the first lady's literacy event at the library," he announced. I was also thrilled to not have to spend another day skulking the halls of this gloomy house that I almost forgot to be annoyed that they had chosen to contact Luke. *Short notice,* I observed, but I refrained from complaining in front of Jesse and Sara.

"Which library? There are several in the city, in case you'd forgotten," I asked in a tone that could almost be called polite. Luke's lips tightened, but he surprisingly did not take the bait. *We must both be getting better at self-control.* The thought made me want to laugh.

"The one off 8th is what they said. We're to arrive at 1:00, and the event starts shortly after. They don't want us there too early in case…" he cast a quick glance at Sara, "well, just in case. Plus, they won't have to worry about us getting in the way during set-up."

"That's a lot of glass," I mused absently, thinking of the library in question.

"We'll be in the Auditorium for the speech. They may want us to stay and mingle afterwards, but that depends on—" Luke stopped short.

"We'll figure it out," I covered, sounding more confident than I felt. Either Luke hadn't gotten a lot of details, or he just wasn't interested in sharing them in front of the Boyle kids. Either way, I was incredibly curious to know the details so that I could start to mentally prepare. *Anything is better to focus on than the fact that I've had nothing to focus on.* Mostly, I was curious as to why they had given us such short notice. Usually logistics were planned out well in advance to avoid any room for error. I knew there had to be a reason, and my mind was spinning as it turned over all of the possibilities.

Who would have thought you'd be chomping at the bit for a chance to be alone with Luke Ryder? My inner voice had a wicked sense of humor, and right now, it felt more wicked than humorous. We had been circling each other like wolves for the past several days, neither of us willing to draw the first blood, but we were overdue for a good spat. We also had something important to talk about now, so I was hoping that would overshadow the ever-present urge for us to throttle each other. I didn't particularly enjoy spending time with Jesse and Sara; Jesse was alright—if quiet and detached— and Sara made up for it by being the complete opposite. Their most annoying qualities became more glaringly obvious to me now that I had a real reason to want them out of the room, but I had to suffer through stunted conversation with them for at least an hour before I was able to pull Luke to the side for a conversation.

"March!" I ordered, sounding for all the world like a drill sergeant. He blinked up at me, amusement and irritation warring in his eyes.

"Ides of or Death?" he asked. I wrinkled my nose at him.

"What?"

"You said March. Ides of March or Death March? With you, I know it's bound to be close to one," he explained in a conversational tone. I rolled my eyes. That was a stretch as a joke, and he had to know it.

"Shut up. Move. We need to coordinate, so I repeat: *MARCH!*" I gave him a nudge.

"You aren't my boss," he began, his feet stubbornly still as he literally dug in his heels.

"Ryder, are you really pulling a 'you aren't the boss of me,' right now? We have limited time already, and we really don't have time for—" I spluttered on the words I was going to say when he put his hand over my mouth. I glared at him, wishing for all the world in that moment that looks could kill.

"I was going to say, 'you aren't my boss, but I guess I can let that slide just this once.' Now, are you going to keep telling me how wrong I am about everything, or can we go somewhere private and discuss this afternoon?" he asked in a way that had only one mature answer, and I hated the fact that he was right. The fight went out of my shoulders.

"That's what I was trying to do," I muttered mutinously, but he ignored me.

"My room or yours," he asked with a twinkle in his eyes. I curled my lip at his innuendo before looking coldly up at him.

"Never, in this or any lifetime," I said frostily.

"Mine it is, then," he answered with a wink. I bit back a retort and climbed the stairs alongside him in resolute silence. I had been beaten in that round, and I knew it. The fact that I knew it did nothing to alleviate the sting of defeat. Once we reached it, I took in his room. It looked lived-in, meaning that I could see his bags and his shoes lined up neatly on the far side of the room, but in all respects, Luke appeared to be a tidy tenant. As I caught sight of his neatly made bed, I thought of my own rumpled bedding and snorted. We were definitely opposites. *Opposites attract,* my inner voice said snidely. I pushed the thought from my mind, catching sight of my reflection in a window and noticing that I had reddened slightly around the ears.

"Alright, so what did they tell you—since, you know, they refuse to communicate with me for some reason?" I pushed past my feelings about our recent banter, determined to finally get down to business.

"And with you being so pleasant to talk to! It's shocking, really," he said lightly. I scowled.

"Ryder, I mean it. What is it we need to know going in?" I asked. The amusement drained from his face, replaced with an expression so serious that it could have belonged to an entirely different person.

"Right. The first lady is giving a speech in the Auditorium of the library. It'll be pretty closed off. Some media presence, some influential philanthropists. It should be a straightforward event, for the most part. We'll go, stay for the speech, let the kids mingle and take photos, and then come home—or back here, I guess." I blinked at his distinction. It was an interesting concept: home. I guess the closest thing I'd had to a home had been the Academy. Now, it was wherever the IPS decided I should be. A few days ago, that was The White House. For now, that meant this house.

"Sounds straightforward enough. Did they send you photos of the event space, or a blueprint or something?" I asked. Luke nodded, whipping out his phone and typing furiously on the screen before passing it over to me. I glanced at him in surprise as he handed over his personal phone, but he shrugged.

"It's encrypted," he explained. *As if I would want to snoop!* I let the indignant thought pass as I took a deep breath.

"Smart choice," I answered, glancing over the blueprints. The room layout had standard entry and exit points, and the facility itself was quite large. I was sure that the others would clear the space before we arrived, but it was disconcerting, given our last encounter with a conspirator.

"I've asked to have an extra set of eyes with us," Luke said quietly as though reading my thoughts.

"Good call. Just in case," I replied casually, zooming in on one of the sections of library and tilting the phone to see at a better angle.

"Think we can handle it?" he asked.

"I guess we'll see," I answered without looking up. I was curious to see if event number two would be as exciting as our first. For the sake of Jesse and Sara, I hoped not.

CHAPTER 17

As we arrived at the front entrance, I realized that the building was larger than I had imagined. I was skeptical the chosen logistics of having the Boyles use the main entrance. I didn't like it, especially after I noticed the photographers that had already gathered out front, holding their cameras at the ready as they waited to pounce. *They had their reasons,* I reminded myself with a sigh.

"Those are a lot of cameras," Jesse said quietly, looking pale.

"You don't like the cameras?" I asked in surprise. Most people his age would kill for the chance to be in front of one on the national level. He shot me a withering look.

"You've never had your entire life on display, I guess." I chewed on the inside of one cheek thoughtfully; I hadn't realized that it bothered him so much.

"Half of the things they all print are untrue anyway. Just looking for something to sell papers," Sara chimed in. Jesse nodded in agreement. I exchanged a look with Luke before glancing out the window of the car once again.

"Makes sense, I guess. All of the ethical reporters must be inside," I tried for a joke to lighten the mood, but nobody laughed. The thought of being on camera—well, let's just say as an agent, the thought of being doxed wasn't a very pleasant one. I knew with a recommendation from a president, I could likely find work wherever I wanted once we finished the job, but that opportunity came with a price: my anonymity. I had not really considered that before Jesse's comment. I barely had time to keep up with the news, and I stayed far away from tabloids, so the thought had never crossed my mind. I scrutinized Jesse and Sara, who looked resigned to the situation but otherwise unfazed. *What had it been like for them, having someone watch their every move?* I was startled as the thought occurred to me that I was doing just that. The thought was unsettling.

"Are you two ready?" Luke directed this at Sara and Jesse, who both nodded with matching glum expressions, and I had the startling realization that they had lived their teenaged years acting just as much the politicians as their father. They'd attended many of the same events, spoken to the same people, been under similar scrutiny, and all the while, they'd known that one wrong move from either of them could impact their whole family's trajectory. It was no wonder that Jesse was so quiet and that Sara had a rebellious streak. Who wouldn't?

They had rearranged their features into accommodating smiles as they waved to the cameras and stepped into their roles. I saw their appeal; Jesse was handsomely quiet and aloof, with a crooked smile and kind eyes, while Sara was bubbly and charming. They balanced each other well, and their presence at the event was an asset. Luke and I moved like shadows in their footsteps as they moved swiftly up to the doors. I was thankful when the doors swung open and we were all ushered inside. That short distance had been suffocating. I looked at the faces of one of the men there to greet us and smiled politely at Katz.

"Agent Katz. Glad to see you," I greeted.

"I'm glad the four of you made it," he replied politely. He passed a glance over the siblings before jerking his head for Luke and I to step to the side. "Bryant will be the third for you two with Oak and Poplar. She'll be mixed in with the rest, but she'll be in your corner should you need her. I'll take them from here. You know where to go?" Katz raised an inquiring eyebrow. Luke and I shared a uniform nod, and just as quickly as he had pulled us, Agent Katz turned away to smile at Jesse and Sara.

"Mr. and Miss Boyle, if you two will follow me, we'll get you settled," he said, and I could hear his voice continue as they stepped further away. Sara cast a backward glance toward us, and Luke gave her a reassuring nod. She took an obvious breath before turning back to follow her brother and the older agent.

"I don't blame her for being nervous after what happened last time," I murmured, only half-conscious that I had spoken the thought aloud.

"Me neither. Shall we go, then?" Luke asked. I glanced up at him and nodded, looking after Jesse and Sara's retreating backs.

"Yeah, I guess we should." I had the sudden urge to rush through the massive building and perform a security sweep myself, but I knew that wasn't feasible at the moment. I had a looming sense of concern that something would happen and that we would be powerless to stop it. Maybe I just had a flair for the dramatic. *You? Never*, the inner voice sneered.

The Auditorium itself was a neatly impressive sort of room. Seats upholstered in crimson fabric stacked from the front of the room to the back. I had a small smile at the fact that the press would be looking down upon the first lady as she spoke, rather than the other way around, since there was no stage. There was, however, a tidy-looking podium at the front, which, since it was placed slightly off-center, appeared to have been brought in for the occasion. As I swept my gaze across the room again, I found my eyes resting on the exits. There were only two possible exit points at the back of the room; it would be all too easy for somebody with the wrong intentions to trap us all in there. The mental image made my insides squirm uncomfortably. After what had happened at the last event, it was hard for me to trust that the security sweep had been thorough enough. They might have been more vigilant after the events of the previous outing, but we were still effectively backed into a corner. I caught sight of Luke wearing an equally displeased expression. *At least we can agree on something.*

Several of the front rows were roped off, and I was relieved to see that one side of the auditorium had been sectioned off as well. I knew the likelihood of maxing out the nearly 300-person capacity of the room was unlikely, but it was reassuring to know that they had been contained to one side.

"I think that one of us should probably hang out near the back rows," Luke said softly. We had initially planned to sit behind Jesse and Sara, who would likely be placed in the front row, but given the layout of the room, it made sense.

"I think that person should probably be me," I whispered back. I much preferred being an observer of things than having my back to the greater crowd, and logically, Luke's larger size would mean that he would be a more effective body shield in the event of…something. Plus, we had Agent Bryant who would be placed nearby. If anything went sideways, she could help too. Luke considered for a moment before nodding.

"I agree," he answered. The admission sounded slightly strangled as it emerged from his throat, and I snickered softly, knowing how I had felt on the rare occasions that I'd had to admit that he made a good point.

"Until the end, then?" I asked. He nodded again before stepping with catlike grace down the set of stairs. I slipped into the back row, behind the area the press and other guests would be occupying shortly, and I waited.

My vantage point gave me the opportunity to survey the event's arrivals as they trickled in. I did my best to blend into the background—which in case you were wondering, is really hard when you're in black and white against bright red upholstery. Somehow, I only caught a few curious glances from the newcomers. I could read the question on each face that noticed me. *What is she doing here?* Some faces screwed up in thought, trying to figure out where they knew me, but most simply shrugged and continued on their way. In a way, my newness to the job was a bit of a blessing; while I stuck out a bit for my age, Luke and I had not been out and about enough with Sara and Jesse for us to be more fully recognizable. To my relief, everyone who had entered seemed to have their mind on the event itself; nobody seemed to have an obvious preoccupation with a conspiracy to kidnap, maim, or otherwise endanger anyone in the First Family. Then again, the day was young; there was plenty of time for someone to get a wild hair and attempt treasonous and felonious activities. Only a few of our newcomers cast their eyes curiously down to where the children and their mother sat, and I did not see anything malicious in the looks, so for now, at least, it seemed as though we were in the clear. I was still surveying the attendees, only half paying attention when a trim, professional-looking woman stepped up to the podium and introduced herself as the Executive Director of the D.C. Public Library system. My attention snapped more fully toward her as she introduced the first lady.

"Please welcome First Lady Allison Boyle," the woman said, stepping aside to lead the crowd in a round of polite applause as Mrs. Boyle stepped gracefully to take her place behind the podium. Her golden-blonde hair, so like her son's, was smoothed behind her ears in an elegant twist, and twin drops of what I assumed were diamonds danced at her ears. *The picture-perfect politician's wife*, I thought without malice.

Her speech, which I loosely gathered was about the importance of funding the library system and accompanying services as a fundamental tier of literacy support, went off without a hitch. It had all of the typical talking points, I took note of the importance of public education and support for adult learning— which this library provided to the community— as I continued to survey the crowd, looking for any of the not-so-subtle movements that had tipped me off to something being wrong at our last event. I noticed Luke, learning from the consequences of his rapt attention to the speaker at the last event, doing the same to those in his general vicinity, subtle enough that the average layperson would not know that he was giving Mrs. Boyle anything less than his utmost attention and thought.

To my surprise, my intense vigilance—while a good practice from a professional standpoint— proved to be unnecessary. The event passed without issue, and the kids had the opportunity for a photo with their mother after she answered a few questions from the press. By all accounts, the event itself went off without a hitch. *Then why do I still feel so uneasy?* My intuition was rarely wrong, and it seemed to sense thunderheads on the horizon. I had the sinking feeling that it would be a major storm when it broke, whenever that proved to be. For now, however, I allowed myself to be grateful for the straightforward event, and I tried to convince myself that it was okay to feel at ease.

CHAPTER 18

I was again surprised at the seamlessness of the day as the rest of the security team cleared the premises, and I moved to stand beside Luke, waiting for Jesse and Sara to say their goodbyes to their mother. First Lady she might be, but it became increasingly obvious as I moved to join them that Allison Boyle was, first and foremost, a mother. You could see it in the way that she hugged her children, and you could see it in the way that worry lines creased her forehead as she looked at Sara, who was sharing something with her animatedly. I wondered briefly if my own parents had ever worried about me in that way, but I pushed the thought away. In our line of work, you had to be able to compartmentalize. It was what kept us—them—alive. Still, I could not fully ignore the looming sense of emptiness that snaked its way in as I watched this particular mother interact with our charges. I glanced up to see Luke watching me with a sympathetic expression, and I realized in horror that what I had been thinking had been written all over my face. I quickly forced my face into a disinterested mask, but I knew the damage had been done.

I was thankful that Luke and I were not forced to be

the ones to interrupt the reunion between the Boyles, as Welsch and Jennings helpfully did so for us. Jennings bent toward Mrs. Boyle's to whisper something, and although I saw the first lady's lips purse with dissatisfaction, she nodded agree with whatever he'd said. While the trio said their goodbyes, I watched as Bryant picked her way down the stairs to join us. I had barely been able to pick her out in the crowd, so well had she blended with the small sea of onlookers that made up the audience. I was impressed. I refocused my attention on those in front of me when Jennings addressed Luke—*because Heaven forbid he acknowledge me.*

"We have the front entrance secured, Ryder. We cleared out the crowd that was there when you arrived. Just go out the way you came, and the car there will take you back to the safe house." Jennings kept his voice low, but I was still able to make out his words, and I blinked in surprise that they would plan such a predictable route. I saw a similar flash of surprise cross Luke's face, but Jennings had already turned to survey the family. Hopefully, they had been as thorough as they had been for the event itself.

"I'll be trailing you in case you need backup," Bryant explained, materializing beside me. She looked faintly amused as she stared at Jennings, and I knew she had not missed the way that he had snubbed me in favor of coordinating with Luke. "It's not just you," she explained in a low voice, a wry smile on her face.

"Well, that's a relief. It's just general misogyny, then," I muttered back, and she huffed out a light laugh. Luke had turned and was regarding us suspiciously, which made the situation all the more entertaining, but we dropped it from there. Jennings said another quick word to Mrs. Boyle before gesturing for Jesse and Sara to follow him. He and Luke flanked the pair as they stepped over to join me and Bryant.

"We've cleared the area," Jennings repeated

unnecessarily, turning to look down his nose at me. "There should be a clear and straightforward path to the car. Try not to get sidetracked again," he said nastily. I felt my face grow hot with rage as he addressed me for the first time. I forced it down, trying to find the humor in the situation—*at least he's acknowledging your existence now.* Luke looked sharply at him and opened his mouth to say something, but I shook my head imperceptibly. Arguing with a superior in front of the Boyle kids was a surefire way to get on his bad side. *Or on his worse side, in my case,* I supposed. He seemed to be waiting for a response, but receiving none, he grunted and then turned to rejoin the first lady.

"*God*, he's such an ass," Sara huffed, and I glanced at her in surprise before Bryant and I shared a knowing smile. *I guess it is all of us,* I thought, turning to watch him interact with the first lady, *except Allison Boyle, apparently.* Jennings's mannerisms were nothing less than perfectly respectful as he spoke to her. I rolled my eyes and let out a sigh.

"Ready to go?" I asked, looking first to Jesse, then to Sara. When both nodded, I turned to Luke. "Same arrangement as last time?" I asked. He didn't look happy about it, but he also didn't argue.

"I guess." He glanced at Bryant curiously.

"She'll be tailing us. You know, just in case," I explained quietly.

"Ah," he replied, and that was the end of it. I felt like every nerve in my body was tingling on high alert as we made our return route through the library. It was empty, as Jennings had promised, and the effect was more than a little creepy in a building of this size. We made quick work of our journey, and before I knew it we were back in the car and I was exchanging a farewell nod to Bryant, who had raised a hand in salute. *Maybe your intuition was wrong.* Sexist Jennings might be, but no one could claim that he neglected his job. It was deserted, giving the appearance of a what I would imagine the city would look like if there had been a mass abduction by aliens. I followed a train of thought along those lines for a considerable part of our drive, and it made the relative silence of the venture much more bearable. That beautiful silence was broken, however, by Sara.

"So, what did *you* do to make Jennings hate you? Other than being a woman, that is," she asked bluntly. I blinked at her in surprise as I returned from my thoughts to reality and lifted my shoulders in a shrug.

"Being a woman? No clue." I shrugged. "I'm sure my age doesn't help," I added as an afterthought. She nodded.

"That tracks." There was a surprising lack of animosity—toward me, that is— in her voice, and I had the distinct impression that this wasn't the first time this had happened.

"I guess it's a pretty constant thing?" I asked, ignoring a warning glance from Luke. I knew that I was blurring the lines between the personal and professional, but after all, Jennings had set himself up for it. He's the one that had made it a conversation piece by snubbing me—and apparently every other woman he's ever worked with— in a public setting.

"Every time," Jesse jumped in.

"Cool. I was beginning to think it was personal," I replied with a humorless laugh. Luke maintained his stoic silence, and I had a hunch that I would hear about this later.

"Maybe he'll get over it one day," Sara said with a long-suffering sigh. Privately, I doubted it, but hey, a girl could dream.

"It is what it is," I answered noncommittally. Luke cleared his throat, and I saw that the driver had looked at us in the rearview mirror, and I realized that he had been hanging on to every word. I sighed. At this point, if it got back to Jennings, I didn't care. He'd made his own bed.

It was not long before we were pulling through the gate of our safe house, and I felt the urge to look behind us with the lurking feeling that we were being followed. To my relief, there was no one else— vehicle or lone person— in sight behind us, and I let out a slow and measured breath. *Why am I so jumpy today?* It had been our first event since the attack, so maybe I could have chalked it up to nerves, but it seemed more like an excuse to me than a valid reason. Something still felt wrong. I reassured myself by reminding myself that we were behind the gate now in a place whose location had been divulged to only a select few. Still, the looming blanket of paranoia did not lift as we got out of the car, said our farewells to the driver, and climbed the porch steps to enter the house.

"Anyone else hungry?" Jesse asked. "I'll make lunch!" I blinked at the offer in surprise.

"Only if it's not peanut butter and jelly sandwiches again. If I never see another jar of grape jelly again, it'll be too soon," Sara answered with a long-suffering roll of her eyes. I couldn't fault her; we'd been snacking on sandwiches for days in lieu of a full lunch.

"Aw, want me to cut the crusts off your bread for you?" Jesse taunted his sister with a wicked grin, and he dodged the arm that went flying up to thump him on the back of the head, leaping through the door to avoid further assault.

"You might want to add extra jelly to Luke's; he's been particularly dry today," I teased, snickering as Luke shot me a mildly offended look.

"What did *I* do?" he asked. *As if either of us had ever needed a reason to rag on each other before. He certainly didn't.*

"Just seeing if you were paying attention. You've been quiet today," I said, instantly regretting letting him know that I had noticed when surprise flashed across his face.

"Not much to say," he replied in non-explanation. I sighed as the sound of a crash came from inside in the general direction of the kitchen.

"Would you guys cut it out?" I called. The sound was unnerving and sent my pulse pumping in my ears. The reply was another thumping noise, and I sighed again.

"Do you want to take this one, or should I?" Luke asked with a resigned sort of voice. At a third pounding noise, I flinched.

"Sounds like it might take us both," I said with a humorless laugh that he echoed. Shaking his head, he led the way into the house and through the kitchen. Luke stopped short before shooting forward again with a shout. The doorway was narrow, so I struggled to see around him. As he bolted into the room, I caught sight of Jesse, collapsed on the floor with a dazed expression and a knot blooming on his head. A sound of alarm ripped from my lungs as I shot forward. Luke was already beside the boy, clasping him on the shoulder.

"Where's Sara?" he demanded. A bloodcurdling scream from upstairs was his answer.

I moved to dart out of the room, but Luke's hand on my arm wrenched me back.

"Stay here," he ordered. I blinked at him for a moment.

"But—" I began.

"They might come back," he overruled me, and without waiting for my rebuttal, he disappeared into the labyrinth of the house. I closed the door behind him, forcing a chair under the knob. With a scrape of the legs on the floor, I labored to push the kitchen table over to it as a reinforcement. I had no way of knowing how many would-be assailants were in the house, rendering an escape a fruitless fantasy, and I needed to protect the Boyle that I knew could be kept safe. Drawing my pistol from its holster, I knelt beside Jesse, whose dazed eyes were—thankfully— starting to clear.

"Sara…?" he asked. I shook my head.

"Luke's with her. I wanted to stay here in case—" I flinched at a banging noise coming from upstairs. Jesse's eyes clouded and he fought to sit up, swaying as he rose and wincing. He glanced to the gun in my hand and the barricaded door.

"What if they need your help? I can stay here. I can—" I held up a hand to cut him off.

"Luke is with her. My job is to stay here and make sure you stay safe. He can handle it," I said with a confidence that I did not fully feel. One or two assailants, he could probably manage, but we had no way of knowing who or what was behind this. *How did they know where we were?* I knew we hadn't been followed. Another crash came from upstairs, followed by several shouts. *Crap.* I had no way of knowing which sounds came from Luke, barricaded as we were, but I felt the blood drain from my face as Sara screamed again.

"Can't you call someone, Artemis?" Jesse demanded desperately. I patted my pockets to find my phone, thinking it was very likely that they had done something to block the signal in and out of the house. A look at the bars on my screen confirmed my theory, and I shoved it under his nose wordlessly.

"It was an ambush, Jesse, all we can do now is wait," I said quietly with a calm I didn't feel. "Move behind the island," I jerked my chin at the kitchen island in question. He looked at me like I'd grown a second head.

"But why—"

"Just do it," I snapped, patience gone. I strained my ears as I heard the approach of thundering footsteps. Was it just one set? Or were there more? At my sharp look, Jesse scooted his way to follow my orders, and I tensed, weapon at the ready, as the footsteps faltered in front of the door. *Just one.* I kept my eye on the door handle as it rattled, and I knew that someone strong would be able to shove past the barricade if they were really determined to. I was waiting for the door to burst open, prepared to fire on whomever or whatever was concealed behind it, when the rattling stopped and the footsteps retreated, first as tentative steps and then with the cadence of a run.

"Are they gone?" Jesse asked, and I shushed him. *Had Luke made it to Sara in time?* The sounds from upstairs had grown silent, and I cursed the fact that we had dropped our radios in the main room before we'd heard the sounds of Jesse's struggle. I would have no way of knowing, unless… I glanced at Jesse, thinking about all of the things I knew about his family.

"You ever shot a handgun?" I asked, questioning the wisdom of giving an untrained, underaged teenager my most effective weapon.

"Yes. Dad and I used to go to the range. Before," he gestured with a hand absently. I took in his now-cleared eyes.

"How many fingers am I holding up?" I asked, holding up two and waving them around.

"Two. What are you….?" Awareness dawned in his eyes. "Won't you need it?" he asked nervously.

"I hope not." I placed it on the floor beside him. "Safety's on," I warned, hoping he would remember to swap it over if the worst happened. He looked down on it in shock, and without waiting for a response, I stood, moving toward the door. I took a deep breath as I shifted the table and then the chair, reaching for the handle when it swung open.

I didn't remember reaching for my knife, but I clearly recalled diving forward with it in my hand as I attacked without seeing. Luke's cry of alarm brought me down to earth, and I froze a hair's breadth away from slicing open the flesh on his arm.

"Are they gone?" I asked, chest heaving as Sara

stepped out from behind him, her pretty face bruised and swollen. Luke nodded, and he spat blood onto the floor.

"Jesse?" he asked.

"Fine." I looked suspiciously past the pair, eyes scanning the shadows. Finding none, I turned to face Luke again. A fresh cut marred one cheek, and his knuckles were split to match his lip.

"We need radios," he began. "Stay here with Richards, Sara, and I'll—" I didn't let him finish before I pushed past him, ignoring as he hissed my name and smiling when he actually called after me with the right one. My face fell back into lines of somber concentration as I crept along from room to room, concealing my knife as I ventured carefully around corners and blind turns. When I returned to the kitchen with my bounty, I saw Luke standing guard. A lump rose above one of his eyebrows. He was right. They were gone.

"Will those even work from this far away?" Jesse questioned, eyeing the radios dubiously. I ignored him, tossing Luke's to him. He caught it easily, and he brought it to his mouth to speak before I beat him to it.

"Idol. I repeat, Idol. Do you read?" I used Jennings's call sign. Hearing no response, I repeated myself. I exchanged worried glances with Luke before the radio crackled to life in reply.

"This is Idol. I read." I had never thought I would be thankful to hear Jennings's nasally voice, but I could not help the rush that whooshed through me at the sound of his voice.

"Idol, we've had a bit of a situation here. Requesting transport. Do you copy?" I kept it vague. It was supposed to be a secure way of communicating, but after the events of the day, I wasn't sure what to expect. The sound of static drew on for what felt like an eternity before Jennings replied.

"Copy that. We're on our way."

CHAPTER 19

The next several hours were a blur. Jennings, Bryant, and Welsch had all shown up to survey the damage to life, property, and limb, while Katz had elected to wait behind for Jesse and Sara to arrive. Jennings had swept the damage with cold eyes before his disappointed gaze rested on me. He shook his head, and somehow, I got the sense that he irrationally blamed me for this mess.

We were peppered with questions, the who, what, and how, and Luke and I had repeated ourselves so many times that I felt sure we were going to explode if we had to do so again. The so-called safe house seemed menacing now, more so as the team that had accompanied them did a sweep of the grounds, searching for any trace evidence that the assailant had left behind. Luke had given a description of the men—plural—who had accosted Jesse and Sara. I, of course, had seen no one, and we had no way of knowing if there had been others with them who had fled upon being discovered. That seemed to solidify Jennings's opinion of me as useless, but I couldn't give a firsthand account if I didn't have one, no matter how much he kept pushing me. Welsch flashed me a sympathetic look when Jennings asked me to repeat the events of the day for the third time.

"Why don't we regroup once we get back to The White House?" Welsch suggested, the silver of a new watch flashing from his wrist as he checked the time. I forced a small smile of gratitude onto my face as Jennings turned away from me to glance at the other agent.

"The White House?" Luke asked. "Not another safe house?" Jennings shot him a withering look.

"Until we can establish how they knew we were using *this* house and what other locations they might have uncovered, The White House is the safest house. I don't expect it will take long for us to find another place, but until then, the Boyles will be safer there," he answered decisively.

"Should we limit their public appearances?" I suggested. Jennings shook his head, surprisingly without condescension.

"The president thinks that would draw attention to the fact that there's an issue. He would prefer to continue business as usual." *Even if that puts his children at risk?* Perhaps President Boyle was more short-sighted than I had thought at our first meeting. Then again, I wasn't the leader of a country; maybe I wasn't in any kind of position to judge.

"Do you have any idea who's behind all of this?" Luke asked. Jennings took a deep breath.

"We'll discuss theories when we get back; we think we have a few leads. For now, go pack up your bags. We'll bring along Jesse and Sara's later. We need to get back as soon as possible." I was thankful for an excuse to leave the room, and I practically ran up the stairs to what had been my room. I hated that it had happened under these circumstances, but I felt a flutter of excitement to be headed back to Pennsylvania Avenue.

* * *

I had lived there for less than 48 hours, but it was a comforting sort of familiarity to stroll the halls of The White House again— and by stroll, I meant stride purposefully to the briefing room. Luke and I had dropped our bags at our old suite, but we hadn't had time to unpack before going to debrief—*again*. I sighed as we made our way toward the room; at least this time, we would be included in the discussions about who to look out for. I was getting tired of feeling like I was going in blind.

I cast a sidelong glance at Luke, who was wearing an inscrutable expression. He'd been quiet since this last attempt on the First Kids, not that we had really had a chance to talk away from listening ears. I had no idea if he was as troubled by it as I was, or if he was shaken up, or anything beyond what he had experienced in the clinical terms in which he had described it. I found the stoicism rattling given the circumstances, but while I wondered what he was thinking, I did not think that my usual method of drawing things out of him was going to be very helpful in this case.

I let him be the one to knock on the door once we reached our destination, and at the prompt to enter, I let him lead the way inside. As the room came into view past his shoulders, I blinked at the number of people in the room. I had been expecting Katz, Jennings, Welsch, and Bryant, and perhaps President Boyle too—although he was surprisingly absent. I hadn't expected the four or five others who crowded into the space.

"Other agents," Jennings waved a dismissive hand in way of introduction. "We can make introductions later if we have time. They know who you are, so we can get on with it." I clenched my teeth as I gave the group a tight smile, and on the edge of my vision, I saw Luke shake his head and roll his eyes. *Well, at least I'm not the only one who's annoyed by it.* What was even more annoying was the realization that each of these people probably knew more about the situation that was threatening Jesse and Sara than we did—and we were the ones who were supposed to protect them from the great unknown. I tried to mask my indignation as Welsch motioned for us to sit at the far end of the large table that now included several more chairs.

"Now," Welsch began, "the time has come to share what we've found out." The murmur of conversation died as he gathered the attention of the group. "A lot has happened in the past several months. Most of you know the details. Some of you," he inclined his head in our direction apologetically, "do not." I felt my face grow hot as several heads turned to appraise us. "We as a collective group have decided that the threat has become great enough that we all be on the lookout for suspicious activity." I covered my snort of derision with a cough—*as if we hadn't been already.* Welsch pulled out a stack of papers—more of a mountain, really— and dropped them on the table with a thud.

"These," Katz said, "are briefs detailing every part of the attacks on and the known threats to the First Family over the past year. Since the unfortunate incident that occurred a few months ago," Jennings's mouth twisted unpleasantly at the mention of the previous in-house conspiracy, "these incidents have increased in number and volatility. It's our job to find out how. It's also our job to keep it from happening again." Bryant stepped forward to address the group now.

"This most recent attack was deeply unsettling, since it occurred in a location that had been relatively undisclosed. One of our safe houses was doxed, and Jesse and Sara Boyle were attacked there. What we need to find out is how they found this information, when many of our own didn't even know it existed." She looked evenly at each of the people occupying the seats, her eyes resting a beat longer on my face and on Luke's.

"It would be helpful to know what all we know," Luke interjected quietly. Bryant blinked at him.

"What do *you* know?" she asked. He shook his head.

"No, I mean it would be helpful for Artemis and I—" he shot me an inquiring look, and I nodded, gratified that he used my chosen name, "to know what we as a collective group know." They stared at him blankly.

"In other words, we have no information, and it would really help us to do our jobs if we did," I interjected bluntly. Heads swung to stare at me in stunned silence.

"I suppose that would be acceptable," Jennings said after a pause.

"For example, why weren't we told that our predecessors betrayed their jobs and tried to kidnap the kids?" I asked pointedly. More stunned silence followed.

"How did you know that?" Welsch asked, caution coloring his voice.

"We were filled in," I answered vaguely, crossing my arms. Hopefully, that made it clear that I was not going to divulge my sources.

"Well," Welsch began uncomfortably, reddening slightly, "we just felt as though it wouldn't be the wisest course of action to share the details past corruption with the new hires."

"It would have been helpful for us to know what we were up against," I pointed out, and Welsch reddened further.

"We didn't feel that it was in anyone's best interests to reopen the doors to that type of thing," he managed, sounding a bit choked.

"In other words, you all didn't want to give us any funny ideas. Ignoring, of course, that we were trained for exactly these scenarios and that our loyalty is and always will be to the job at hand," I answered pleasantly. To that, Welsch had no response. Luke stared at me as though he hadn't really seen me before.

"In any case, now you know," Jennings salvaged, sounding put out.

"Anyone want to tell us who these scumbags *are?*" I emphasized. Jennings stared hard in my direction.

"It's irrelevant." I barked out a laugh.

"In what possible world is it irrelevant?" I asked.

"Most of them were neutralized." I blinked at him several times in quick succession.

"Neutra—? Oh." I fell silent.

"And the others?" Luke asked.

"As far as we can tell, they haven't been involved since. So, it really doesn't matter who they were. They're just another dead end." Jennings said.

"I assume you looked into their contacts?" Luke put in. Jennings looked down at him coldly, which I thought was bold of him, considering that Luke was less than half his age and currently sporting war wounds from his earlier encounter. Then again, Jennings had who knew how many years of experience, so he probably was not intimidated.

"Naturally, we took care of that," Jennings answered icily.

"And?" Luke challenged.

"There was nothing. They covered their tracks well. I saw the investigation through myself," Katz spoke up, smiling apologetically. "We left no stone unturned."

"I see. So there really aren't any leads?" Luke asked.

"I'm afraid not," Katz said, firmly though not unkindly.

"Then what *do* we know?" I asked, eyeing the leaning tower of paperwork that Jennings had dropped to the table.

"It's not so much what we know; it's a matter of where we begin," Jennings replied with a wry smile. I realized with a start that it might have been the only time I had seen Jennings smile at all.

CHAPTER 20

My head was spinning as Luke and I made our way back to our suite. The other agents had given us a surplus of information, and it was incredibly hard to digest it all at once. Then again, we had asked for it; I just hadn't been prepared to absorb it in one fell swoop.

They had figured out the identity of the man who had accosted me at the museum. Max Branford hadn't had an easy upbringing. His home life had been as inconsistent as his schooling, and somewhere along the line, he had fallen into a plot to harm the First Family. *Such a waste.* The group behind the initial attacks was still a mystery, as were their motivations. It had been initially assumed that the attacks were aimed at the president and had been poorly planned. After a surprising number of them, however, it became evident that Sara and Jesse were the intended targets. Jesse had been targeted more early on, but it seemed that they were starting to shift their focus to include Sara too. What they wanted with either of the children, no one could say. My guess was ransom or blackmail, which Katz had more or less confirmed was his suspicion too, but we had no real way of knowing. Branford had been imprisoned since the fateful day of our encounter, but he wasn't talking, and because this was the United States and his capture had been covered by the press, there were only so many ways of trying to convince him to spill his secrets. All that they had really gotten out of him was that he did not know the identity of the one in charge of the whole operation, although whether he was or was not to be believed was really anyone's guess.

Luke had remained quiet throughout the meeting, asking a question here or there, but mostly just absorbing the information. I was anxious to pick his brain and compare notes. All that I really processed was that this had been going on since just before President Boyle had assumed office. It felt like an important timeline.

That was part of what made it so interesting: this had begun well before he'd had time to make too many enemies as the leader of a world superpower. Who would preemptively target someone before they had any real power? It was anyone's guess. I pushed open the door to our suite, still thinking and barely noticing the darkness as I beelined for the couch. Behind me, Luke cleared his throat and, in one deliberate motion, turned on a lamp.

"You'd think you'd be more open to seeing things, given the circumstances," he complained halfheartedly. I chuckled.

"What, you mean me being jumped and the kids being attacked under our nose? Those circumstances, you mean?" I asked with a laugh, which Luke did not return.

"Yes," he answered dryly, raising an unamused eyebrow.

"We're in The White House; that's probably the safest place to be," I reasoned.

"Not safe enough for Jesse and Sara to stay here," he

countered.

"We aren't the targets anyway," I pointed out.

"For now," he replied carefully. "What about when they figure out we're all that's between them and their prize?" I rounded on him, glowering.

"Stop trying to talk down to me," I demanded threateningly. He did not look affronted. If anything, he doubled down.

"I'm not trying to talk down to you, Richards, but we need to be smart. This involves all of us now. We are all that stands between them and who knows what. We have to watch our own backs so that we can watch theirs." I opened and shut my mouth, but honestly, he made sense, and I had no rebuttal.

"So, what did you make of all of that mess?" I asked, changing the subject at the speed of light. He blinked at me for several seconds, clearly taken off guard by the change in trajectory, before shaking his head.

"It was a lot," he finally admitted.

"That's one way to describe it," I said darkly. "I can't believe they didn't fill us in before. It would have been nice to take it in stages instead of all at once. We could have been more prepared." Luke looked as though he was battling with himself before he replied.

"Well, at least we know now," he said.

"We sure do," I said softly. "What we do with it is another thing. I'm not quite sure how to process it all," I admitted before immediately second-guessing my decision to speak. Could I really trust Luke Ryder with a vulnerable admission? Surprisingly, after all that we had been through over the past week, I was inclined to say yes.

"Me neither," he murmured an assent. If possible, that shocked me even more. Seven days ago, we would have been at each other's throats and frequently were. Now, here we were swapping uncertainties and feelings. *What is the world coming to?* I asked myself incredulously. We sat in silence for a moment, and I wondered if he was thinking the same thing about me. I was not even remotely tempted to ask.

"So, what do we want to do with all of this? Do you feel like talking about it and sorting out what we remember from that mess?" I asked tentatively. I looked closely at him and noticed the way that his eyes were shadowed underneath. He was probably just as exhausted as I was. *More, probably. He* did *have to beat up the bad guy today*, I reminded myself.

"We can if you want to, but not really, if I'm being honest," came the admission. I was actually relieved.

"You look exhausted," I commented. He looked up at me sharply, but there was no malice behind my observation, and he apparently sensed that.

"I am a picture of beauty," he mocked proudly. "I *am* exhausted. You look pretty worn out yourself," he amended finally.

"So, bed?" I asked. He nodded.

"Are we sleeping in our actual rooms, or are we going to crash on the couch again?" he asked innocently, and I was somewhere between mortified and amused at the teasing spark that lit up his face.

"Good *night*, Ryder," I announced dryly, turning pointedly toward my room. He laughed tiredly behind me as I left the common area without looking back.

A bed had never felt so good to me, though, and within moments, I was asleep—as the cliche goes—without even fully realizing that my head had hit the pillow. I hoped for a dreamless, restful sleep, but of course, I knew that it was a highly unlikely possibility.

I was not planning on dreaming about work, but as it stands to follow with dreams, we rarely get to choose the things that haunt us while we sleep. There was some resignation mixed in with the jolt of panic that shot through my veins as I sat straight up in bed, chest heaving as my heart pounded with a sudden thought.

"What if it's still one of us?" I whispered the words aloud. *Here's to another sleepless night.*

CHAPTER 21

"You think it's someone that's still *here*?" Luke hissed in shock, keeping his voice down and looking warily around the common area of our suite. Despite my first inclination, I'd had the self-control to wait until the morning to share my new theory with Luke. The first reason was because I thought that one of us should get a full night's sleep before a busy day's work—which was very considerate of me if I did say so myself. The second reason was that I wanted to turn the theory over and over in my mind to make sure that it wasn't only my intuition guiding me, and the third—well—the third was that I needed to decide if Luke was someone that I could trust with the information. It was not that I thought he could possibly be part of the plot; I may not have always liked Luke Ryder—heck, most of the time, I still wasn't sure if I really *liked* Luke Ryder—but I knew that he wasn't a traitor. What really held me up was the question of whether or not he would run to Jennings and the others and shout my new theory to the high heavens. I eventually decided that it was a risk I needed to take, and since he hadn't laughed in my face immediately, I felt that it was going rather well.

"That makes the most sense to me. How else would they have known about the safe house?" I reasoned. He blinked at me as he considered it.

"A bug?"

"Not likely."

"Eavesdropper?"

"Less likely."

"Accidental leak?"

"With their training? No way."

"So that leaves—"

"A traitor." I finished for him. He seemed thunderstruck for a moment, and I understood. On top of everything we had learned the previous evening, this was a lot to process, and it probably seemed a lot more far-fetched than files and research in black and white.

"And why wouldn't the ones who have been here through the whole thing have thought of this?" he asked.

"Maybe they have and couldn't talk about it because the person they suspected was in the room. Maybe it's more than one of them in on the thing, although I don't think that's likely. Maybe they're just too close to it and don't want to see the possibility of it being one of their own." *Again,* I added silently before continuing. "Either way, it's worth investigating… right?" I was a little breathless as I finished. I did not realize how much I needed for him to agree that it was a possibility until we sat there with the words hanging in the balance between us. *It's not something that we should even be considering, it's probably ridiculous, but—*

"It's possible." I was not sure if Luke knew that he had finished my thought in exactly the right way at exactly the right moment, but at that moment, I was just glad that we were on the same page.

"So, what do we do with that?" I asked. "Do we watch and wait? Do we tell somebody? I'm kind of at a loss here." The admission was startling to say out loud, but to his credit, Luke concealed whatever surprise he might have felt.

"I think we should wait. We'll need to look through the things that have happened, to figure out who we *can* tell if it comes to that. Mostly, we need to be careful. If we choose the wrong person or are wrong entirely, this could get very bad very fast." Luke spoke slowly, like he was choosing every word carefully.

"And not just for us," I agreed. "Sara and Jesse too," I agreed. He nodded.

"I'll see if we can get ahold of some of the files from the previous incidents, because we'll have to be able to prove it. It might not work, but if I can get Jennings to hand them over even for a little while, maybe we can find something useful," he mused.

"Better you than me, my friend," I said. His green eyes twinkled with amusement as they met mine.

"We're friends now, then?" he asked.

"I guess we kind of have to be, don't we?" I countered.

"I guess we kind of do." His lips parted against his teeth in a devilish grin. "Or at least allies."

We decided that Luke should be the one to ask Jennings for access to the files again, since he was not very fond of me. Since Luke had agreed that we should wait to include the other agents until we could figure out who to trust, I wondered how he would explain our renewed interest to Jennings. Then again, he was Luke, and he had a way of getting what he wanted. A week ago, that trait had driven me absolutely nuts, but it was less annoying now that it was being wielded to help me.

The task had fallen to me, then, to secure breakfast, which I hated on principle but agreed to because I was starving. I had plenty of time to let my appetite build further as I got turned around more than once on my way to find the kitchens. Then came the fun task; staring at the spread in front of me and trying to figure out what Ryder would eat. My stomach grumbled at the sight of the table laden with pastries and toast and jams galore, but it was the smell of freshly brewed coffee that called to me like a siren song. My feet carried me over to the large coffee urn, and I fumbled with the flimsy cups as I peeled them apart and filled one for myself. I was half-tempted to forego the food altogether just to carry a second cup, but I discarded the idea, picturing the look on Luke's face if I showed up empty-handed. Still, there were worse vices to have in our line of work, and I found myself contemplating how to carry plates for us along with the spare cup. *It's basically Tetris, right?* As it turned out, the game was not as easy when you were stacking unevenly made plates of food on top of precariously full cups of hot coffee, so it was with a forlorn look backwards that I took what bounty I could and had to forego my extra caffeine boost. *On the bright side, Ryder's probably beaten me back to the suite, so I probably won't have to wait.*

My instincts were right. As I balanced the unsteadily piled plates and fought to open the latch, Luke was seated on the couch with a spread of papers in front of him. *I guess it worked,* I thought. He barely glanced up when I entered, and I tried once, twice, three times to close the door with a hook of my foot before I cleared my throat loudly.

"Hey, Ryder. A little help?" He looked up, seeming to see me for the first time. Luke jumped to his feet and hurried over.

"Sorry. I was just—" he gestured vaguely to the pile of papers before shutting the door behind me.

"Thanks," I said, slightly out of breath. I delivered the piled-high plates to one of the end tables with a flourish, since the coffee table was currently occupied by a mountain of paperwork.

"I guess Jennings said yes?" I observed, taking in the mess.

"After a valiant effort," he answered. "He wasn't

happy about it, but he understood why I was asking, and I don't think he could really figure out how to argue against it." One cheek dimpled as he grinned, and I found myself smiling slightly in return.

"Huzzah," I held up a muffin in a toast. "Cheers to your brave efforts on our behalf." He gave me a funny look, but he compliantly grabbed a scone of his own, lifting it in salute before taking a massive bite.

"Cheers," he said with his mouth full. I devoured my muffin as I surveyed the pages that littered the table.

"Where do we start?" I asked. He held up a finger as he finished chewing. He swallowed thickly and reached for a muffin.

"It's not all here, but these are the most recently documented incidents. If we can find some sort of commonality in who was working, or which communications were being monitored, I figure that maybe that will give us a good idea of where to start… before, you know, we have to start hurling accusations," he finished with a small grimace. The thought weighted my stomach. I had a strong conviction that I was right, and I knew that I shouldn't doubt my intuition, but the idea of tackling senior agents if it came to that was daunting.

"Probably wise," I answered absently, turning over the possibilities in my mind. I felt Luke lay his hand on my arm reassuringly, and I looked at it blankly in surprise.

"If there's something there, we'll find it." I wished that I shared his certainty, but I was not in any type of position to make an argument, which was a pretty strange position to be in when it came to interacting with Luke.

"I guess we should get started," I suggested, uncomfortably aware that he was still touching me. As though sensing the same thing, he removed his hand and looked away.

"I guess we should."

CHAPTER 22

I tossed another file onto the table, feeling a flash of irritation as it bounced off another and slid onto the floor. We had been at it for hours, trying to pull the threads of this tangled web to see if we could find our way to the center. Somehow, after hours of trudging through paperwork, we were no closer to making sense of it all than we had been when we started. I let out a low hiss of frustration from between clenched teeth as I bent to pick it up and replace it on the table. As I did, two more files slid onto the floor.

"Oh, for the *love* of—" I picked them up and shoved them back into place, barely preventing the first file from reclaiming its place on the floor. "Stay!" I ordered, holding my hands back and at the ready in case they tried to pitch themselves to the floor again. When they didn't I let out a sigh of relief and turned to see Luke smirking from behind his own file. As he sensed me looking at him, his eyebrows raised above green eyes that still looked frustratingly bright. I put my hands to my face, pressing my fingers into my exhausted eyes before dropping them to see that he was still studying.

"Need a break?" he asked, the smirk widening. I

scowled in his direction without looking at him.

"No. I need any of this to make sense," I huffed with annoyance, casting a dark look back on the files.

"Well, there is *one* part of it that makes sense," Luke said. He closed his folder with a snap and tossed it onto the table. My scowl deepened as I stared at him.

"What?" he asked. I closed my eyes and took a deep breath before opening them again.

"What makes sense?" I asked, changing the subject.

"Whoever's behind this is really good at covering their tracks and making each incident look like an isolated event," he said.

"Which, unfortunately for us, does nothing to narrow down our suspect list," I reminded him dryly. He shrugged.

"I don't know about that," he said slowly. I felt one eye twitch. *Could he* be *any more vague?*

"Okay, as much as I enjoy the building anticipation, would you just tell me what you mean?" I asked rudely.

"Well, if we're right, then someone covered their tracks really well. These all look like disconnected issues, but they always happen in the same way and with the same targets. That means whoever's in charge of this is smart enough not to get caught. And…" he trailed off, furrowing his brow in thought.

"And what?" I prompted.

"I don't have any way of proving it, but something about the way these have all been laid out in the files makes me think that they missed documenting the details that could have tied it all together. There are just some things they don't describe in the files, which makes me think…" he trailed off again, gesturing vaguely.

"Meaning that whoever is behind it must have a pretty thorough knowledge of our procedures," I finished for him, and he nodded sheepishly.

"I have no way of proving I'm right," he countered

his own theory.

"But it makes sense if something's being concealed. And there are enough of these things," I gestured wildly to the mess of files littering the room, "that after enough time has passed, no one would notice if there were details missing."

"Well, yes." He blinked at me, seeming surprised that I was trying to convince him of his own suspicions, and I was taken aback by it myself. Still, I agreed with his assessment, and there was no sense in pretending otherwise.

"Like there's still not much of a mention of the agents that had our jobs before us. And that wasn't so far in the past," I pointed out. It was true, the situation had been spoken of in the loosest of terms, but so many of the details—their contacts, family, prior associations—had been left out of their suspect profiles. They weren't even mentioned by their names, only their initials.

"I guess we could find out their names from Sara and Jesse," he offered halfheartedly.

"I'd hate to involve them, though. They're already at risk enough from whoever it is," I said, biting on the corner of my lip as I racked my brain.

"Do you have any other ideas?" he asked. My eyes jumped up to meet his with a hostile retort ready on my tongue, but to my surprise, it seemed as though the question hadn't been sharply meant. I thought for a moment.

"I really don't," I admitted finally.

"Well...." he trailed off.

"We probably should see what they have to tell us," I allowed. I saw his shoulders shift as he inhaled deeply, blowing out the breath a moment later.

"Now we just have to figure out when. We'll have to find a time when the four of us can be alone," he said thoughtfully. I nodded my agreement. That should not be hard. We'd spent the previous day away from the

Boyle kids to be briefed, but I knew that it was unlikely we would be away from them for long. Even in The White House, we would be expected to keep an eye on things. Luke glanced down at his watch and let out a low groan.

"What?" I asked. He twisted his arm to show me the time, and I jumped. "No way, it can't already be noon." We really had been at it for hours. Much more time, and they would assume that *we* had been kidnapped.

"We're going to be late," he groaned.

"To what?" I asked tentatively.

"Jennings wanted us to have these back by now." I squinted at him.

"He thought we would be able to get through all of this by *noon*?" I asked. I mean, we had, but barely.

"Apparently, he had just the right amount of faith in us," Luke said, snorting as though he had amused himself.

"There's a first time for everything, I guess," I muttered. With a slight sigh, I rose, and Luke and I slowly gathered the folders into piles. As we started to combine them, I hesitated, shooting Luke a questioning look.

"They weren't really in any order," he said apologetically. "It wasn't exactly a testament to their record-keeping." He had a point there, and I thought personally that it was further evidence—however circumstantial—that someone was deliberately concealing information that could help get to the bottom of things.

"How in the world did you get all of this by yourself," I grunted, hefting a sizable chunk of the files into my arms.

"Very carefully." I knew that we looked completely ridiculous as we made our way to the briefing room at Luke's direction with our arms laden with folders and dog-eared pages. *Someone should tell them that the future is digital.* The thought made me smile before another sobered me. *Then again, at this rate I'm not sure I would trust their cybersecurity.* I wondered what the rush was for Jennings to have us return the documents. We had made it through an initial skim of the pertinent information, but it would have been nice to have been given the time to cross-reference pieces of it.

I thought of Jennings's attitude toward us throughout our investigation, and a niggling suspicion wormed its way through me. In a sequence that seemed outside of my control, I thought of all of the instances of his hostility, and the fact that he had seemed to be in control of the goings-on related to Jesse and Sara's security detail, and then the fact that he seemed to be in charge of how the records were kept and organized followed it. With a creeping horror, I wondered if he had been behind it all along. *Surely, he wouldn't be so stupid enough to be openly hostile and so openly conceal information if he was,* a voice in my head reasoned. *But he operates at the top of the hierarchy here. What's to stop him?* The horror was sinking like a dead weight in the pit of my stomach as I realized that if he was behind this, nothing and nobody really could. *Unless someone figured it out and outed him,* I finished the thought. My heart thudded its pulse in my ears as my hands and feet started to tingle. *This is* not *the time to panic. Have some self-control,* I scoffed at myself with a nervous glance at Luke. My eyes darted back and forth involuntarily for a few moments before I focused on the flooring in front of me and willed my mind to concentrate on taking one step at a time. Slowly, the tingling receded, and my pulse evened out. It was just in time; we had arrived. I glanced down at the watch on Luke's wrist, and thought, *not a moment too soon.* Luke raised a still-scraped fist, and as his damaged knuckles rapped on the door, I winced. He shot me a curious look.

"Does that not *hurt*?" I asked, looking pointedly down at his still-balled fist. He relaxed his hand, and flexed his fingers, but as he opened his mouth to respond, the door swung open, and we were greeted by Welsch, who looked unsurprised to see us.

"Come on in and set them down," he said without a greeting. I blinked at his briskness, thinking that we must have interrupted something. Nevertheless, Luke and I stepped into the room with the files in tow. I stopped short when I saw Jennings, eyeglasses perched on his nose, sitting in the chair at the far end of the table as he reviewed data of his own. He looked for all the world like the evil genius in a children's movie, and again, I had the flash of thought that he might well be the villain of our story as well.

"You're late," Jennings said without looking up. *Yep, saw that coming.* It was 12:07.

"We brought back the files we borrowed," I ventured.

"You can set them on the table with the rest," he replied, still not looking up at us. I exchanged confused glances with Luke.

"You don't want to make sure that they're all accounted for?" I could not keep the surprise out of my tone, and Jennings finally looked up, staring at me with eyes that were hard with dislike.

"If they're not, I'll know who to fire, won't I? You can set them on the table with the rest," he repeated coldly before looking back down at the papers spread out in front of him. Luke and I exchanged uncertain glances, and I let him be the first to step forward and replace the files on the table. I followed suit, and then we both stepped back. *Should I expect a dismissal from his highness?* I bit back the words and arranged my features into a neutral expression. There was an awkward silence that stretched beyond social acceptability, and Welsch was making me nervous, glancing between us and Jennings, back and forth, back and forth until I thought that his head might pop off. *How did he ever become an agent with* that *poker face?*

I wondered. When Jennings did not speak, I nudged Luke, who was standing with his hands clasped behind his back. His green eyes met mine, and I jerked my head in the direction of the door. He shrugged, considered for a heartbeat, and then nodded. At that, I turned, my earlier suspicions clamoring in my head once again.

"Before you go, Ryder," Jennings said, "take one of these for you and Richards." We turned just in time to see something small and black hurtling through the air, followed by another. With impressive agility that could only be achieved from years of training, Luke caught one and nearly had to dive to catch the other before it crashed to the floor. Luke handed, rather than hefted, one of the missiles at me, and I looked at it in disbelief.

"Flip phones?" I asked aloud before I could stop myself.

"We've set these up so that they're not traceable. Use them. All of the numbers you'll need have been programmed in." Jennings said in a tone that did not allow for argument.

"Instead of the radios?" Luke asked in surprise.

"Exclusively," he answered firmly. Luke paused, and I shot him a look of confusion that he answered with a half-shrug.

"Do you want those back?" he asked.

"They can travel with you," Jennings said.

"Uh…" Luke began.

"Use the phones until we tell you otherwise. One way or another, we're going to figure out how this keeps happening." It was the first admission from Jennings that the scope of the problem was beyond him, but given my newfound suspicions, I was not sure that I could trust what he was saying. He fell silent again, and we waited a few more moments before I cleared my throat.

"Is there anything else we should know?" I asked

with the hint of a challenge. To my annoyance, Jennings still refused to look at me. *What is with that guy?*

"You can go," Jennings dismissed with an absent wave of his hand. Feeling as though I had just been snubbed—probably because I had— I turned on my heel and left without a backward glance. Luke's footsteps behind me told me that he had followed me, and I resisted the urge to barge back through the door and give Jennings a piece of my mind. Could be pretty dangerous, actually. If he is behind all of this, it's probably better for him to keep underestimating you, my inner voice reasoned. I shook my head; I hated when the mature side of me was right, which I supposed was most of the time.

"We should probably go check in with Jesse and Sara. You know, just so they don't think we've fallen off the face of the earth. And maybe to see if they can add anything to what we know now?" Luke suggested as we closed the door on our suite. I heard him without really listening, twisting the end of my ponytail as I thought about how to express what I had been turning over in my head.

"I think Jennings might be the one behind all of this," I blurted. Okay, so that probably wasn't the best way to say that, I thought as soon as the words left my mouth. I forced myself to look Luke in the face, and his expression told me that he was thoroughly taken aback.

"You think that.... Jennings?" he asked incredulously. I felt a self-conscious heat rush to my face, but now that I had said it aloud, there was no turning back.

"I do," I said firmly.

"But... why?" he asked. I wondered briefly if I had been off-track. Plainly, the thought had never crossed Luke's mind.

"Think about it, Ryder. He's the talking head for the

rest of the agents, he pushes the buttons. He's the one that divvies out responsibilities. He's the one who was in control of the records that we both agreed were missing information," I looked at him pointedly, "and there's the fact that he was so reluctant to give us the details in the first place. It makes me think that he's worried about us figuring him out."

"Or it could be because the last agents he trusted betrayed the job and the Boyles," Luke pointed out. "Artemis, he may be the main point of communication for us, but that doesn't mean someone else couldn't go rogue. He may be an ass, but I don't think that means he's our guy."

"What about these?" I held my new phone aloft. Luke blinked at me.

"The phones?"

"Yes. Another thing he's been put in charge of. Now, he's changing the whole way we have to communicate?" I said stubbornly.

"Yes, because they're less likely to be compromised. If he wanted to tap into how we communicate, he could do it better with these." Luke held up his personal cell phone. He had a point there.

"I don't know. I just… I don't trust him, Luke. There's something about him that I just don't trust." Luke nodded in reply.

"I get that. I don't really trust him either. Granted, I don't distrust him, I just…" he trailed off, scratching at the back of his neck. "I just don't think we have enough proof to go around throwing those kinds of accusations in his face. Not yet," he added as I opened my mouth to argue.

"I wasn't planning on having a big, dramatic 'gotcha' moment," I muttered.

"I didn't think you were. I just think we need to be really careful here," he replied mildly. The vote of confidence was a pleasant surprise. It wasn't that long ago that he would have readily assumed the worst of me.

"I still think we should talk to Jesse and Sara about what they've seen; I just wanted you to know where my head was at," I answered. He seemed surprised by that, although I wasn't entirely sure why; we may drive each other nuts, but we were a team the second we arrived. The surprise faded into a curl of a smirk.

"You know, there are people you can talk to if you feel like you've lost your head," he teased.

"Is that from personal experience?" I fired back with a dramatic roll of my eyes. He doesn't miss a beat. Luke threw his head back and laughed, and I stared at him for a moment, caught up in the sight of the dimples that the laughter carved into his cheeks. A second later I joined in, the stress of the day dissolving into mirth as I cackled alongside him. Luke paused, glancing at me as he did, but something in my face kept the surge of his giggles coming apparently, because a heartbeat later, his laughter continued.

"We must be stressed, this w-wasn't that…. wasn't that f-funny," he said between peals of laughter.

"Maybe we've b-both lost our h-h-heads," I cackled, sending us down the rabbit hole of merriment again. It took a while for the laughter to stop, and I was almost disappointed when it did. I wiped my watering eyes with the back of my hand, letting out a long, slow breath as my abdomen stopped cramping.

"So, before we devolve into total insanity, we should probably go talk to Sara and Jesse," I suggested once we had caught our breath. The smile on Luke's face slowly faded as reality set in once again. I was sorry to see it go. He had a nice smile. It was like a patch of bright blue amidst all the thunderheads: refreshing and unexpected. Nice, Artemis. Now you're waxing poetic. I snorted at myself, making Luke's expression shift into concern—probably for my sanity. I waved it off so that we could return to the subject at hand.

"Today?" he asked, seeming surprised.

"No time like the present. I can't justify sitting idle while someone is out there plotting to hurt them or kidnap them or whatever it is, can you?" I asked. He shrugged.

"I guess not, when you put it that way. I wish we knew what they were after," he admitted, looking away as he said so.

"Me too. But our best shots at finding out are in the same building. Let's go see what they know."

CHAPTER 23

We found the Boyle siblings in one of the sitting rooms on the second floor, sitting with their heads bent low as they discussed something that was obviously important. I felt a little bit like an intruder, but in my defense, they had left the door open. Whatever they were discussing could not have been *that* private—that, or they were worse at protecting themselves than I had thought. Clearly, they weren't as practiced as Luke or I at sensing an intrusion, because they kept their heads bent low in conversation for several seconds until Luke cleared his throat. The siblings jumped, clacking their foreheads together with an audible sound, and I winced in sympathy.

"Ow!" Sara complained, rubbing the spot where her head had hit her brother's. "When did you get so hard-headed?"

"You're one to talk," Jesse grumbled. "Haven't I been beaten up enough for the week?" Jesse still bore a few bruises from our encounter at the last safe house, but thankfully, his visible injuries were healing more quickly than Luke's.

"Are we interrupting something important?" I asked with one raised eyebrow. Sara narrowed her eyes at me and looked at the floor, and Jesse looked as though he wanted to evaporate where he sat.

"No! I mean, yes! I mean…. we were just talking about… everything." He gestured wildly with his hands, and I assumed he meant everything to do with the most recent incident at the safe house.

"Well, if everything means the last attack, that's what we were hoping to talk to you two about as well," I answered conversationally. Jesse continued to look acutely uncomfortable, but Sara looked evenly at me.

"I guess that's fine," she said, and I blinked at her in surprise. She was actually addressing me in something other than a condescending tone, and she hadn't hit on Luke at all in the sixty seconds she'd been aware of his presence. This was progress.

"Really?" I asked, unable to hide my shock in time.

"Really?" Jesse seemed as surprised as I was.

"If she was trying to kill us or kidnap us or whatever those pieces of—-whatever those people were trying to do, they'd have done it there, not helped rescue us," Sara said reasonably to her brother, as though she were explaining primary colors to a five-year-old. Jesse seemed to struggle with himself for a moment—my assumption was that he was deciding whether or not to be offended by her tone—before he shrugged.

"That's fair," he answered.

"What would you like to know," she asked.

"First, I think we need to know more about the last agents who were here. The ones before us who, well…" Luke trailed off.

"The records we reviewed don't have much information on them personally, which I found surprising. I think they're our best shot on linking these attacks to whoever is orchestrating them," I felt my eyes wander over to Luke, who gave me the smallest of shakes of his head, "since they were such a major part of it from what we understand," I finished, and Luke looked relieved that I hadn't brought up

Jennings. I didn't know why he was worried, though. The last thing I wanted to do was tell the siblings at all that we suspected one of our own of being behind it. It would only make them panic, and that would make our jobs much, much harder.

"I know you might not have known a whole lot about them; we're trained to separate our personal and professional lives, but—" Luke was interrupted.

"We didn't know everything, but we did know some things. They were like you guys. Not young, but a man and a woman. Older than you. Probably around Agent Bryant's age?" Jesse recalled. I was surprised that he spoke up; I had expected Sara to offer the most information to us. In all honesty, I had not expected Jesse to contribute much at all.

"And their names?" Luke asked. Sara looked thunderstruck.

"They didn't even have their *names* in the records?" she demanded. *Oops.* Maybe we shouldn't have told her that.

"Not in the ones we were given," Luke answered carefully. I knew we both had to be careful of what we said to the pair, and I had to admit that Luke was doing the job admirably.

"Agent Hughes and Agent Bradshaw," Sara interrupted, screwing her mouth up with displeasure at the names.

"You weren't fond of them, I take it?" I said mildly. She shook her head violently.

"Not at all. They barely gave us the time of day; I guess I should have known something was wrong," she said frustratedly.

"You had no way of knowing that," I reassured her. "Now, is there anything in particular you two remember about them? Anything that could help us link them to whoever's behind all of this?" I prompted. Sara shook her head again.

"Nothing, really. I don't even remember their first

names," she admitted.

"John and Victoria," Jesse quipped, and Sara shot him a surprised look.

"You remember that?" she asked, stating the obvious. Jesse rolled his eyes.

"I *do* pay attention to things, you know," he replied, sounding slightly offended. I let out a breath of relief. Names were something to go on, and if another man-woman pairing had been unreliable in our jobs, maybe it explained why Jennings was so skeptical of me? Unless, of course, he was behind the whole thing, which I still had a strong feeling about.

"Do you remember anything else? Anything they said, anyone they talked to?" Luke redirected the two back to the topic at hand, and I flashed him a grateful look. This would have been difficult to do on my own and still put the pieces of information into place. It was nice to not have to do it alone.

"Hughes was on his phone a lot, always talking to someone, but I thought that he was probably just trying to figure out what to do with us or getting instructions, so I didn't pay much attention to it," Sara divulged. There was no telling where that phone was now, so we likely had no way of knowing who his contacts had been. I sighed again. It was nice to get at least some information, but unfortunately, it hadn't been anything that we could use so far.

"They had a lot of meetings," Jesse commented. I swiveled my head to stare at him.

"Meetings?" I asked, waiting for him to explain further.

"Yeah. I mean, you guys have had a lot of meetings because it's your first week, but they had a lot of meetings… after," he finished, with a wave of one of his hands.

"Do you know who they were meeting with?" I asked cautiously. Jesse shrugged.

"They never really said; they were just gone. I

figured it was probably the rest of the team, though," he answered. "Sorry," he added as an afterthought.

Thought, figured, assumed. This was a long way from the cold, hard proof that I had hoped we would have after talking to Jesse and Sara. Then again, our predecessors had been professionals, even if they weren't—and I didn't think they were—agents of the IPS. The likelihood of them slipping up around a couple of teenagers, even one that they had underestimated, was small.

"Can you walk us through what happened that day? The day they were found out?" I heard my voice ask the question before I had made it a tangible thought in my mind. Jesse and Sara exchanged a thoughtful look before Sara shrugged.

"Yeah, but I'm not sure how helpful it'll be. Was that not in the record either?" she asked with an edge to her voice. I couldn't say that I blamed her.

"No, it was," Luke assured, "but we want to hear it from you two."

"Well, we were at a school," Sara began, "Franklin Prep. We were reading to the kids," she explained, "so they had us split up and going to different classes. I was in first grade, and Jesse was in…." she trailed off as she tried to remember.

"Third. I was in the next hall," Jesse filled in helpfully. "I remember us both thinking it was weird that they'd split us up for something like that. Usually, only one of us would go at a time, or a split like that would be preplanned."

"It wasn't preplanned?" That surprised me, but it made sense if the head of whatever operation this was had been giving the other agents orders.

"No, not really. We had thought we were going to visit the classes together and then take turns reading. Then we got there, and Agent Bradshaw told us that the plan had changed," Sara's face darkened with dislike again at the mention of Bradshaw's name. I wondered what exactly had happened between them to make her so vehemently despise her, but then I reasoned that outright betrayal and the endangerment of life and limb was probably enough to put a sour taste in anyone's mouth.

"I wonder who changed that at the last minute," I wondered aloud, drawing a sharp glance from Luke, "like what made one of them decide to change it," I covered.

"I don't know. Agent Hughes was on the phone a lot that day, but that was normal for him," Jesse said.

"Anyway, we were separated, and after I finished reading to my first class, I had to use the bathroom. So I asked the teacher in that room where the nearest one was—I figured that it wouldn't be a big deal to slip in and out. Agent Bradshaw walked me out, but she kind of shoved me past the bathroom and told me to keep walking. Her voice had changed," Sara's face clouded as she recounted the memory, and I could only imagine that the other agent's tone had turned dark and threatening.

"I guess I was still in my class at that time. The kids had a lot of questions," Jesse half-smiled faintly at the memory, but it didn't quite reach his eyes.

"You were," Sara said, and I blinked at her in surprise. "I asked Agent Bradshaw where he was, and she said he was finishing up, and then we would leave. I remember that I thought it was strange, because we hadn't said goodbye to the principal, and I hadn't quite finished with my class yet."

"I wasn't far behind you, though. I finished up with my kids, and then Agent Hughes told me that we had to leave right after," he added.

"So, they split you up for a reason," Luke said quietly, and I could practically see the wheels of his mind turning.

"I guess they figured if they did it that way, they could get at least one of us if they got caught," Sara said bitterly. I couldn't blame her for her bitterness.

"But they didn't get either of you?" I prompted. She shook her head, her auburn hair dancing before it came to rest on her shoulders.

"No. I realized something was wrong when I didn't recognize the driver," she smiled apologetically. "After a while, you can recognize everyone; there are only a few of them." Luke smiled reassuringly, and her eyes lit up. *Even when recounting a traumatic experience? Really?* I wasn't sure why it bothered me.

"Go on," I urged, mostly to keep myself from going down that rabbit hole of self-analysis.

"Well, I..." she smiled sheepishly. "I argued. The driver tipped me off, but then when I didn't see Jesse... I just kind of refused to cooperate." With a grim smile of my own, I understood exactly how a refusal to cooperate from Sara Boyle must have looked.

"I was still inside, so I didn't know any of this until after," Jesse interjected again, and I nodded at him before my eyes returned to Sara's face.

"What happened next?" Luke asked. She took a deep breath.

"Well, Agent Jennings and Agent Katz were there. It was our first time doing an event by ourselves, so they had wanted extra hands." Privately, I knew that this was because there had been other attempts on the siblings, but I was not sure just how much of that they knew, so I decided that it wasn't the right time to share that particular nugget of information.

"And then?" I prompted.

"Well, it's all kind of a blur. Agent Jennings came sprinting out of the school— I remember that clearly because it was the fastest I had ever seen him move— Agent Katz was behind him. There was a lot of shouting, and a couple of pulled guns. The driver made a run for it. Agent Bradshaw pushed me, and I fell on the ground." Her face twisted in distaste at the memory. "There were some shots fired, so I crawled under the car." That was probably just as dangerous, in retrospect, but I kept that opinion to myself. "And then Agent Katz was helping me up, and it was over."

"And Agent Hughes?" I asked, turning to Jesse.

"We heard the gunshots from the hallway. He ran," Jesse said simply.

"Because he knew that he was caught too," I reasoned, and Jesse shrugged.

"I guess. At the time, I thought it was because he was a coward. I filled in the blanks later," he said, looking at the ground.

"He got away." It wasn't a question that sprouted from Luke's lips, and I met his eyes.

"He got away," I affirmed. Sara looked between the two of us suspiciously.

"You're not going to tell anyone we told you that, are you? Mom doesn't like it when we talk about it, and Agent Jennings told us to keep the details to ourselves until they figured out how something like that had happened." I shook my head.

"No, we can keep that between us," Luke assured her, and she looked slightly less troubled.

So, Jennings had stopped the whole thing, I thought. That really put a hole in my theory that he was the mastermind behind it all. Still, I couldn't shake my uneasy feeling. If it hadn't been Jennings, then who? Who else would have had that kind of pull, to hide the details and change up the logistics? I studied the wall behind Sara's head, chewing on the inside of my lip as I thought. *Unless it hadn't gotten approval?* It was possible that Jennings had noticed that the information in the records was lacking. If he wasn't behind the conspiracy, it was likely that the change in logistics had not been approved at all or that the agents had simply gone rogue. It would have been foolish to attempt something like that with both Jennings and Katz there, though, unless there had been another moving part. *Maybe something was supposed to distract them so they could get away? Maybe some part of the plan failed.* I huffed out a breath. We may have gained more of an understanding about what had happened to our predecessors, but we were no closer to getting to the bottom of the mystery. We were still missing something big.

We made stunted conversation with the siblings for a few minutes before a twin buzzing emanated from the phones in our pockets. Our eyes met as we wordlessly reached into our pockets and pulled out the phones. Mine had a text on it, and I assumed that Luke's phone had received the same.

Briefing. Ten minutes.

"Seriously? Flip phones?" At Sara's indignant observation, I let out a chuckle.

"Apparently untraceable," I explained with a snort. It was true that they were more secure than their more computerized counterparts, but the technology felt dated.

"We have to go," Luke said suddenly, looking troubled. I glanced over at him in concern, but his face gave nothing away. We made our goodbyes to Jesse and Sara, who were both wide-eyed as owls at the sudden shift in tone. Luke and I walked beside each other in silence, and I wondered what he could possibly be thinking; I got the sense that it wasn't a need for punctuality that had made him want to leave so abruptly. When we were out of earshot of the room, I let out a startled yelp as he grabbed my arm and pulled hard, seizing the knob to a door, and pitching me inside. I twisted when the darkness swallowed me whole as he pulled the door shut behind us.

"What the—" I exclaimed before he clapped a hand over my mouth. I stuck out my tongue, and he made a noise that sounded somewhere between a croak and a gag.

"Shut up," he hissed. I complied for a moment, but he said nothing in the way of explanation.

"Is there a reason you dragged me into a closet? I don't appreciate being manhandled." I whispered fiercely. I wasn't sure why we were whispering, but if he was insistent on it, I didn't want to find out what he had seen or heard.

"I didn't want to be overheard," he said. I tensed.

"Was there someone—" I began.

"No, but there are ears all over the place around here," he admitted grudgingly. "I didn't want to take a chance." I rolled my eyes, although he couldn't see in the darkness. *He could have just said that.*

"And here I thought I was about to be murdered with no witnesses," I whispered. As my eyes adjusted to the gloom, I saw Luke run a hand through his hair, making it stand on end.

"Not yet," he muttered back.

"What, then? Were you about to confess your secret, undying love for me?" I teased. My joke was met with silence, and my heart pounded as a flush crept up my throat. *Wait, no. I take it back!*

"I just knew you'd understand." Luke's voice, dripping with sarcasm, brought me down to earth.

"Well, spit it out then, before we're late," I said roughly.

"Blythe Artemis Richards," he began theatrically, and I smacked him in the stomach. His responding grunt was satisfying.

"Be serious," I snapped, unnerved. He let out a light laugh, and I felt his breath, warm on my face. "You need mouthwash," I muttered, not meaning it.

"We learned something today," he changed the subject, ignoring my recommendation.

"Yes, I was there," I answered.

"We know that there are two people we can trust now," he said. He was right. We could effectively rule out Jennings and Katz as being involved in the conspiracy; they had been there to stop one of the incidents.

"I don't know that I'll ever trust Jennings," I complained, following his train of thought.

"*Meaning*, we can tell someone our theory. We don't have to go at it alone anymore. We'll be able to find out more with help," he said emphatically. "We're a little in over our heads. We need all of the help we can get," he added. I hated that he was right.

"You think *Jennings* is going to listen to what we have to say? He'll think I've corrupted you with my squirrel-sized female brain or something," I said bitterly. I felt Luke's shoulders shake with silent laughter, and I smacked him hard on the shoulder. Luke's breath was hot against my cheek again as he leaned in close.

"Well, Agent Katz, then. He'd never be tactless enough to mention your squirrel-sized brain," Luke said.

"You *absolute*–" What I had been about to say was cut off by a loud crash from the end of the hall and a screech of alarm. Luke and I stiffened, and I leapt forward, grasping the door handle and flinging open the closet door in time to see a girl with rich, auburn hair fall to the ground, clutching her side. I raced to her side, conscious of Luke beside me. Blood poured from the young woman's fingers, sticky, hot, and scarlet. I ripped off my blazer when I reached her side and crouched, bundling the fabric and clutching it to the wound. Luke danced from one foot to the other as I applied more and more pressure.

"Don't just stand there. Go after them; I've got this." I barked at him. Without a response, Luke dashed around the corner in the only direction where the assailant could have fled.

"I'm going to die. Oh, God. I'm going to die," the young woman moaned, pale-faced and shaking now. Her eyelashes fluttered against her cheeks as she nearly fainted.

"No you're not. What's your name?" I asked. She looked up at me with startling gray eyes.

"Lena. Lena Jacobs," she said with quivering lips, and then she promptly fainted. Cursing under my breath, I continued applying pressure with one hand before fumbling for my phone, bloodied hands slipping across the keys as I pressed the first number that popped up.

"What?" Jennings's voice crackled to life on the first ring. "You're late."

"Get here now. There's been another incident." I gave him a quick rundown of our location before dialing 9-1-1 as Lena fluttered into consciousness again. She looked down at my blood-soaked blazer, still pressed firmly into her side, and let out another bloodcurdling scream as I had to repeat to the operator that we would need an ambulance at The White House.

CHAPTER 24

"…just had to call about the intern and rouse the public, didn't you?" Jennings had been lecturing me for the past quarter of an hour, and I'd had enough.

"Would you rather me have waited and then called the coroner?" I snapped. "You saw her condition. Her name is Lena, by the way, in case you want to send flowers or a card or demonstrate that you have *some* compassion." Somehow, he'd not thought to lecture Luke on not catching the person responsible; it was only my perceived failings that warranted a verbal lashing. Jennings put two fingers to the bridge of his nose and massaged up toward his forehead. I braced myself for a scolding or a punishment for the way I'd spoken.

"No," he growled, ignoring my attitude entirely. "How did this happen?" he asked, mostly to himself.

"My guess is that they thought she was Sara and panicked when she wasn't," I offered helpfully. He glared at me, his glasses magnifying his sharp, blue eyes.

"I know *that*, Richards. I mean, how did they manage to do this at The White House?" I, of course, had known that he had meant that, and I decided that it would be a smart choice not to antagonize him further. I turned to the opposite end of the room, where Agent Katz was having Luke describe his pursuit of the attacker in vivid detail. Unfortunately, it didn't seem as though Luke had managed to catch up to them—either that, or his target had slipped out of sight, which was even more chilling to think about.

"I suppose we'll be moving Sara and Jesse to a new safe house, then?" I asked, not taking my eyes from Luke and Katz as they seemed to finish up. Luke glanced up, seeming to ask if it was safe to rejoin us, and I gave a subtle nod in response.

"We'll have to," Jennings said through gritted teeth, "if we can find a place they don't already have on their radar."

"Has the president been briefed yet?" I asked. To my surprise, Jennings did not sneer at the question; he simply nodded.

"Bryant and Welsch are with the family now. They're shaken," he replied.

"Understandably so," Katz offered as he and Luke joined us.

"They could have had inside help," I offered casually. All three men blinked at me in response, the shock crackling like lightning in the air.

"What?" Jennings demanded in a hiss. The color drained from Katz's face.

"You think there's someone else here who's a traitor?" he asked. "Who?" I shrugged, a motion which felt a little casual and dismissive, given the weight of the circumstances.

"I have no idea, but it makes sense," I said. Luke glanced between the two older agents, but he apparently had nothing to add, because he stayed silent.

"It's impossible," Jennings said coldly. I blinked at him several times before answering, and even Katz shot him an uneasy look.

"Is it though? I mean, if it was possible for them to infiltrate The White House and stab a girl, doesn't that mean they could have had inside help?" I reasoned. "The only people who've known the exact movements of the Boyles have been agents. I think we have to consider that one of us is in on it." The casual nature of my tone felt very discordant with the context of the conversation, and I felt a little bit like I was watching it all happen from outside of my body. Jennings leaned forward, and I resisted the urge to take a step back.

"I vetted every single one of our agents. Every single one of our new hires, including *you*. It's impossible. Corruption this deep doesn't happen twice. We learned from what happened last time. It did *not* happen again," Jennings spat in a dangerous tone. He jerked suddenly, and I flinched, half-expecting to be hit. I saw Luke tense from beside Katz, but Jennings simply turned on his heel and stalked back toward his chair.

"There are things missing," I tentatively added now that Jennings was a safe distance away. "From the files, I mean." Katz glanced at me in warning, but I ignored the look.

"It's true," Luke moved to stand beside me, "she's right. Those files you gave us don't have the whole story. They didn't even have the names of those agents. Hughes and Bradshaw, weren't they?" I was surprised to see him goading Jennings, especially after we had told the Boyle siblings that we would not share what they had told us, but it seemed to be working. Jennings's face turned an ugly sort of purple, and I was surprised. *What did we do to rattle this man enough that his self-control is gone?* I wondered. Jennings, like us, would have been trained to conceal his emotions. What had terrified him so much that he was letting us see? I watched, fascinated, as Jennings seemed to wrestle with himself for a moment. His color returned to normal, and his usual, frosty expression returned to his face. Had it not been for the white-hot anger that still burned in his eyes, I would have thought that I had imagined the whole thing.

"I should have known better than to give you access to those. I knew that they would go over your head," he sat, adjusting his glasses on his nose.

"I think you two are way off base… and out of line," Katz said quietly. I was a bit surprised to hear that he agreed so wholeheartedly with Jennings. I had expected him to at least hear us out before casting judgment.

"But—" I began, but Katz shook his head.

"Do not bring this up again. You're wrong. There's another answer," he said forcefully.

"Question us like this again, and you can find a new job. There are plenty of competent agents who can do yours," Jennings said with the hint of a snarl. I wheeled around and looked to Luke for help, but he shook his head.

"Agent Jennings, I…" I began again.

"Get out. You'll receive information about your next safe house as soon as I select the place." I looked wildly between the men in the room, feeling helpless and very small, but there was nothing that I could do. There was also apparently nothing that Luke would do. Feeling the slightest bit hysterical, I spun around and was out of the room in just a few quick strides.

CHAPTER 25

How can they not even consider the possibility? I was still reeling from our earlier encounter with Jennings and Katz. They had completely dismissed our very valid points, and for what? The sake of Jennings's ego? In what world was suggesting the possibility of foul play—in Katz's words— "out of line?" Wouldn't they rather eliminate any shadow of a doubt than completely disregard the possibility that we had been right?

I paced the suite I shared with Luke, every nerve ending in my body crackling with tension. I had managed to keep my calm in the moment, but now, every bit of adrenaline from the earlier situation was coursing through me at once, leaving me with what I imagined it would feel like to have three days' worth of caffeine injected straight into my heart. Upon our return to our suite, Luke had said he needed air, and he had vanished out into the hallway. I had no idea if he blamed me for how Jennings had taken the suggestion or if he was just as rattled by it as I had been, but he had been gone long enough that I was on edge.

And what if he went back to Katz and Jennings behind

your back? What if he's been playing you all along? It would have been just like the Luke Ryder I had known from before to make me out to be a fool, but this would have been an uncharacteristically long con, even for him. *No, he would never turn on an assignment, though. Unless he's —* I pushed the thought from my brain. Luke was *not* responsible for these attacks. There was no way; they had been happening since before we had arrived, and I did *not* need to let my mind go down that road. With a growl of annoyance, I ripped a throw pillow off of the couch and flung it across the room, watching unsatisfied as it sailed across the living area and plopped softly to the floor. What had been the point of the Academy's Placement Board assigning us to this job? We were underestimated and under-respected, which had already had an almost catastrophic impact on our ability to do our job. How many more times would we be able to get lucky and skate by before something tragic happened?

"Because Heaven forbid Jennings consider that he might have made a *mistake*," I snarled aloud. The explosion of temper had not made me feel any better, so with a sigh, I walked across the room to pick up the pillow I had thrown. As I bent over to retrieve it, I heard the latch of the door click, and I whirled around, pillow held aloft, to see that Luke had finally returned. A bit sheepishly, I lowered the pillow, and he looked me up and down with an expression of tired amusement.

"Could do some real damage with that thing." He nodded at the pillow, and with a scowl, I tossed it haphazardly onto the couch.

"Where have you been?" I challenged, hearing and hating the accusatory inflection of my words. Luke raised an eyebrow.

"Thinking. And then making myself stop thinking. Mostly, calming down though, which it seems like you need to do," he observed. I threw myself down into a seat on the couch, burying my face in the pillow and letting out a long scream. When I looked up, Luke was staring at me.

"What?" I asked through gritted teeth. I thought that if his eyebrows got any higher, they would disappear into his tousled hairline.

"Feel better?" One corner of his mouth turned upward.

"Not particularly," I answered stiffly. "What are we supposed to do now?" Luke shrugged, looking infuriatingly unbothered.

"The same thing that we have been, I guess: our jobs." He ducked as I launched the pillow at him. He dodged, but he was caught off-balance, and he stumbled. "Hey!" he exclaimed. "What was that for?"

"It's hard to do our jobs, when we keep getting cut off at the knees," I complained hotly. Luke nodded.

"I know, but the nature of our assignment was never to figure out who was behind all of this; our job is to protect Sara and Jesse," he said sympathetically. I shook my head, my brown hair swinging around my face. I clawed at it madly before jerking it into a sloppy bun.

"The best way we can protect Sara and Jesse," I fired back, "is to figure out who is doing all of this and why, so we can stop them." There was sympathy in Luke's eyes, and in that moment, I hated him more than I ever had.

"You're passionate. That's part of why they chose you. I'm passionate too. But right now, we need to channel our focus into what we *can* do. Right now, we can't change Jennings's or Katz's minds. We can't force an investigation," he reasoned.

"It's just so senseless," I huffed. He nodded, tightening his lips.

"It is," he agreed. Suddenly, a thought popped into my head, blazing like a beacon as it overshadowed whatever I had been about to say. I straightened, eyes wide, and stared at Luke, who backed away slowly, as though he was worried that he might become the target of another projectile.

"There *is* a way we can change their minds," I breathed. Luke squinted at me, and I could tell he had thought I had finally lost my mind.

"I don't follow," he replied. I could see the confusion clouding his eyes, so I summed up quickly.

"There's one person whose orders can change their minds," I clarified. Luke squinted harder at me before his eyes shot open wide.

"*No!*" he exclaimed.

"Yes," I replied.

"Richards, we can't do that! We can't go over their heads. Not that far over their heads, at least," he amended.

"And why not? Didn't he say he'd reviewed our files personally," I shot back. "He chose us to do a job. How do you think he'd feel if he knew his own heads of security, agents from across organizations, weren't doing everything in their power to keep his children safe?" I demanded. Luke blinked furiously at me before shaking his head.

"He'd be furious," he said.

"Exactly!" I said triumphantly.

"Maybe furious enough to get rid of them, especially if he blamed all of them for what keeps happening. Don't you think that would put all four members of the First Family in more danger?" he asked. I opened and shut my mouth a few times, feeling for all the world like a gaping fish, but I could not seem to get the words I wanted to say out. *Who cares if he gets rid of them?* Part of me screamed. *You will if it gets worse because they get replaced with people who don't know what's going on or what to expect.* I sucked in a deep breath and blew it out quickly.

"Probably," I agreed, sounding and feeling strangled in the response.

"That's what I thought," he answered.

"Couldn't we at least tell him what we've figured out? We don't have to mention our last conversation with Jennings and Katz. We can let him draw his own conclusions. Maybe, he'll decide to do nothing with it, but he has the right to have a full picture and make an informed decision from there." I knew it was a Hail Mary argument, but I had to try. I knew that there was nothing stopping me from finding President Boyle without Luke, but we were a team, and for him not to come with me to share the theory with the president would place him under suspicion too. I could see him thinking carefully, clearly pondering along the same lines, and I held my breath.

"Well, maybe we can—" Whatever Luke had been about to say was interrupted by a loud buzzing from both of our phones. I had been concentrating so hard on watching Luke's face that the noise startled me, and I jolted in surprise at the unexpected sound.

Pack a bag. New safe house. Meet in Briefing Room.
You have 15 minutes.

The message came from Jennings, and I stared at it for a moment, torn between reacting with hysterical laughter or outright dismay. I glanced up at Luke to see him looking likewise conflicted.

"Well," I began dryly, "I guess that answers that question." Luke narrowed his eyes, and one corner of his mouth worked furiously as he pulled his cheek between his teeth in thought.

"Think we can sum up what we know in fifteen minutes?" he asked finally, his expression telling me that he did not hold out much hope.

"Not likely, if we want to keep our jobs," I answered, shaking my head with a sigh. His dark eyebrows scrunched together with thought for a few seconds before they parted once more.

"I guess it wouldn't do Sara or Jesse any good to risk it," he muttered.

"We'll figure it out. Right now, we have bags to pack," I said, sighing again. We went our separate ways in silence, and I tried my best to focus on the future, rather than the dismal present. Jennings had made quick work of finding a safe house, and the fact that we were not meeting as a group beforehand told me that either he was still outraged by our suggestions that there could be an inside man, or the location of this particular house was even more of a secret than the one that had come before. From what I had observed of Jennings at work, I thought it was likely the latter, although the former might have still carried some weight. I emerged from my room a few minutes later, haphazardly packed bag in tow, to see Luke's was already waiting on the coffee table, its owner nowhere to be seen. *How does he keep doing that?* I asked myself with a flicker of annoyance, wondering briefly where Luke had gone. A flushing noise from the bathroom gave me my answer, and he emerged a second later.

"You didn't wash your hands," I said critically, wrinkling my nose in disgust.

"Were you eavesdropping?" he asked in disbelief. I noticed that he did not deny the accusation.

"Of course not," I said impatiently. "I heard the flush."

"Ah," he answered blandly, making a move for his bag. I let out a sound of revulsion, and he paused, glancing back at me quizzically. "*What?*"

"You're seriously not going to go back in? Men are disgusting," I said. He raised an arm, holding aloft a small bottle and wiggling it between his fingers with a smug expression. I squinted to read the small, moving text. *Oh. Hand sanitizer.* I dropped the disgusted look, and his lips split open to reveal a knowing grin.

"You were saying?" he asked, his eyes widening in mock-innocence.

"Shut up," I grumbled, hefting my bag onto my shoulder without another word, wincing as the strap tugged at a loose strand of my hair.

"Oh, come on. You had plenty to say a second ago," Luke teased. I turned decisively away from him and made for the door as the sound of his laughter tickled my ears and made me smile in spite of myself. I shook my head imperceptibly as I opened the door and left our suite, conscious of Luke hurrying behind me as he scrambled to catch up.

We were the first to reach the briefing room, and that surprised me. Jennings had become a fixture of the room in my mind, so being in there without him glaring at me from his normal post at the end of the table gave me the distinct feeling of having been sucked into an alternate universe. I dropped my bag on the table, where the thud it made echoed through the empty room.

"Weird," I murmured, mostly to myself, still conscious of Luke behind me. The look he gave me had a question in it, but I pretended that I hadn't seen. I did not even understand the feeling myself; I doubted I would be able to find the words to explain it.

"I guess we're early," he tried. I nodded silently, and that silence stretched for several seconds before the door crashed open behind us. I wheeled around just as Luke's head snapped to face the direction of the door, the sudden noise shocking after the serenity of the quiet, but my alarm dissipated as Jennings strode into the room, flanked by Katz and Bryant. *Strutting in like a high school clique,* I thought to myself, barely repressing a smirk. The trio stopped short when they saw us, plainly taken aback that we had beaten them there. Jennings quickly covered his surprise with a grim-faced neutrality, but the other two apparently didn't see the need.

"You're ready then?" he asked shortly, looking at our bags.

"You said fifteen minutes," Luke pointed out. Jennings did nothing to acknowledge his reply as he turned to Katz.

"Is their car ready?" he asked the other man. Katz nodded, and Jennings turned to address us again.

"You two are leaving now. Jesse and Sara will follow. You're to perform a sweep of the premises when you arrive. Once you have performed this check, you are to contact us so we can send the Boyle siblings to meet you," he said without emotion, looking each of us evenly in the face in turns.

"And how many will be made aware of this location?" I asked coolly. Jennings turned his frosty gaze on me and fixed it there in uncomfortable silence until I thought the ground might rise up and swallow me whole. *If looks could kill,* I thought, *then I would have been dead a long time ago,* I amended the thought. From behind Jennings, Bryant shot me a knowing look, her dark features arranged in an expression of sympathy.

"Just enough," came the reluctant reply. "There's a car waiting for you at the East Gate. We'll wait to hear from you." Without waiting for a response, Jennings turned on his heel and left the room with Bryant and Katz following closely, leaving Luke and I staring after him in bewilderment.

"Is it just me, or does he seem more like a cartoon villain every time we see him?" I mused in spite of myself. Luke let out a dark chuckle, and I had my answer.

CHAPTER 26

I lost track of the time as the car twisted and turned through the maze of streets, but I knew that it had to have been a long drive based upon the fact that I really, *really* had to pee. I crossed my legs, hoping and praying with every fiber of my being that we would arrive soon. The driver was surprisingly silent for the duration of the trip— most of our drivers in the past had at least exchanged pleasantries before lapsing into the quiet of the journey— and Luke had been likewise disinclined toward conversation, so that left me with nothing to focus on but my uncomfortably-full bladder. Thankfully, the next few minutes provided a distraction.

The car slowed as it passed by a series of townhouses, lined severely along the side street, windows dark and full of secrets. I wondered briefly about the people who might have chosen to live in such close proximity to other families, but I figured that housing was hard enough to come by these days without being picky about space and privacy. Some people—not me, but some—might feel more at ease with the closeness, and probably wasn't in a position to judge. *To each their own.* I broke from this train of thought as our driver screeched the car to a halt in front of a townhouse in the dead center of the line of homes. I sat, stunned, for a moment before clearing my throat.

"Why are we stopping?" I asked suspiciously. Was this another trick?

"We're here," the driver answered in a rasp. I wondered privately if the rasp in his voice came from its disuse as I glanced skeptically out the window.

"Are you sure?" I asked, exchanging a surprised look with Luke. To my relief, he seemed just as taken aback as I was. Given that the last safe house had featured an iron gate and several other obvious security features, I wondered at the choice. Then again, maybe Jennings was going for the unexpected. Who would expect the First Kids to be sequestered smack dab in the middle of other residents?

"I'm sure." Came the gruff reply. I shook my head, still taken off-guard. *At least it will be less for us to sweep.* It would be harder for an assailant to lurk in the shadows of a townhouse, and it would be even harder for them to sneak up on us. *One way in, one way out.* I frowned at the thought. That meant that there were fewer avenues of escape if we did get taken by surprise.

Luke and I stood side by side, staring dubiously up at the looming face of the building with our bags by our side as the driver drove quietly away without a word of farewell. I shook my head, still adjusting my expectations to meet reality.

"Think they left the front door unlocked for us?" A muscle in Luke's cheek twitched as he asked the question, and I smiled ironically at the thought of a safe house being left unlocked and vulnerable to the outside world.

"Hope so, because I don't have a key." I shrugged. We certainly were not going to find out by standing outside and staring up at it. Hefting my bag onto my shoulder, I stepped up to the front door and tried the handle. *Locked.*

"No good?" The question came from behind me. Turning, I shot Luke a dismayed look and shook my head.

"No good. Should we call someone?" I asked, thinking out loud before I snorted at the thought. That was all we needed, for Jennings to know that we had been defeated by a locked door. I raked my eyes across the frame of the door, looking for any sort of hidden latch that I had perhaps missed.

"Is the alternative to break in?" I heard Luke's footsteps approaching.

"I feel like if we can break into a safe house without tools, then said house probably isn't very safe. Jennings wouldn't have forgotten to give us a key; we must be missing something," I said absently, still surveying the entrance. The door was standard, heavy and dark and painted black. The knob was nothing special, and I could see where a key could be inserted. I scrutinized the lock carefully before I realized that the space where a key would have been placed was filled in.

"Hmm," I made the noise without thinking. *I'm definitely missing something.*

"Jennings couldn't have told us how to actually get in," Luke said with an annoyed roll of his eyes. I nodded.

"He must have trusted us to figure it out." *And it can't be too difficult to figure out, given his oh-so-high opinion of us.* The fact that it had to be something simple, coupled with the fact that I hadn't figured it out immediately, did nothing to diminish my growing annoyance. *Standard knob, standard frame, standard doorbell—* My thoughts stopped short at the thought. Seized by either madness or inspiration, I placed my thumb on the doorbell and pressed hard.

I nearly jumped backward off the steps as a strong vibration zapped into my thumb, but I found myself fixed to the doorbell. I watched, fascinated, as a bar of white light started from the bottom of the button and scanned toward the top of my thumb before returning to its original position. Of course, we had learned about security technology in the Institute's academy, but I had not expected to find that here. *When did they have time to install this?* A turn of my head brought into focus Luke, who was watching the process with a mixture of interest and wariness. I jumped again when a clear voice spoke.

"Details confirmed. Blythe Richards. Temperature: ninety-eight point seven degrees Fahrenheit. Heart rate: sixty-three beats per minute. Signs of life confirmed." There was an audible click from the door, and I felt the pressure on my thumb release, leaving a tingling sensation on the pad of my finger. I rubbed it, glowering at the machine.

"Glad to know I'm alive," I muttered, before grasping the knob of the door. I twisted it with a slight movement of my wrist, and there was no resistance this time as I pulled open the door.

"Fascinating." I turned my head again to see Luke's face inches away from the doorbell button, studying it carefully.

"Careful; you won't want that thing to get your face," I advised, and with a startled glance at me, he straightened and backed away. I cast a glance down the street, which I realized then had remained suspiciously devoid of traffic during the whole debacle. "We should get inside," I added, unnecessarily as Luke stepped past me and entered the home.

The reason for the deserted nature of the short street was obvious almost immediately. What had seemed to be a series of quiet townhomes was actually one connected space that was carefully hidden behind an outward facade. I dropped my bag to the floor with a thud, letting out a low whistle as I took in the sight.

"Clever. Very clever, Jennings." I was not sure where or how he had been able to find this place, much less install such high-tech security features, in such a short amount of time, but I was grudgingly impressed.

"I guess we should do our sweep," Luke said, breaking our mutual silence. I nodded in swift agreement, although how anyone could possibly get past the AI features at the door, I had no idea. *I wonder what happens if someone who isn't us rings?* If it reacted to others the same way it responded to me, there would be no doubting that it would pique the interest of any surprise visitors. *So, no take-out orders for us then.*

We dropped our bags at the entrance, and Luke and I set off in different directions. Despite the convincing facade outside, the bottom floor held a relatively open floor plan, with a spacious kitchen and dining area that flowed seamlessly into a minimally decorated living space. The sparse decor did little to detract from the warm-wood accents and complementary colors of the wall, and I found myself admiring the taste of whomever had been responsible. I felt a small smile of approval creep onto my face. *I could get used to being stuck somewhere like this.* Then I remembered that being in a townhouse meant that our access to the outdoors would be slim to none, and my smile dimmed. Maybe we could open a window or something. Considering the doorbell security, however, I dismissed that as unlikely. Sensing nothing out of the ordinary, I returned to the place where we had left our bags, staring curiously at the doorway through which Luke had disappeared before shrugging. There would be plenty of time to take the grand tour later. I turned to face the stairs, admiring again the rich wood touches of the steps themselves and the artfully carved handrail before making the decision to move on to the upstairs.

I had an eerie sense of foreboding as I climbed the elegant staircase, but I tried my best to put it from my mind and focus on the task at hand. The events of the past several days had set me on edge, and that was natural. I needed to give myself a little bit of grace, but I also needed to stop pretending as though I was in a position in which my emotions could be allowed to take over my poise. I had two options once I reached the landing at the top of the stairs; I had the option of turning to the left or the right. I was unsure of why my mind was applying so much pressure and bravado to the decision. Annoyed with myself, I hissed out a breath and turned to the door on the left, shaking my head as I pushed it open. The door was lighter than I had expected, and as it swung open smoothly, I put too much weight behind it and stumbled, letting out a shriek of alarm as I tumbled to the floor in a heap. I laid flat on my back for a moment, shocked for a moment by the fact that I could have been so monumentally stupid, cursing as I heard the thundering of footsteps on the stairs.

"Richards?" I scrambled to my feet as Luke appeared on the landing, barely visible from my position inside the door. I poked my head out, smiling sheepishly.

"I'm fine," I chirped. He squinted at me suspiciously, thick eyebrows pushed together.

"What happened?" he asked.

"Me. I happened," I said vaguely, trying to move past the situation.

"Yes, I gathered it was you that shrieked. I'm asking why," he said obviously, as though he was explaining it to a toddler.

"I tripped," I admitted, embarrassment flooding into my face as a flush. The suspicious look on his face gave way to a smirk at the admission.

"She is beauty, she is grace…" he said, barely concealing the laugh behind the words.

"She will punch you in the face," I finished under my breath. That *did* inspire his laugh to break free, and

I turned my back on the good-natured mockery with what little dignity I had left. Fumbling on the wall next to the door, I found the light switch and flicked it on, illuminating a very basic bedroom. Through the cracked door on the other side of the room, I could see a basic bathroom set-up, and I turned to convey my observations to Luke. Something electric jolted through me as I realized that we were suddenly very, very close. I could see the roughness of the stubble poking out from his cheeks—he must not have had time to shave— and the tight spread of smooth flesh across his high-cut cheekbones. I finished my appraisal at his eyes, intense and—as always— incredibly, vibrantly green. It was strange; we had spent so much time at each other's throats and on the go that I hadn't looked at Luke—really looked at him— without dislike or panic in, well, ever.

"Find anything exciting?" It took me a moment to register that Luke had spoken, and I somewhat reluctantly tore my eyes away. *What the Hell is the matter with you?* I scolded myself, pushing thoughts of Luke's closeness from my brain. I had kept my head through years of torment, being stuck in the same job immediately following said years of torment, and even accidentally falling asleep with this man, and somehow him sneaking up behind me was what made me pause to take in the scenery. I shook my head at my own madness. Maybe I had finally cracked.

"Uh, bathroom," I stammered, my mouth suddenly dry. I had no idea why I was suddenly struggling to string two words together, but it rattled me.

"Convenient," he said lightly, in a way that made me question whether or not he had even noticed my obvious social ineptitude. From the way that his head tilted curio "If you're not being horrifically attacked, I'll finish up the other side if you want to sweep the bathroom," he finished. We stood there in silence for several seconds before I realized that he was waiting for me to respond. A renewed heat crept up my throat and threatened to flood my face in a flush, and I turned away to hide it. *Stop being such a girl,* I ordered myself.

"Yep, that works," I answered, letting my feet carry me away as quickly as possible without being obvious. It was unnerving, this feeling, and I would be relieved when we were no longer alone in the house.

CHAPTER 27

Thankfully, the upstairs was small—although not cramped— so Luke and I made quick work of checking it out. When we regrouped, I had the sense that he was watching me very closely, but I tried my hardest to ignore it. It was more likely that I was imagining it anyway. It was possible that he didn't notice the awkwardness; maybe I was still self-conscious from the moment we'd shared upstairs. Still, I couldn't shake the sense that I was being watched, and the thought of my innermost thoughts being obvious, especially when I did not understand them myself, was terrifying. I was relieved when we finally regrouped to discuss our findings, even though they wound up amounting to nothing of interest.

The floor plan made the house simple enough to sweep, but we spent long time—mostly because I kept pushing the issue to fill the silence— discussing the layout. The second floor contained two bedrooms, one on each side of the landing and with their own bathroom. One room had attic access, but there had been nothing of interest there. We had decided that it made the most sense to put Sara and Jesse upstairs, further away from any obvious potential access points. The bottom floor, as I had found out, was mostly open, and for one wild moment, I had felt a flash of panic at the thought that there might be only one more bedroom. Luke quickly informed me that there were two smaller rooms in the area he had investigated. One was a traditional bedroom, and one was an office space. The second, he informed me, had a futon, which he politely offered to take so I could have the actual bed. Once this was established, it didn't take long for us to run out of things to discuss on the subject, so we sat in silence for a few moments before Luke stepped away to give Jennings the all-clear. Then there was nothing to do but wait for Sara and Jesse to arrive.

"It's a nice place," Luke broke the uncomfortable silence. We had taken up reference on one of the couches in the living room, and although we sat on opposite ends, I was painfully aware of our proximity.

"Very. Bigger than I expected," I answered shortly.

"They did a nice job with the facade out front. No one would ever know this was just one big place," he commented somewhat lamely.

"Excellent design. Very spacious," I answered, and then I winced. *Are we really talking about interior design?* There was a reason that I hated small talk. It was painful for me—and probably for whomever else had to suffer through it talking to me, since it was apparently impossible for me to do it well. Luke seemed to find my awkwardness entertaining because his mouth was slanted in a smirk that was on its way to being a permanent fixture on his face.

"Artemis," he began.

"Hmm?" I asked, suddenly finding the patterns of the rug fascinating.

"Are you okay?" he asked.

"Hmm? Fine. I'm just fine," I answered, not convincing myself, let alone Luke.

"Really? Because you've been acting strange since

we were upstairs." *Let it go Ryder*, I thought savagely, wishing desperately that the floor would open up and swallow me whole.

"I really don't know what you're talking about," I managed coldly, dragging my eyes from the floor to see Luke looking hard at my face. He seemed to be choosing his next words carefully, his face as guarded as the front door to the townhouse had been.

"It seemed like we had a… moment earlier," he said carefully. In a rush of brief hysteria, I let out a laugh.

"A moment? What, when I tripped? A moment of clumsiness for me, sure." I covered my growing panic with another hard laugh, and I didn't miss the brief confusion that flitted across his face.

"Are you sure, because—" He began again, pushing, and I rolled my eyes, taking a deep breath as I stared at the ceiling for a moment, fighting to control the renewed sense of embarrassment that I was sure was written all over my face. *Why can't we ever be attacked when it's convenient?* Our attackers had *no* sense of timing.

"I'm sure. I tripped in the dark, and I didn't expect you to be behind me," I said firmly. *Don't push it Ryder*, I warned in my head. I put my hands to my face, pressing my fingers into my eyelids in exasperation, before glancing up to see that he still looked unconvinced.

"I mean, it really *seemed* like we had a moment, and I feel like we should…" he trailed off, seeming uncertain. Like a shark in the water at the scent of blood, I attacked.

"We should what? I don't know what you think happened; all I know is that I tripped, and then somehow you were in my face when I turned around." He opened his mouth to interject again, but I pressed on, ignoring him. "Not everyone goes weak at the knees just because you grace them with your oh-so-dreamy presence, Ryder," I ended savagely. He blinked at me, clearly taken aback, and I felt a prickle of guilt at the hurt that flashed faintly in his eyes. Cool anger replaced it so quickly that I thought I must have imagined it.

"I guess that's good, then. I would have hated to break your heart," he answered with a cold sneer. Anger, hot and violent, rushed through me, and I narrowed my eyes for the kill-shot.

"This isn't the Academy; this is the real world, and some of us have better things to do than to stoke your ego. Not every girl is falling all over themselves starved for your attention, Ryder; most of us have standards." Now, it was his turn to flush, his hands curling into fists at his sides. He stood suddenly, moving as though he couldn't get far enough away from me, and I saw the tension in his barely shaking shoulders. When he turned again, his mask of control had returned, and the only thing in his eyes was cool disinterest. He opened his mouth to say something else, before he could, the sound of the front door unlatching made him freeze.

"Richards? Ryder?" Jennings's voice called. Luke looked at me for a moment more, and I was seized by the intense urge to apologize. Before I could, he turned away, leaving me sitting on the couch as he left to greet the Boyles. I covered my face with my hands and let out a low grown of exasperation before rising to follow him. It was just our usual banter. We'd recovered from worse than this at the Academy; there would be time for it to blow over. *This time was different.* He'd been sincere, trying to ask me about something, and I had attacked him. A flicker of guilt sparked in my gut, but there was nothing that I could do about it now. We had a job to do.

Jennings stood in front of Sara and Jesse, who were surveying their new home with appraising eyes. Bryant and Welsch stood behind, looking stoic. I blinked in surprise, wondering who was with the president and his wife if the three of them were here. Katz could not be expected to cover both of them at once. Then again, it was becoming clear that the younger Boyles were the main targets at present, so maybe that trumped their usual roles—at least for now.

"Richards," Jennings greeted coldly. "Nice of you to join us." I opened my mouth to point out that I was only a few seconds behind Luke, but sensing the overall mood, I decided against it. The transition happened quickly enough, with Jennings filling us in about a few potential events coming up in the less-than-distant future, but it felt like only minutes before the trio of agents had disappeared through the front door, leaving the four of us alone. Luke did not speak, and I was not inclined to either, so we stood in silence, with Sara's eyes darting suspiciously between the two of us before Jesse spoke.

"So, uh. Where are we staying?" he asked, reaching down to pick up a bag that could only be his. I realized that we had left our own piled near the entrance as well, distracted as we had been by our conversation, and I blinked for a second before answering.

"Upstairs," I managed finally.

"I'll escort you," Luke said briskly, moving to box me out of the group. Sara's eyes widened for a moment, giving her the startling appearance of a blue-eyed owl before she squinted at me again. To my relief, she did not comment on the subject, and moments later, they had ascended the stairs and were out of sight. I sighed deeply as I eyed my bag. I would have loved to go ahead and move it out of the main room, but I had serious doubts about whether or not Luke still planned to take the futon, and I didn't want to make the wrong assumption given everything. With a sigh, I decided to make my way into the kitchen, hoping that the fridge and pantry were as fully stocked as the house before it had been. To my relief, there was some food, although the selection was slim. The energy drained from my bones as I contemplated cooking for four, and I pulled out a pound of ground beef, placing it on the counter as I turned to the pantry. *Looks like it's spaghetti night,* I mused. That would be easy enough. I felt like there was a metaphor in that, something about messy food in a messy situation, but I decided not to think too hard about that particular comparison. As I set a pot of water to boil for the noodles, I knew that I would need to make amends somehow; I knew that Luke and I couldn't work as a team if we were at each other's throats. It was the *how* of the matter that stubbornly escaped me. I sighed again. I would figure it out; neither of us was going anywhere anytime soon, and I didn't have another choice.

CHAPTER 28

As it turned out, Luke decided not to go back on his offer to sleep in the office—not that he'd actually told me that in words. I gathered this from the fact that he had snatched up his bag, which I could still see from the kitchen, and disappeared in the direction of the room. *Alright… So, there's that,* I thought with another heavy sigh. *You'll have time to figure out how to fix things later.* Dinner with the Boyle siblings probably was not the appropriate time for that. The ongoing tension meant that there was a stunted sort of silence as the four of us sat around the kitchen table, staring into our food. Sara had tried to ask questions about our stay, while Jesse had read the room and stayed nobly silent, but Luke had answered her inquiries, for the most part, in grunts and noncommittal shrugs. As for me, I followed Jesse's approach and stayed silent, twirling my pasta absently on my fork. About fifteen minutes into the meal, Sara slapped her palms on the table, and I looked up, startled to see her squinting hard between me and Luke.

"Did you two sleep together?" she demanded. I recoiled with a blink of shock; she might as well have slapped me. Luke choked on a bite of his pasta, red-faced as he coughed and spluttered. Jesse faced his sister openmouthed, his jaw hanging open like a door on broken hinges.

"Sara!" Jesse exclaimed.

"What? Of course not." I asked, shocked. I winced slightly as Luke shot me a disgruntled look.

"Are you sure? Something's wrong here. You're both being weird," Sara pressed.

"Sara," Jesse groaned this time, covering his face with his hands.

"I think I'd remember," I answered dryly.

"I'm *sure* you would," Sara retorted suggestively. Luke barked a short laugh, and I closed my eyes, taking a deep breath as I fought for restraint.

"I don't know, maybe she wouldn't," Luke interjected conversationally once his initial laughter had died. Sara looked at him curiously, but his eyes were fixed on me, dark and stormy now. "After all, she has *standards*." You could have heard a pin drop as the table fell into stunned silence, and I felt the blood rush from my face. Without another word, Luke pushed back his chair and took his half-empty bowl to the sink before leaving the room without another glance in my direction. I stared after him in silence long after he disappeared out of sight, flinching at the sound of his bedroom door slamming shut.

"What the hell was that about?" Sara asked. My eyes snapped toward her, and I fought with the wild urge to tell her to mind her own business. Luke had made it everyone's business, although I still didn't really understand what 'it' was. With that in mind, instead of rounding on Sara and taking out my frustration on her, I rose quietly, shaking my head with a half-hearted shrug, and left my bowl where it sat as I made to follow Luke. As I left the room, I heard Jesse's voice quietly follow me.

"You can give me shit all you want, Sara, but that's why I don't take my love life off-line," he said. She made a further scathing innuendo, but the last half of it was lost to me as Luke's door materialized in front of my face. I raised my knuckles with a sigh before dropping them uncertainly. *What am I even going to say? I don't know what the problem is,* I thought desperately.

Yes, you do. You're not that dumb, my ever-infuriating inner voice argued back instantly. I sighed and lifted my hand again, following through with a gentle knock this time.

"Go away, Richards," came the reply.

"No," I said firmly, grabbing the doorknob and twisting. *Locked… Of course it is.*

"I don't want to talk to you right now," he reinforced, and I huffed.

"I could break it down," I offered, not really serious. "Jennings might bill us for repairs though." *He put up a boundary. You should probably respect it,* came the nagging voice again. I ignored it. There was no further response from either my snide inner voice or Luke's very audible one.

"I could apologize?" I offered, this time more helpfully. The silence stretched on, and I stared at the uneven grains of wood on the planks that made up the floor. I sighed, prepared to turn and leave him alone for the evening as requested when the sound of the twisting knob fixed me in place. My eyes reluctantly crept from the floor to his shoes, tracing the frame of his body where it came to lean against the frame of the door. Something in his jaw worked furiously as he stared down at me with crossed arms and hard eyes.

"Do you even know what you're planning to apologize for, or were you just saying that to get me to open the door?" he asked. He lifted his eyebrows expectantly. I brushed a strand of hair out of my face and forced myself to hold his gaze.

"No, I was out of line with the standards comment. I knew that when I said it, I just didn't quite know how to…" I trailed off as the tumble of words reached the precipice of uncertainty. I took a deep breath. "We *did* have a moment earlier," I admitted quietly. That familiar thread of panic threatened to worm its way through my stomach; I couldn't read his face at all.

"That's all I was asking," he said conversationally; we might have been talking about the weather, for all his neutral tone implied.

"Why?" The incredulous word slipped out before I could catch it, and I winced at the flair of caution that crossed his face. He sighed, running his hands through his hair before he crossed his arms again, leaning even more heavily on the edge of the door frame now.

"I thought it was interesting," he replied, as though it should have been obvious.

"What was interesting?" I asked, still feeling clueless in spite of the fact that my heart was now beating a staccato in my chest. I saw his chest rise as he took a deep breath.

"That it's mutual," came the reply. I blinked several times before staring at him, convinced I had misheard.

"Mutual?" I couldn't help it; I burst into laughter. It was not the polite kind of laughter, or the light, pleasant sort of chuckle that one might use to defuse this kind of situation. No, this was the kind of hysterical laughter that you'd expect from somebody suffering from severe sleep deprivation or who was under the effects of laughing gas. It certainly wasn't what you would expect to hear from someone who had just heard a confession of attraction from a years-long enemy. Mutinous disbelief replaced the careful neutrality on his face, and he backed up slowly, moving to swing the door shut before I stepped forward, eyes glistening with tears of mirth as I held up my hands in truce.

"No! No, wait! I didn't mean—it's not—" I broke off, still cackling, and Luke scowled at me.

"Do you want to share what you *do* mean? Because laughter isn't the most flattering response," he said stiffly.

"I just—I didn't think—*mutual*." I answered nonsensically, still gasping. With a huff of annoyance, Luke rolled his eyes and gestured for me to enter the room, and I acquiesced, barely noticing as the door clicked shut behind us. *Dear Lord, I am an idiot.* The thought was half confession, half realization. Despite my best efforts, I had actually caved to the attraction, and I had become just like every other weak-kneed girl who had ever met Luke Ryder. It was a tale as old as time. The irony—and my internalized misogyny—was not lost on me, which made the whole thing worse.

"So, what *did* you think?" he asked curiously once my cackling had begun to subside. The thought sobered me for a moment as I remembered the years of banter and visceral rage.

"Don't you hate me?" I asked. He snorted in amusement.

"Yes," he said bluntly. I squinted hard at him. "And no," he amended.

"Well, that clears it up," I answered dryly. He shook his head, dark hair settling on his forehead once he stopped. It had grown longer in the past few weeks. It was strange that I had not noticed it before.

"You are infuriating," he began. I opened my mouth to retort, but I sheepishly shut it again, realizing that it was probably true. "You are also fierce, and smart, and brave, and… competent," he added.

"Competent, eh?" I asked, lips twitching as I fought to conceal another chuckle. He sounded more like a hiring manager than somebody expressing his attraction.

"Self-sufficient? Independent? Capable? Choose a synonym, Richards," he scowled at me as he stuffed his hands into the pockets of his pants. "I'm trying to give you a compliment."

"So, we're back to 'infuriating' then?" I teased with another snicker. He half-smiled, and then his face was serious again as he leaned forward. My laughter stilled as my heart leaped, and the world around me seemed to still. The room around me faded, as though I was in a tunnel and the light at the end of it was Luke's bright eyes and the curve of his lips as he smiled.

"I don't know that we ever really left," he replied. My mind sluggishly tried to work out what he meant, but it gave up the venture, because in the next heartbeat, Luke had crushed his mouth to mine. I panicked for a brief second, my heart doing a sort of tap-dance in my chest before I gave in to the sea of emotion and let myself be swept away.

There were no fireworks, not in the traditional sense, and given the passionate, bickering nature of our relationship, I had half-expected there to be. Instead, the sensation was warm, more like candlelight or a fire in the hearth of home. Luke was surprisingly gentle as his mouth moved softly against mine, and I felt myself melting into the moment as his hands came around to weave his fingers through the strands of my hair. Heat rose through my body, starting in my toes and working its way up to the tips of my ears.

A loud crash from the direction of the door startled me, and we sprang apart, breathless. Jesse stood in the doorway, panic wild in his eyes and chest heaving as he looked between Luke and I in disbelief. I had the sudden, crashing sense that something was terribly wrong.

"Are you serious right now?" Jesse demanded.

"Jesse, what's wrong?" I asked, noticing that Luke had moved several strides away. Jesse wasn't looking at me; his eyes were fixed furiously on Luke.

"You had a job to do," his voice rose furiously. Luke stared silently back, but I saw the uncertainty on his face. It was the first time I had ever seen Luke Ryder speechless.

"Jesse, what happened?" I tried again, stepping between them to block their view of each other. His eyes focused and met mine, blazing with an odd combination of fury and fear.

"Sara's gone."

Whatever spell had come over me in that room with Luke dissipated as I pushed past Jesse before either of them could speak. I was not aware that I was running until I reached the landing at the top of the stairs, feeling for all the world like I had flown there as my stomach pitched and rolled like a ship on stormy seas. Sara couldn't be gone. I hadn't waited for Jesse to explain himself, but maybe she'd just stepped out of the room and didn't tell him? Even to myself, it seemed unlikely; Jesse was quiet by nature, and for him to barge into Luke's personal space—well, that meant that he had done his due diligence. Still, I was trying to be optimistic as I approached Sara's room, hoping that I would push open the door to see her sitting on her bed or hear the shower in her bathroom running. As you can probably guess, neither of those things happened. I pushed open the door to see that it was empty, devoid of any movement except the subtle swinging of the string that attached to the attic door overhead. Sara had never been the tidiest of people, but the knocked-askew lamp on the bedside table and the tossed-about bedding told me that there had been a struggle. *No!* I crossed the room in a few bounds and bounded onto the bed to seize the dangling cord. I flexed my arm, ready to pull down the door, when arms wrapped around my waist from behind. I screeched in alarm and twisted, thrashing wildly and prepared to do battle with my assailant. The arms dropped me, and as I spun furiously to face the person head on, I realized it was Luke, his green eyes grim.

"Not alone," he said firmly, taking my place on the bed and opening the door with a tug. The door dropped to reveal a creaking ladder that folded down, and without a backward glance, Luke disappeared into the yawning black hole that appeared in the ceiling.

Conscious of Jesse standing by the door, I motioned for him to stay put as I scrambled up after him.

I nearly smacked into Luke's back as he stood on the edge of the hole, and if it hadn't been for the light from his cell phone flashlight, I would not have seen more than his faint outline. From the light cast by his phone, I could see what he had discovered: the attic was empty. For a minute, I thought about questioning whether Sara had even disappeared this way, but he adjusted his light, scanning the room, and I saw where a previously boarded-up opening, which I had assumed on our initial sweep was another facade, had been knocked loose. *Gone.* Luke stepped forward to grasp the haphazardly replaced piece of wood, and he pulled easily to reveal an opening to the outside world. It was obvious that they must have climbed through and gotten onto the roof somehow. From there, there was no telling where they had gone. A bubble of panic threatened to burst in my chest, and I had the sudden, terrified realization that Jesse had been left alone. I hastily scurried back to join him where, to my relief, he still stood by the doorway.

"Explain." The words rasped in my throat, and I was surprised that I had not been at a total loss for them.

"We cleaned up from dinner. We came upstairs. I heard sounds coming from her room. When I got here, she was gone," he said blankly, as though he was trying to make his point in as few words as possible.

"Gone," I repeated, still struggling to process.

"Gone," he replied firmly.

"And you didn't see anything?" I asked. He shook his head.

"I would have told you if I had. I came in here and saw that string on the ceiling swinging. I was going to follow them up, but then I realized I didn't know how many there were, so I came to find you and Luke instead. I'm glad I did; there's no telling how long it would have taken you two to notice we were gone," he finished with uncharacteristic venom, and I flinched.

"You did the right thing," I said quietly.

"I know I did!" he snapped, and Luke made a noise of warning in the back of his throat. "It's you two who got it all wrong."

"That was a one-time thing, and it will *not* be happening again," I answered firmly. If this had been the result of our lapse, then we could not afford for another moment of distraction. We had been foolish. In our position, it would be impossible to work together and maintain any type of relationship or attraction or whatever this was. Our job required clear priorities; we wouldn't be allowed to keep it if those priorities seemed in any way clouded or misplaced.

"I believe you," Jesse said, the anger dimming slightly from his face as he looked at me. As Luke's steps creaked over our heads, he glared, and I nearly expected the expression to burn a hole in the ceiling. I fought the urge to interfere. He was handling the situation remarkably well, in my opinion, for someone so young and untrained. *How many times has something like this almost happened? How many times has he prepared himself for the fact that his sister could just be gone… or that he could be taken? Why does Sara always seem to be the more heavily targeted of the two?* The thoughts raced through my head like thoroughbreds at the Kentucky Derby, one right after the other and each pounding full force.

"No sign of anything outside," Luke said as his head popped down through the opening. In another moment, he had climbed down the ladder and was standing beside us before I could blink. I struggled to look at him as the memory of the kiss flashed in my mind, and I felt the tips of my ears burn.

"I guess we need to call it in," I said, turning away. I dreaded the thought of Jennings's reaction, but I dreaded not pulling out all of the resources to find Sara more. Luke nodded.

"Want me to do it?" he offered casually, and I shook my head without looking at him as I pulled my phone out of my pocket. I dialed and took a deep breath before putting the phone to my ear.

"Jennings? This is Richards. We've had a bit of a situation with Oak."

CHAPTER 29

"...don't know how you could leave them alone, even for a second," Jennings said, as the other agents he had brought to help investigate milled around, obviously trying not to look at us as he finished his very thorough dressing-down.

"She was in her room, Agent Jennings. I was in mine. We were on the second floor; they couldn't have known that this would happen," Jesse interjected bravely from a few paces away. Jennings shook as he took a deep breath before turning to the president's son.

"It's their job to know," he said. I shot Jesse a grateful look. He hadn't divulged our indiscretion to any of the agents who had asked him for his recollection of events, and that had been kind enough without him sticking up for us with Agent Jennings as we were—I admit rightfully— disciplined.

"So where do we go from here?" I ventured. "How do we track down whoever's responsible for this?" Jennings's eyes snapped up to meet mine, and the sharpness of his glare almost made me drop my eyes to the floor. Instead, I held his gaze evenly, feeling as though I was undergoing some sort of test.

"I don't know that '*we*' should do anything given how you bungled today," Jennings spat. "As it is, whoever was behind this was good at their job. Other than the signs of struggle in the room, they didn't leave a trace of them being here. Whoever is behind it is a professional."

"Then it sounds like you'll need all hands on deck," Jesse interjected again, with a cool sweep of his eyes that reminded me startlingly of his father. To that, Jennings had no response, and he instead inclined his head to the president's son before lowering his voice.

"There are only a few people who knew this place existed. This shouldn't have happened," he said darkly. I exchanged a knowing look with Luke, wondering if it would be the wrong time to revisit my theory of it being an inside job. I wondered who *had* known about our location. Jennings certainly had, of course. I assumed that the other heads of security— Katz, Bryant, and Welsch— did as well, but who else? Bryant and Welsch were conducting their own investigation of the house, so I would need to be careful before bringing up their name in conversation. That left Katz, who so far had not appeared, but I was reluctant to accuse one person.

"Who knew?" Luke asked, cutting across my thoughts as he posed the question to the older agent. Jennings blinked at him slowly, like a big cat appraising a piece of meat and deciding whether or not to pounce, before he sighed.

"There were the four of us. Plus you two and the kids. And the one driver. Even the president didn't know the details. We thought it was better if he and Mrs. Boyle were kept at a distance from all of this to avoid any slip-ups." The explanation was short, but it confirmed what I had thought; it didn't take a genius to figure out who was encompassed by 'the four of us.'

"Do they know yet?" I asked, watching Jesse

carefully. He had managed the situation with a surprising amount of poise, but I knew that he had to be reeling internally. He would need the support of his family. Jennings sighed again.

"We filled them in. It was a very difficult conversation to have to have," he answered cautiously. I was impressed—this was the closest that Jennings had come to admitting he experienced normal human reactions to tough situations since we had arrived. *I guess maybe he doesn't blame us too much?* The thought was probably unrealistic, but it lingered in my head nonetheless.

We resigned ourselves to waiting downstairs as a flurry of additional personnel surveyed the area, looking for any trace of evidence, which we already knew they wouldn't find. It was tedious, and it set me on edge. Every moment of time that they spent in the house was another moment that Sara could be getting further away and be in even more danger. The waiting was maddening, and even though there was nothing productive that either Luke or I could do to help her, any action would have made us feel saner than the emptiness of seemingly endless waiting.

To my surprise, Jennings joined us in the living room and chose to wait alongside us. He didn't talk to us much, really only speaking at all when one of the other investigators came to ask him a question or to clarify something, but the fact that he remained was— while strange—oddly reassuring. *He could just be keeping an eye on you,* my inner voice warned, but I shook the thought away. We would have made for easy scapegoats. The fact that he hadn't openly accused us of being involved yet told me that it wasn't his intention. *That's something, at least.*

I turned at the sound of the door opening, slightly surprised to see Katz step over the threshold looking rather the worse for wear. His normally well-pressed clothing was rumpled, and he had a hurried air around him. Without a word of greeting to us, he stepped over to Jennings, and the pair lowered their heads in private conversation. I turned my head slightly to look at Luke, who met my eyes with a curiously raised eyebrow. A few moments passed before Katz turned away from Jennings, and as he seemed to notice us for the first time, his eyes darkened suspiciously.

"How did this happen?" he demanded. I took a deep breath, preparing to explain the events of the day for what felt like the thousandth time, but before I could, Jennings put his hand on Katz's shoulder.

"It wasn't them." There was a certainty in his voice that made me blink, but I definitely wasn't planning to argue the point. Katz turned to face the other man, seeming surprised by the declaration, but he inclined his head respectfully before turning to face us again.

"Jesse is safe?" he said, sounding marginally less hostile as he posed the question.

"Very. He's upstairs." Jesse had declined to wait with us, instead returning to his room alone—well, as alone as one could be under now-constant supervision.

"And the elder Boyles?" Luke asked. Katz paused, seeming not to understand what he was asking at first.

"They've been briefed. With as much information as I had to give them," he answered shortly. "Mrs. Boyle is distraught."

"I'm sure she is," I murmured. Katz scowled at me, the expression uncharacteristically harsh on his normally friendly face, and he turned again to Jennings.

"You're sure we don't know anything more?" he asked. Jennings shook his head.

"I'm afraid not. Whoever is responsible for this made no mistakes this time; it was a clean job." At his words, Katz nodded slowly, and the madness of inaction finally overcame me.

"What do we do from here? She can't just be *gone*,"

I said emphatically. The heads of both men snapped up to stare at me with wide eyes.

"What do you expect us to do?" Katz asked cautiously.

"You're the senior agents; you tell us." I was surprised when Luke snapped a challenge. It was unlike him to challenge his superiors—it was especially unlike him to do so with such hostility.

"There's not much we *can* do right now if they didn't leave any clues behind. Our leads have all led to nothing. We just have to wait and see if they'll make contact with us," Jennings answered shortly.

"You're just giving up?" Luke fired back.

"As opposed to what? Aimlessly wandering the streets and hoping someone will be dragging her down the sidewalk in plain sight? They want something, Ryder, more than just to take her from here. They're going to use her to get to the president; that's the only thing that makes sense. It won't take long for them to make contact. At this point, our best bet is to just be ready when they do." Jennings suddenly sounded very, very tired.

"And where will we be waiting with Jesse until they do?" I heard myself ask. Jennings barked out a short laugh. The sound echoed around the room, sounding painfully rough against his throat.

"Back to The White House, of course. That's where contact will be made," he answered, as though it should have been obvious. I thought of Lena, the girl who had been stabbed merely a hallway away from where Luke and I had been, and my blood ran cold. My skepticism about the wisdom of that plan must have shown on my face, because Jennings rubbed a hand over his face wearily.

"Further security arrangements will be made upon our return," he allowed, sounding as though the day had aged him a decade.

"Meaning?" I asked, unwilling to let the point rest.

Jennings stared at me coolly, with an expression that told me to let the matter rest. I looked at him curiously, tilting my head as his eyes darted imperceptibly toward Katz, who was conveniently looking in the opposite direction. Jennings's chin dipped a centimeter in a nod. My eyes widened, but I forced my expression into one of careful neutrality as Katz turned back around to ask Jennings a question.

Internally, my mind was racing. *What was he implying with that little head nod? Does he think that* Katz *could be behind it?* I struggled to make sense of the thought as it passed through my head. Katz had been the most welcoming, the most *human* of all the agents we had met from the start—with the exception, of course, of Bryant. Katz did not strike me as the type. More than that, he always seemed to be off doing something related to his position; I wondered wildly where he would have found the time to spearhead a conspiratorial campaign of terror. *No, Jennings must have meant something else.* I looked across the conversing men to see if Luke was following a similar train of thought, but did not look my way, instead appearing absorbed in their conversation. I would have to keep my musings to myself.

CHAPTER 30

When we returned to The White House, we were whisked away from the car in a flurry of movement, and for the first time, the weight of what had happened threatened to come crashing down. How could we face the Boyles, all the while knowing that our lapse in concentration had led to their daughter being taken by God knew who? Bile rose in the back of my throat, and I swallowed roughly, staring hard at the back of Luke's head, taking in his hairline where it met the back of his neck, barely visible above the high collar of his button-down shirt. *That's one way to distract yourself. And it ended so well last time,* my inner voice said snidely, and the bile surged again with a vengeance.

To my relief, we passed by the president's office without stopping, and I released tension that I hadn't noticed I was holding in my shoulders. The tension returned when I realized that he might have been relocated to the briefing room for information such as this. *Don't be ridiculous. Nowhere would be more secure from prying eyes than the Oval Office.* I shook my head; I was on edge, and more than any other time, I needed to stay in the present moment.

The nameless escorts around us screeched to a halt

in front of a door that I could only assume led to a small closet from its size. I shot a curious glance at the person to my left, but he stood facing resolutely forward, doing an admirable impersonation of a statue. Were we being crammed into a closet as punishment for the fact that the kidnapping had happened on our watch? I glanced ahead in case Luke was experiencing similar uncertainty, but he, like the man beside me, was fixed on what was ahead. Thankfully, I did not have to wait long to find out what was behind the door. It swung open seemingly of its own accord, and a dim sort of yellow light spilled onto the floor, in stark contrast to the sharp whiteness of the lights above. Luke stepped inside without hesitation, and after the briefest of uncertain glances at our hulking escorts, I followed him, a sense of foreboding looming behind me even as the uncertainty loomed ahead. I was still staring at the back of Luke's head when the door slammed shut behind me, and I jumped at the sound. Peering around Luke's broad shoulders, I saw that the room was small and nearly empty— it currently housed only a small table and Agent Jennings, who was sitting in a wing-backed chair with his fingers interlocked atop the table. *Lord, is he about to start monologuing?* His similarity to a cartoon villain grew more and more prevalent the longer I knew him.

"Ah, you've made it," he said in a chilly greeting. I stepped out from behind Luke when I realized that I was still half-hidden behind him.

"Where are we?" I asked curiously. I had never ventured into this room, and by the look of curiosity that had taken up residence on Luke's face, he hadn't either.

"My private meeting space. We won't be overheard here," he assured. I squinted at him skeptically. *This is definitely giving off supervillain energy.*

"And the armed escort?" I asked dryly. Jennings shrugged nonchalantly.

"I couldn't very well text you two. They don't know what this room is either, only that I asked them to bring you here," he said with a casualness that chilled me.

"A whole goon squad, then?" I murmured. Jennings's raised eyebrows told me that he had heard my under-the-breath commentary, but if he had a response to it, he did not make it aloud.

"And who are you worried will overhear us?" Luke asked. *Well, I guess one of us should be responsible for getting directly to the point.*

"I don't know yet," Jennings said, seeming to stiffen as he leaned forward. "Do you?" The question, although it sounded loaded, wasn't; I could hear the barely-concealed hope cracking through in his voice. Luke shook his head, and I reluctantly followed suit a moment later.

"Only my suspicions that it might be an inside man—or woman," I amended a moment later. Jennings inclined his head.

"Then we're on the same page." He leaned back again, seeming both tired and more at ease all at once. It hit me how tightly wound he must be to function as the de facto leader of such a high-stakes security team with all of the additional pressures of the job still growing.

"And the reason we're here?" Luke asked with a casualness I wished I could master.

"We need to discuss Mr. Boyle," he replied as though it should be obvious. I sighed; I had hoped that he had received at least some news of what had happened to Sara. Outside of the somber tone of the team, it was almost as though she had never been taken. *Almost.*

"Where will he be hidden next?" I asked, and Jennings shot me a look from narrowed eyes. I sighed again. *And here I was beginning to think maybe he didn't hate me so much after all.*

"In plain sight," he replied, and I wondered if he

was being deliberately vague.

"Meaning?" I prodded.

"Meaning with you two." I blinked at him.

"With us?" I asked.

"Yes."

"In plain sight?" I clarified.

"Yes." I paused, turning to look at Luke, whose mouth appeared to be wrestling between lines of seriousness and amusement.

"What am I missing here?" I said at last. Jennings leaned forward again, looking intently between us with a glint in his eyes.

"You three will not be leaving The White House again, at least not for now. Jesse Boyle will be hidden in plain sight. Your suite is well-concealed. He'll be staying with you until the danger has passed." Looking particularly proud of himself for his plan, Jennings looked between us as though expecting an argument.

"Until the danger has passed? For the President's son?" I couldn't resist the subtle tease, and to my delight, a flicker of amusement crossed Jennings's face.

"Diminished, then," he amended. There was a pause, and I saw Luke's mouth twitch as though he was deciding how to word a thought.

"And how many people will know about this plan?" he managed delicately. Jennings raised an eyebrow in a manner that revealed his answer before he gave it.

"You're looking at them," he replied, gesturing to the three of us.

CHAPTER 31

For being a standard-issue, teenaged boy, Jesse Boyle was surprisingly easy to live with as a roommate. Of course, we weren't actually sharing a room; that was an honor we had collectively decided should go to Luke, but overall, the suite hadn't been trashed and it didn't smell too much like feet, so I felt like we had gotten lucky overall. It had been no trouble at all for Jennings to procure a cot with secrecy, and somehow, a bag with Jesse's belongings from the most recent safe house had materialized in the living room.

Apparently, our suite's location was a well-kept secret though. Even Jesse had been stunned when we'd brought him in. Of course, the door was visible from the hallway, despite the subtlety with which it was crafted, but Jesse said that he had assumed it had led to something about as interesting as a utility room. Unassuming as the door was, I remembered my own surprise at the fact that the suite had been hidden behind the door, and I had laughed in spite of myself. The three of us got along well enough, which I attributed to so many days in a row spent hunkering down in various safe houses with the threat of our own impending doom looming nearby. Regardless of the circumstances, it made things easier. What I was less pleased with was the fact that there had not been any word of Sara Boyle. The three of us—Jennings, Luke, and myself—had assumed that her captors would reach out quickly, wanting money, power, or favors from the Oval Office, but 48 hours had passed since our return to Pennsylvania Avenue without a word.

While it wasn't something that we openly discussed with Jesse, it was obvious that the lack of news about Sara was wearing on him too. In the evenings, one of us—Luke or me— brought in food, and we ate together. More than once during those times, Jesse had faded out of the conversation and into silence. He spent night after night slumped quietly against the couch as thought the weight of the world was crushing down upon his young shoulders. The fact that his cell phone, so often a distraction for him, had been taken upon our return to The White House—Jennings thought it was a liability— gave him extra time to just sit around and think. I understood the helpless tension that came with waiting, and I was beginning to wonder if we had been wrong about the motives behind Sara's kidnapping. A thousand possibilities ran through my mind, one following the other like a hound after a pack of rabbits, and each one was more disturbing than the last. I was thankful when the 49th hour announced itself with a text buzzing in an alert on both Luke's and my flip phones.

Our hands leapt to our pockets simultaneously, and out of the corner of my eye as I fished out my phone, I saw Jesse glance between us with carefully guarded curiosity. There was, naturally, no news contained within the message. As usual, there were only instructions.

Briefing. Five minutes.

The message was from Jennings, and that meant that he'd had news. I stood quickly, nearly spilling my plate out of my lap as I got to my feet. I kept my leftovers from toppling over by changing the direction of my momentum so that the plate skidded to a rest on the coffee table instead. The sound echoed in the small room.

"You've heard something?" Jesse asked, and I could hear the barely concealed strain in his voice.

"No details. Not yet," Luke said shortly, although not unkindly. Still, Jesse looked slightly crestfallen.

"I hope it's about your sister, although we won't know until later," I allowed, drawing a warning glance from Luke. I returned his look with a squint. *I know better than to give too much away*, I thought mutinously. That being said, I had compassion for Jesse; it was hard enough knowing what we knew, which was next to nothing. This was his sister, and he had even less information than we did. Jesse's shoulders drooped heavily as he slumped forward, putting his face in his hands.

"What are the chances that you can tell me what they tell you if there's news?" Jesse asked in a dull voice, his voice muffled slightly behind his palms. I knew that he already knew the answer, and I sighed.

"Sorry, Jesse," I answered. He nodded once, averting eye contact and staring away with dread and desperation warring on his face. I hoped desperately that whatever Jennings was calling us for would lead us in the right direction.

It was hard for me not to break into a run on the way to the briefing room, but this was not just because I was anxious to get there. Luke also seemed like he was in a hurry, and with his longer stride, it was all I could do to keep from running to keep up. The benefit to our mutually shared urgency, though, was that it made for a quick trip through the maze of hallways. We were not the first to arrive, but I was relieved to see that we were not the last. I was amused to see that the one we were waiting on was Agent Jennings. Welsch and Bryant had their heads buried together, while Katz sat to their left, seeming lost in thought. They all looked up when we entered, but they returned to their respective activities without any words of greeting. Luke and I took seats on opposite sides of the table, and I tried to catch his eye. He didn't look at me and instead struck up a conversation with Agent Katz, leaving me to silently ponder about the state of things.

One of these people has betrayed us. The thought hit me again. Was it Katz, who was keeping to himself now, but who had been so warm and welcoming our first days on the job? Was it Welsch, who was easily flustered in personal conversation, but who was generally good-natured? Or was it Bryant, who had commiserated with me about being underestimated for having the "wrong" reproductive parts, who had fought tooth and nail against the status quo to achieve her current rank? Could it be more than one of them? The thoughts slammed against each other like hailstones in a storm. Who could put on an act like this, so convincing and for so long? We were all trained agents, but the thought still boggled my mind. I was almost grateful for the reprieve from my thoughts when the door swung open, and Jennings swept into the room. Then, I realized that whatever information he had would likely just send my mind into a rapturous flurry again.

"They've made contact," he announced, striding across the room to take his normal seat at the head of the table. I shot to the edge of my seat, waiting anxiously for him to continue, all thoughts of the other agents and met suspicions forgotten for a moment.

"Is she okay?" I asked breathlessly, unable to hide the concern in my voice. Jennings looked over at me sharply, and for a minute, I thought I might be chastised before he nodded. He seemed to choose his next words carefully.

"I was able to confirm proof of life. She seems, for the most part, fine. Shaken up, but unharmed," he said cautiously. I nodded in reply; that was a positive, even if it wasn't the entire picture of what she had endured.

"You talked to her, then?" Welsch piped up. Jennings nodded again.

"I did. We were unable to trace the phone's exact location, but we were able to pinpoint the area of the device. And more than that, they told me what they wanted." *Money, power, or influence? Money, power, or influence?* The thoughts repeated themselves in my head in a kind of chant.

"Is it a ransom situation, or is it blackmail?" Katz asked curiously. It was the first time he'd spoken out since we had entered the room, aside from his small talk with Luke, and I was a bit taken aback to hear him ask the question.

"Both." Jennings said.

"Meaning?" Katz raised an eyebrow.

"They want President Boyle to block sanctions against Russia at the upcoming summit." Katz considered Jennings's reply for a moment before leaning forward. It was a mark of how distracted I'd been that I had no idea what he was talking about.

"And then they said they'll return Miss Boyle?" he asked.

"So they say," Jennings said frostily.

"So, if we can just get the president to give his word, then…?" Bryant began slowly and then trailed off, her dark eyebrows rising skeptically. Her coils of hair were tamed into a tight bun, and the effect was such that it looked as though the pull of her hair was lifting her eyebrows into her hairline. Jennings shook his head.

"No good. You know they'll want confirmation through action," he said.

"Which could take months," Welsch added.

"Precisely."

"And what are their interests in Russia? That seems like a bold ask." Until this point, Luke had been silent, and I had been so engrossed in what the others were saying, I'd almost forgotten the depth of our involvement.

"They kidnapped the president's daughter. Bold doesn't even begin to cover it," Katz pointed out. I looked sharply at him to see the older man's eyes glittering with intrigue and—was it admiration? Russia was a powerful player on the world stage, and they had been flexing their military muscles along their European borders. If the one behind all of this was in league with a world superpower, or working on behalf of one, we had a lot to figure out, and they would be a force to be reckoned with. They could have backers, powerful backers who would not be easily dissuaded from pursuing their goal. In other words, this was a very precarious situation for Sara Boyle.

"They didn't mention any specific connection with the Russians, only that they wanted any sanctions that are discussed to be blocked," Jennings answered Luke's question as though Katz hadn't spoken, but I didn't miss the way that his eyes raked across the other agent. Maybe I *hadn't* been imagining the tone of eagerness after all... or Jennings just didn't trust anyone.

"So, what? They just want us to wait until the Russian government hypothetically commits war crimes or something so we can block hypothetical sanctions before they give her back to us? Doesn't that seem a little...? I mean, they could just keep her indefinitely at this point and use her for leverage. What's the point in offering to give her back to her family?" I asked, struggling to word the question sensitively. Sara was a job—and sometimes more work than even a job should be—but she was a person. It felt wrong to talk about her as though she was some type of commodity. I almost immediately wished that I had not spoken at all, because Katz turned those same, glittering eyes on me next, and I felt for all the world like a bug under a microscope.

"An interesting perspective. Why *would* they give her back?" Katz mused thoughtfully.

"I suppose they might not actually have the deep connections that we initially thought. If they merely had a shallow interest in the topic…" Jennings trailed off now, and I glanced at him curiously, wondering exactly what the wheels of his mind were spinning into gold.

"So, there's a possibility that they won't actually return her, and of course we can't compromise the president for the whims of someone who is unlikely to hold up their end of the bargain," Welsch added, surprisingly calm—I had seen him flustered over lesser situations. "So where do we go from here?" To that question, no one had a response—at least, no one gave one out loud. I was sure that many of us had a lot of things on our mind, but either none of them were feasible or none of them could be shared with this particular group, because the silence loomed on, and the thoughtful expression on Jennings's face did not change.

"It seems like negotiation is really the only option here," Katz broke the silence carefully. "Unless they make contact again and provide us with other leads, of course," he added.

"If they make contact again," Bryant pointed out. "Who's to say that they will?"

"I mean, they'll have to have an answer. Their hypothetical sanctions situation might not happen for a long time; surely, they'd want reassurance before then," Luke pointed out. Bryant inclined her head in response, and I privately agreed with Luke. The thought made sense.

"Agent Jennings, did they give you any way to contact them?" I asked, knowing what the answer would be before the words left my mouth. Without looking up at me, Jennings shook his head slowly. *I guess he was paying attention after all.* His silence and lack of movement had almost convinced me otherwise.

"The voice on the other end did say they'd be in touch. I think we can expect them to make contact again," he shot a wry smile in Bryant's direction, but his tone was missing the characteristic barb it usually held when he was correcting someone.

"So, for now—" Luke began.

"We wait," Jennings finished.

CHAPTER 32

The next twenty-four hours were tense. Luke and I snapped at each other more than once, leaving Jesse woefully confused. We had kept our agreement not to tell him anything beyond the essentials—not that we had much to tell. That was actually the source of the first in our new round of arguments. Luke had all but ordered me to keep my mouth shut—in much less professional words—and the order had chaffed at my temper. I knew how to be discreet and keep classified information to myself. Jesse had been quiet for the duration of our fight, still lost in his thoughts—and likely still lost without access to his phone—and I was beginning to worry about him more and more. He had been cooped up in the suite, allowed to leave for only short periods of time to alleviate the suspicion that anything in his routine was different, and I could tell that it was wearing on him. The fact that he hadn't complained, which any normal person would have done under the circumstances, was especially concerning. The three of us had the collective sensation of being trapped in a fishbowl; we could see the rest of the world, but we existed largely in isolation. That's why the knock at our door was so disconcerting.

"What the hell?" Luke muttered, jumping at the pounding sound. Our eyes met, and I imagined that my face wore a similar expression of wide-eyed wariness. The pounding came again, and my eyes darted toward Jesse, who look equally startled.

"In my room, now," I hissed, and confusion joined his startled expression. Separating him from his belongings may have seemed irrational, but I had my suspicions that if someone *was* looking for him, they would be less likely to look for him in my room first. He complied quickly, casting a confused glance back over his shoulder as he went. When the door was closed, I took a deep breath and nodded for Luke to answer the door.

"Took you long enough," Jennings's annoyed voice floated in from the hallway, and seconds later, the agent was pushing his way into the suite, gesturing for Luke to shut the door behind him. He stopped short, seeing my tense shoulders, and then glanced around the suite curiously. "And Mr. Boyle?" he asked, seeming amused.

"All clear, Jesse," I called without taking my eyes off of Jennings. The door to my room creaked open, and Jesse emerged. The amusement on the other agent's face only grew, but to my relief, he didn't comment on the subject. Still, my face grew warm, and I resisted the urge to defend my decision to send him into my room.

"You have news?" I said instead, and out of the corner of my eye, I saw Luke's mouth twitch in a half-smile, as though he knew exactly what I'd been thinking. To my relief, Jennings chose not to comment on the matter; he nodded his response and continued as though the moment hadn't happened.

"They called," he said. "Speaking of calls, let me see your phones." I blinked at that, and a glance in Luke's direction showed that he was equally taken aback. Luke caught my eye, and his shoulders moved up and down in a halfhearted shrug. I reached into the pocket of my pants, struggling with the fitted fabric and internally cursing whoever had had the brilliant idea to make women's clothing so inconvenient.

"What did they say?" I asked with a cautious glance at Jesse. To his credit, the president's son had dropped a careful mask of neutrality over his features.

"Renewed demands, proof of life," Jesse jerked at the mention of Sara's life, but he did not otherwise react. "The phones," Jennings urged. I dropped my phone into his waiting hand, but Luke did not. Instead, he stood back, arms crossed as he surveyed Jennings with an inscrutable expression.

"What aren't you telling us?" he asked impassively. Jennings huffed impatiently, but he didn't respond as he looked sharply at my device. I bit back a sound of protest as he popped open the back of the phone, where the battery was housed. Seeming to find nothing suspicious, he snapped the cover back into place and held it out to me. I gingerly took the phone from him and wiggled it back into my pocket, thoroughly confused.

"Have you two had any unusual contact with anyone?" he asked. I blinked in surprise at the fact that he would ask such a question in front of Jesse, but I shook my head nevertheless. Jennings turned an expectant gaze toward Luke, who looked disgruntled at the fact that his question had been ignored. Still, he shook his head.

"Why do you ask?" I ventured. I wasn't sure how much Jennings would be willing to discuss in Jesse's presence, but it was worth a try. To my surprise, Agent Jennings actually answered.

"Just something the caller had said. Something about all of us waiting for his next call. Said we should keep an eye on our phones." His tone was short, barely concealing the strain that I knew he must have felt.

"So, you wanted to check the phones for...?" I

prompted with a raised eyebrow. Jennings glanced very deliberately in Luke's direction, and I gestured for him to hand over his own phone. With a huff of annoyance, Luke complied, the lines of annoyance on his face growing more pronounced.

"I just wanted to make sure that there weren't any extra features added to them," Jennings returned the device to Luke's waiting hand after a short inspection. At this, Jesse looked startled.

"Like a tracker or something?" he asked boldly. Jennings widened his eyes in faint surprise at the interjection, but he nodded.

"Something like that," he answered softly. I was still unsure of exactly what Jennings had thought he would find, but I was thankful that whatever his hunch had been had not been proven right.

"But there wasn't one?" Jesse prodded, obviously fishing for any sort of insight into the situation. Agent Jennings quelled him with a look.

"No." The agent's tone left no room for further inquiry, and Jesse's brow furrowed in frustration. Sympathy swelled somewhere in my stomach. As helpless as I felt in this situation, I knew that Jesse was feeling it even more. Jennings turned suddenly, the movement startling me as he made for the door.

"Where are *you* going?" I blurted out, surprised at his sudden departure. He paused and turned, his eyes passing over all three of us before clouding with thought.

"There's something in that comment. It was as though he was taunting us when he said it. It meant something. I just need to figure out what." Then, as quickly as he had arrived in our suite, Jennings was gone.

"He'd do well on a TV drama," I murmured, looking thoughtfully after him.

"He does seem to like a good cliffhanger," Jesse agreed, and a glance in his direction showed that his brow was still creased with lines of frustration. Luke said nothing, but as I let my eyes wander to rest on his face, I saw that the wheels of his mind were hard at work. If there was a puzzle in the caller's taunt, we would figure it out. We would have to.

CHAPTER 33

There's nothing quite like the sensation of being shaken violently awake from a deep sleep, particularly if you're trained to react to a physical attack at a moment's notice. I credit that instinct as the reason that I came to be sitting on top of Luke's back with one of his arms twisted dangerously at the shoulder.

"Richards, what the—" The rug muffled his voice, and as the awareness of the waking world flooded into my brain to replace the sleepy dream-state that had been inhabiting it, I sheepishly released his arm and climbed off.

"God, Ryder. Even you should know better than to wake a sleeping agent," I said in annoyance, the initial surge of adrenaline fading now. I rubbed at my eyes, scowling into the dark. "What do you want?"

"I couldn't sleep," he began, and I scoffed.

"So what? Misery wanted company?" I snorted. A glance at the clock beside my bed showed that we were still in the wee hours of the morning. Combining that with a late night of tossing and turning, I was running on about three hours of sleep at the moment, which did nothing to improve my mood.

"I had a thought," he said with a dignified huff. I

snorted again.

"Well, it was bound to happen sometime, Ryder. Don't worry; it's pretty normal for the rest of us. I'm sure you'll get used to it." My retort was answered with a long-suffering sigh, and I couldn't help the snicker that slipped out.

"It was about how they kept finding us," he said seriously, and the I sobered instantly. If Luke's theory was so pressing that it had gotten him out of bed and led him to sneak into my room to wake me up at this hour, I knew that it had to be one he felt confident in—which meant that I really couldn't fault him for waking me. I'd have done the same thing.

"What are you thinking?" I asked. There was a lengthy pause, and I realized that I couldn't see his face, since it was still too dark in the room for me to see more than Luke's faint outline. I toed my way over to the table where the alarm clock glowed faintly and blinked at the sudden flood of light as I turned on the lamp that shared its table. Turning, I saw that Luke's brow was furrowed deeply in thought, and it looked as though he was trying to choose his next words carefully.

"I'm thinking that Jennings showed up here yesterday to check the back of the phones for any extra hardware," he said cautiously. I nodded.

"Correct. And?" I prompted.

"Well, the thought occurred to me that if he felt as though he had to check, and he knew that we've kept them on us since they were given to us, that he might not have been the one to set them up," Luke reasoned.

"Following the thought down the rabbit hole," I commented quietly. When I looked up, Luke was staring at me.

"Huh?" he asked eloquently.

"I just mean that he had a theory he didn't share. He was following a hunch. So, if you're right that he wasn't the one who set them up and he was suspicious enough to look at them, that means he also had an idea who was behind all of this," I reasoned.

"Exactly," Luke said. A thought hit me.

"Which he didn't share with us..." I trailed off, mildly annoyed at the prospect that Jennings was hiding things from us. *Unless he thinks that we—no, I'm sure he just wants to have a clear picture before he includes anyone else.* After all, if he had doubted us, he hardly would have made us the only agents who knew about Jesse's current location. He would have had no trouble outing us if that was his actual suspicion.

"I'm wondering who set up the phones to make them supposedly untraceable," Luke finished.

"We could always ask," I offered. "But are we sure it's the phones? The attacks happened before we got them."

"Not exactly," Luke admitted. "But the first attack happened at a public event. The one with that intern was a chance encounter. The two in the safe houses happened after we had the devices in-hand. And if Jennings thinks there's a lead there..." he trailed off.

"And how many of the previous attempts on Jesse and Sara happened in public versus in a safe house?" I wondered aloud.

"And how many times has whoever Jennings is suspecting been in charge of setting up 'untraceable' communications? How many times have the attacks in safe houses happened after those phones were assigned?" Luke asked, making air quotes with his fingers.

"It's a stretch," I said with a tilt of my head.

"But it's a possibility," Luke said firmly. We both fell silent then, each of us swimming through the cesspool of our own tangled thoughts.

"So... Who, then?" I broke the silence, unable to fully investigate the possibilities on my own.

"That *is* the question," Luke murmured.

"And there's the fact that he didn't find anything,"

I pointed out reluctantly. "So we might have just wasted our chance to sleep even thinking about it." Luke's lips tightened at that thought.

"He only checked the back," Luke pointed out.

"Which would be the standard place to bug a device," I replied, raising an eyebrow at him.

"But not the only one," Luke pressed, a stubborn gleam rising into his eyes, which—even in the gloom of early-morning exhaustion were somehow still vibrant. I rubbed my own, feeling the bags of fatigue beneath my hands.

"Come on, Ryder. Surely you don't mean to take apart the entire phone at—" I glanced at the clock. "—three in the morning." My statement was met with silence, and I felt the weight of resigned exhaustion sink onto my shoulders. *Clearly, he does.* I sighed heavily.

"It's the one way we'll know," Luke said, earning an unenthusiastic nod from me.

"Yep," I said gruffly.

"And we'll know what to look for, since it's unlikely to be a software issue," he pressed.

"Mm-hmm." I pulled out my phone and tossed it at him. He narrowly caught the unexpected throw and blinked at me in surprise.

"I would have thought you'd demand we use mine, since this is my idea and all," he commented, his mouth twisting into a wry smile.

"This may be your wild goose chase, but you and I both know that if Jennings or the other agents need something, you're the one they'll send a message to. Do your worst," I said wearily.

I did not have to prompt him a second time. Without asking, Luke flicked on the overhead light, much to the dismay of my still-tired eyes, and sat on the floor, pulling off the back cover and doing his own examination of the place where the battery rested. With a forlorn glance back toward the rumpled covers of my warm, cozy bed, I shuffled over to where Luke sat and sank down to join him.

"You may as well go ahead and pop out the battery completely," I advised tiredly, "so you don't electrocute yourself when you pull it apart." He nodded without looking up at me and then promptly followed my advice before proceeding to dismantle the rest. I watched him work from my position on the floor, noting the way that the corner of his mouth tugged toward his cheek as he focused on his task. His eyes were downcast, darkened in the shadow of concentration. I observed the way his fingers, long and agile, manipulated the pieces of the device to pull them apart with impressive speed and efficiency. Most of all, I noticed that this was the first time that we'd been alone and in close proximity since we had kissed. The fact that I *was* conscious of this fact made me feel a bit like a ridiculous schoolgirl, but once the realization was there, I was unable to push it from my mind.

"Sorry for waking you up," Luke murmured a bit belatedly, still fixated on the task in front of him.

"If you're right, it was for a good cause." *And if you're wrong, I'll never let you live it down.* The unspoken thought hung in the air, but he made no further comment on the subject, so I let it rest. It was strange that I was content to simply watch him as he worked; normally, I had this intense need to be a part of every aspect of solving a puzzle. This was a one-person job, and for some reason, I was content to let him be the one person. I stopped myself from reminding him to check the back side of the buttons on the keypad. *He knows what he's looking for.* The thought surprised me. *I guess this is trust.* It was a foreign concept, and the realization made me smile. The expression died on my lips when I remembered how dangerous trust could be in our line of work. I didn't have a chance to think about what that meant for too long, though, because in the next second, Luke had found something.

"Is this where I'm supposed to say 'eureka?'" he asked, finally meeting my eyes with a smile.

"Depends on what you think you found, I guess," I answered with a forced sort of blandness. He was not deterred, because in the next second, he tilted the back of the keypad in my direction. I blinked the tiredness from my eyes, trying to figure out what it was that I was supposed to be seeing. Then I saw the extra wire, and my eyes followed it to where it rested against a tiny chip-like addition to the body of the device. It was the picture-perfect example of an old-school tracker.

"There's that," I said softly.

"There's that," he confirmed. What the purpose of this wired-in chip was, I couldn't be sure, but it did mean that the device had been tampered with.

"It could be what made it untraceable," I suggested lamely. Luke shot me a withering look, and I shrugged. "Just saying."

"I don't think it is," he countered, inspecting it more closely.

"I don't either," I clarified, and Luke nodded.

"What now?" he asked, although I knew that we both knew the answer.

"Can I borrow your phone? I need to make a call, and mine isn't working for some reason," I said, my lips twitching as I repressed a smile. Luke made no such effort, and I felt my heart lighten at the wide grin that split onto his face.

"I guess I can do that. What's up with yours?" he asked innocently. I rolled my eyes.

"Some lunatic did a science experiment," I answered. He laughed again as I snatched the phone that he extended to me. After a moment of debate, I dialed Jennings; this wasn't the time for a text. As the other man picked up, I thought of how to word what I had to tell him in a way that whoever might be listening on the other end wouldn't pick up. *It looks like a tracker, but you never know,* I reasoned.

"What?" Jennings's weary voice asked on the other end. With an amused glance at Luke, I returned my attention to the call.

"Briefing Room. Five minutes," I said, and then I hung up.

CHAPTER 34

"Yeah, that's a tracker for sure," Jennings confirmed what we had already known, yawning as he did. "I don't know how I missed it." I opened my mouth to remind him that he had only popped open the back cover of the phone, but I quickly thought better of it. He was admitting a flaw; for Jennings, that was progress. He leaned back in his chair, leaving the pieces of the phone detached on the table like a dismembered corpse.

"No listening capabilities, right?" Luke asked shortly.

"I don't think so," Jennings confirmed what we had hoped.

"Well, that's a plus at least," I said softly. Neither man looked up, and the three of us sat in contemplative silence for several seconds. Luke seemed to wrestle with himself for a moment before he broke it.

"So, what now?" Luke asked. Jennings looked up at him and his features darkened.

"Well, since I highly doubt you two planted a tracker on yourselves, I suppose we need to figure out a way to arrest Agent Katz," he answered acidly. I reeled backward in shock, nearly toppling over my chair as I pulled it back to its normal position with a last-minute grab at the table.

"*Katz?*" I asked incredulously. The man had been the most welcoming, the most informative, the agent I had felt we could trust the most when we had arrived.

"Katz," Jennings said, and the tone that he used might have been the same one he used to discuss the weather.

"Make it make sense," I demanded. He blinked at me, and I half-expected a reproof, but the corner of his mouth twitched upward in a gesture that was almost a smile.

"I'm not sure I can do that, Richards. But I *can* tell you that he's the one who set up the devices to be untraceable. I can tell you that he had pulled me for some sort of wild goose chase when the kids were accosted at the school before you two were hired on. I can tell you any number of suspicious actions he's taken that—while they're circumstantial at best— make him the most likely candidate. Shall I go on?" he raised an eyebrow, and I thought back, still reeling. Sara and Jesse had said that Katz was with Jennings at the elementary school. He *had* been late to the last safe house. I thought back to the almost admiring expression he had worn when we were discussing the professionalism of Sara's kidnappers. Jennings was right; it was circumstantial at best, but it made the most sense.

"So, where do we go from here?" Luke asked rationally, seeming annoyingly unfazed by the situation. I scowled in his direction, rubbing at my temples with both hands as I fought to center my thoughts on the actions that we could realistically take now.

"Tail him?" I asked hopefully. Jennings shrugged.

"He's experienced. He would probably see that coming," he pointed out.

"We could bug *him*," Luke suggested, glaring down at the tracker that still sat menacingly in front of us. Suddenly, a horrifying thought occurred to me.

"Won't he notice that both of our phones are in the same room at—" I estimated quickly "—four in the morning?" Luke shook his head with a small smile.

"I left mine in the room." I pursed my lips with grudging approval, slightly envious of his forethought, given the sleepless circumstances.

"Smart thinking," I muttered reluctantly.

"So, bugging him?" Luke repeated, turning to gage Jennings's reaction. Jennings nodded slowly; his lips drew tightly against his teeth.

"Probably our best option. Some sort of tracker anyway. Meanwhile, I'll see if I can get ahold of call records in the vicinity of the White House and near his apartment. It won't be easy to trudge through, but it'll give us something to work with in the meantime." Jennings seemed to struggle to get the words out, and I realized that, much more than simply realizing that he had overlooked a bug, this situation was forcing him to admit that I had been right, and that he had miscalculated the ethics of his team. It was likely a hard blow to hit the man a second time. The thought made me wonder again about our predecessors.

"Was there any connection between the agents who were here before and Agent Katz?" I asked. Jennings glanced at me with an inscrutable expression, but I took the fact that he did not immediately disregard the suggestion as a sign that I could be on to something.

"It would be something for us to look in to," he managed, sounding a bit strangled in his reply.

"They escaped, right?" I asked, just for the sake of clarity. There was still so much about that situation that I did not know. I winced as Jennings's expression darkened; I hadn't meant for that question to be a dig.

"One of them escaped," he confirmed gruffly. I nodded in response, feeling that for diplomacy's sake,

I should not press him further on the issue.

"So what now?" Luke asked, changing the subject to refocus on the present.

"I suppose we wait. I'm sure to get another call soon; I've been stringing them along so they keep making contact. When I get the call, we'll want to watch Katz. See what he does. I have an idea."

"And until then?" I asked, feeling bold.

"Keep an eye on Jesse. But don't tell him anything about what we've discussed. He has enough on his plate as it is, and I don't trust him to keep his trap shut if he's convinced that someone here has hurt his sister." It was a reasonable request, although it was a bit of a harshly worded one, so Luke and I agreed. Now, all we could do was wait. Unfortunately, that was never something that had come easily to me. It would be a good exercise.

We did not have to wait long. We were summoned to the briefing room the next morning, and the tension hung in the air like a thick fog, impenetrable and ominous. I allowed my eyes to pass over each of the room's occupants as I took my seat. There was Bryant, poised and politely intrigued. Welsch was beside her, characteristically on edge. Jennings, as usual, sat at the head of the table, his eyes narrowed in a knowing, catlike expression, and Luke seemed wary. Then, of course, there was Katz, whose face gave nothing away. Like any of the rest of us, he might have been awaiting brand new information. *He's good*, I allowed reluctantly.

"Have you heard from them again?" I asked as soon as I lowered myself into my seat. Jennings and Luke seemed unsurprised at my question, but the three other agents whipped their heads around to stare at me. I shrugged; there was no sense in dragging it out.

"I did," Jennings answered gravely, with such a somber tone that the heads swiveled back in his direction. *And that's how you get whiplash. Workman's comp?* I snorted at the thought, surprisingly not drawing any return glances. The pull of Jennings's insight was too strong for them to be concerned with me.

"And?" Bryant asked sharply. It hit me that she was just as worried as I had been.

"We have to approach this delicately," Jennings began. "I was unable to obtain proof of life from this call." The shocked silence hung heavily in the air, and my heart began to pound as a dull ringing clamored in my ears. My shock must have shown on my face, because Luke kicked me under the table. *Was this his plan? Or was he serious?* I glanced at Katz, remembering why we had needed to meet in the first place, and saw that the color had drained from the older man's face, his horror obvious. It could have been the expression of a concerned party, but in a job where objectivity was often key, I knew that this could be taken as further evidence of his involvement.

"No proof of life?" Katz asked, sounding slightly strangled. The tone could have been my imagination, but as I exchanged a knowing glance with Luke, I didn't think that was the case.

"They were unable—or unwilling—to provide it," Jennings said, maintaining the grave tone of voice as he leveled his gaze at the other man. To that, Katz seemed to have no response. I noticed that Jennings did not mention the other context of the conversation, and I wondered for one, wild moment whether he had made the whole call up. *That would be an interesting plan,* I reasoned, but I quickly discarded the thought. If he had made up the call and Katz had been involved, he would have been equally horrified by the fact that they had made contact without his knowledge or consent… or he would have sniffed out the lie.

"What did they want?" Welsch asked, seeming surprisingly calm in the face of Jennings's admission.

"They want a public statement to be released,

promising that the United States will not support an sanctions, regardless of what happens in the near future." The threat of their words was obvious, even through Jennings's relatively neutral tone.

"But there was no proof of life? Kind of throws off their leverage a bit," I said boldly, darting my eyes toward Katz, who still retained that ugly, colorless shade.

"Were we able to get a trace on the call?" Luke said, finally speaking up. He had been surprisingly quiet throughout the ordeal, and I wondered what he was thinking.

"We have an idea of where they were coming from, but nothing there's definitive yet," Jennings admitted after a pause. The words did nothing to relieve the obvious horror still written across Katz's face. If anything, they intensified it.

"Did they mention why they wouldn't provide proof of life?" Katz asked, his expression suddenly deadpan as all of us turned to face him. Jennings raised an eyebrow and shrugged in a way that would have been appropriate for a casual disagreement about a football team, rather than the fate of the daughter of the president.

"Only that they were unable to comply," he said mildly.

"And has the president been informed of this?" Bryant piped up. "Or his wife?" Jennings scowled and rounded back to face her.

"Of course not. I felt our team should be briefed first." The hostility in his voice made me blink in surprise; Jennings had—for the most part—dropped the overt aggression with me. Apparently, I was now the exception to his rule. Bryant's eyes darkened dangerously, but I was impressed to see that she didn't rise to take the bait.

"And now we have been," she answered coldly, tilting her head to the side. It was obvious that she was waiting for Jennings to adjourn the meeting so that she could pass along the news, and I found myself holding my breath. *Wouldn't Jennings want to be the one, since he had the direct contact?* Then again, Bryant was assigned to cover the first lady often. Perhaps they had bonded as women in a man's world or something like that. I shook my head; that side of group politics was the least of my concerns. I probably should have felt guilty at how readily I disregarded how a mother was told that there was no way to verify her daughter's life, but since my primary focus was trying to figure out how we could retrieve said daughter, I wasn't too bothered. In any case, Katz was where I should be directing my attention; he was the one that we couldn't trust.

I was jolted out of my thoughts by the scraping of chairs as Welsch, Katz, Bryant, and Luke stood. I had clearly missed the meeting dismissal, and I rose belatedly, the loud scrape of my own chair on the floor drawing a reproving glance from Welsch.

"Ryder, Richards, if you'll stay behind." It was not a request. I felt my left eyebrow twitch at Jennings's order, but I fought to keep the rest of my expression composed. It was no surprise that Katz was the first to exit the room, shoulders hunched as he disappeared through the door.

"I suppose the plan worked. Shouldn't we be following him?" Luke asked, and I turned from where the door had clicked to a shut behind the last agent to see amusement and concern at war on his face.

"I have that taken care of. He'll call. They won't know what he's talking about, and then he'll feel the need to check on things himself," Jennings said.

"And you're sure he'll go check? If he talks to Sara himself, won't he think you lied? And won't he wonder why?" I asked. Despite the back-to-back questions I asked, there was no challenge in them; I was genuinely curious.

"He has no reason to think I would lie. This was an

official briefing. More likely, he'll be distrustful of whoever he has watching her. He'll want to know why they failed in their duty to keep stringing us along," he replied carefully. *If he's involved.* The unspoken words hung heavily in the air, but none of the three of us took the chance of saying them out loud.

"When you say you've got following him taken care of…" Luke trailed off in a way that invited Jennings to respond.

"I do." The man made no effort to do so, and I resisted the urge to roll my eyes in annoyance. After all, we were in this together at this point.

"I thought you said he was too experienced not to see a tail," Luke squinted at the other man skeptically.

"I did," came the same, infuriating non-response. I could see that even Luke, the master of self-control himself, was growing irritated.

"Then how—" he began, and Jennings waved him off.

"Surely even you know by now that there are other ways of finding someone's location," Jennings snapped, and Luke gritted his teeth.

"A tracker?" I offered helpfully, and Luke—it seemed— did not have my same control to keep from rolling his eyes.

"Yes. Are there any other questions?" Jennings asked, sounding more like he had when we had first arrived, before this mess had started and he had been forced to trust us.

"I don't know, you told *us* to hang back," I pointed out, drawing a snort from Luke. *Well there's that. He's had the personality of cardboard for the past few days.*

"Yes, but not so you could harass me about details that don't matter. I asked you here to tell you that things are about to move rather quickly here, and you should be ready." I resisted the urge to ask for what, since I had gathered that this situation was all fairly unprecedented.

"What does that mean for Jesse? When…things… start to happen, will one of us remain here with him?" Luke asked. I tightened my lips slightly as I realized that I had not even been thinking of what we would do with Jesse during this entire fiasco. Selfishly, I had hoped that we would both get the chance to be part of the action in rescuing Sara. For my part, I wanted to be there because I felt responsible for the situation. My distraction had led us here. As for Luke—I stole a glance in his direction—I wanted someone I trusted to have my back, and I didn't think there would be any more distractions from him any time soon. I turned back to face Jennings and saw that he was frowning thoughtfully, and my stomach dropped.

"No." The response to Luke's question made me reel back slightly.

"No?" I repeated, the word flying from my mouth before I could stop them.

"No." Jennings leveled his eyes at me. "You should both be there. After all, it's your mess." I flinched at that, and I opened my mouth to reply that he was right, but before I could, Jennings continued. "It's also my mess. It was a mess that was here before you were, and it's a mess that everyone involved should clean up." I closed my mouth again, unsure now of how to respond to Jennings taking responsibility for the situation.

"And Jesse?" Luke pressed again. Jennings turned to face him now, the thoughtful expression still on his face.

"I'll be entrusting Bryant with the safety of the first lady while we're… away. I think she'll be able to handle the younger Mr. Boyle as well." I could not help the small smile that wormed its way onto my face. It was a shame that Bryant was not in the room to hear the compliment that Jennings had just given her; it was likely to be the only one he would give her aloud. She would never believe me if I told her. Then, a thought struck me.

"And the president? Surely you won't be leaving Bryant alone with all three of them?" Both men looked at me in surprise, and I backtracked furiously. "I only mean... she's very capable, but nobody should have that job alone given the circumstances." I stumbled over my words, but apparently my meaning was clear, because Jennings nodded.

"It's handled," he said without explanation, and I did not think that it was worth it to wheedle one from him.

"So, we should go then?" Luke asked. Jennings nodded.

"You should go. Don't let Jesse know what's about to happen, but it won't be long before something does. I'm sure he'll work it out; he's been part of this world for long enough. Until then, sit tight and don't do anything stupid." He looked sharply at me as he said the last part, but I was only half-offended. If anything, the more prominent feeling was one of foreboding as I realized that we were about to embark on a very risky mission. The consequences, far beyond my own safety, would extend past Sara's wellbeing. Wars were started over things like these. Alliances were broken, and governments were toppled. We would have to succeed.

CHAPTER 35

I'm still not sure why I underestimated Agent Jennings when he told us that things would move quickly, but the man certainly wasn't wrong about that, as infuriating as the fact continued to be. Luke and I had been able to return to our suite and convey to Jesse that he would be paired with Agent Bryant for a while in a short time, fend off his seemingly endless barrage of questions that we were not allowed to answer, and very nearly see his annoyance and desperation teeter on the threshold of rage before our phones buzzed and we were being summoned once more. My stomach growled, and I scowled at the very human reminder of my own mortality as Jesse peppered us with renewed and demanding questions.

"Where are you going?" he asked.

"We still don't know," Luke said, rubbing a hand over one cheek wearily as he glanced at the phone and gave me a swift nod. It was time.

"Who's going with you?" he demanded again.

"No idea," Luke said neutrally.

"Why can't I go with you?" At that, Luke's eyes flicked up to meet mine in a very "is-he-serious" expression before raising an eyebrow at the president's son.

"I'm not even going to pretend to answer that," Luke replied mildly, and Jesse's bright, blue eyes, usually so calm and clear, clouded in anger.

"As if you have been anything else," he grumbled. I sighed.

"Jesse, we won't know a lot until we're on our way there. That's for our safety and yours. All we know is that we have orders for you to go to your mother's office and stay there with Agent Bryant until we get back," I said. I had begun the interjection calmly, but my words had an edge as I finished the thought, fueled in part by the still-obstinate expression on the younger Boyle's face.

"It's something to do with Sara, right?" he assumed, turning back to Luke.

"I can't answer that either," Luke said, drawing a humorless laugh from Jesse.

"Whatever. Try not to get so distracted with each other that you mess things up again," he snarled. I took a step back as Jesse turned his ferocity on me, surprised by the uncharacteristic fury that had washed over the mild-mannered politician's son. Luke's shoulders tensed, and he moved as though to step between us, but I moved to block the motion.

"I know you're worried. We care about Sara too. Not in the same way of course; she's *your* sister," I added hastily as Jesse opened his mouth again. "But we really can't tell you any more than what we already have. We do, however, need to go. So, *move.*" I ordered. Surprise broke through the storm clouds in Jesse's blue eyes, and to my relief, he didn't argue. Instead, he stormed from the room, shoulders still tense and angry as he made his way up the maze of hallways toward the first lady's office with Luke and I trailing closely behind him.

Allison Boyle seemed equally perturbed by whatever Bryant had shared with her about our plans, although she lacked the angry set to her shoulders that was so very present in her son's. Bryant stood at the corner of the room, grim-faced as we followed Jesse into the office without the formality of an announcement. Her curls had been freed from their characteristic bun, and they sprang to life around her sharp cheekbones, softening them slightly. The first lady, to her credit, smiled politely at us as we entered, but her worry-lined eyes were fixated on her son.

"Agent Bryant filled me in. Jesse will be with me until you return?" Mrs. Boyle asked softly. Her voice had a light, airy quality to it that was fresh without being too breathy. I had not given it much thought before, but some detached part of me recognized that the old me would have dismissed it as a small, weak voice. Right now, I was admiring its composure.

"He will," Luke answered her when I was silent. She nodded, looking back at her son for a moment before meeting each of our eyes deliberately. *I guess Bryant filled her in quite a bit after all.* It was a little bit disconcerting to have that even, blue gaze leveled at me, and I felt the sudden urge to squirm beneath it. *Is this what they call a "mom look?"* My own mother had surely given it to me before, but that had been many years before, and it had been several since I had seen her. I half-expected a lecture from the woman, but instead, she smiled softly.

"Be careful, will you?" I blinked in surprise. I had not been face-to-face with the woman since her daughter had been kidnapped under my watch, and here she was telling us to be careful.

"Yes, ma'am," I managed, swallowing. Luke expressed a similar sentiment, naturally with more poise than I had managed, and in the next moment, we had left the room and returned to the hallway.

Luke's eyes darted my way with annoying frequency as we stalked back up the hallway in silence. Once the moment had passed, Mrs. Boyle's mothering had set my teeth on edge; the last thing I needed to be thinking about before a potentially life-threatening altercation with a conspirator was the fact that my own mother hadn't been around, regardless of her reasons. As Luke's darting gaze flickered to me and away again, I knew that the second-to-last thing I needed to be thinking about was him, at least in the context of whatever confusing relationship dynamic we hadn't had time to confront yet.

"Stop looking at me," I hissed. Luke flinched at the ferocity in my voice, but he complied, his green eyes fixed stonily ahead as we continued our silent journey to join the rest of the agents. From the corner of my eye, I saw the muscle in his jaw twitching, but that was my only hint that something was still bothering him. The fact that I noticed it meant that it was bothering me too, and the fact that neither of us had clear heads for what was about to come bothered me most of all. That's why, when the opportunity came, I grabbed Luke's arm and yanked *hard*, ripping us both out of the hallway and into a conveniently placed closet. I breathed heavily from the exertion as the door snapped shut behind us, and I extended my free hand blindly, groping for any switch that might give us some light.

"Uh, Richards?" Luke asked. I only half-heard him, and I didn't bother to correct him this time as I cursed the darkness.

"Mmm?" I managed, feeling triumphant as I located what felt like a light switch and flicked it upward.

"You're still holding my arm." I froze for a moment as the light flooded the closet and I realized that I was, indeed, practically holding Luke's hand. I dropped it hastily and crossed my arms, ignoring the comment. My mortification did nothing to help the breathless feeling that was continuing to tighten my chest.

"Why are we in a closet?" he tried again, wariness clouding his face.

"We need to talk," I said, my chest tightening further.

"We need to *go*," Luke emphasized. I felt my cheeks heat as a flush crept up my throat. I really couldn't have picked a worse time to have this conversation, but it needed to be had.

"We do. But when we do, I need to know that nothing else is going to distract us from our job," I began awkwardly. Luke blinked at me.

"I can be professional," he said coolly, something turning frosty in his eyes.

"I know you can," I corrected quickly, "I just... I don't know. I know that we..." The words I wanted to say battered in my mind too quickly for me to say, and my tongue felt like a deadweight in my mouth as I tried to say what I meant.

"We made a mess," Luke said for me. I nodded, falling silent. "And we need to clean it up without distractions," he finished.

"Yes," I said softly.

"And we need to talk about what happened to cause the mess," he added. I felt my eyes grow round as they widened, and I shook my head.

"That's not what I—" I protested weakly.

"That wasn't a question. It was a statement. We need to talk about it. It shouldn't be hard for you. After all, it was just a one-time thing, right?" he added with a pointed look in my direction through cloudy eyes. My heart thundered in my chest. *Is that regret in his voice?* I hadn't realized he'd paid attention to what I'd said to Jesse when we were in the safe house.

"We can't let it happen again," I ventured, feeling for all of the world like I was walking on the edge of a precipice. His face tightened at my confirmation, and my heart dropped somewhere in the vicinity of my stomach.

"We need to talk about it," he repeated, "and we will. But not right now." His expression cleared to the mask that I had known for years, and I matched it as I nodded briskly.

"Right. I just wanted to make sure that we were on the same page moving forward. We need to focus on Sara. Getting her back. Fixing our mess," I said, trying not to sound as small as I felt. I winced inwardly at referring to what had happened between us as a mess, but it had, in fact, been messy.

"No distractions. Clean job," he murmured, his eyes searching my face. I felt a sense of longing to say something to unpack what I was feeling, because we were treading on dangerous ground, but in the end, I simply nodded again and turned away.

"As long as that's settled." I seized the handle of the door and fled back into the hallway, forcing myself not to turn around as I listened for Luke's footsteps behind me.

I didn't like this, going into a high stakes situation with unresolved feelings for a colleague. After all, that's what Luke was: a colleague. Somehow, we had moved from enemies to friends, and then even that line had been crossed, but at the end of the day, this was a job, and right now, it was one that could have dire consequences if we got distracted. *Unprofessional. Emotional. Typical.* I heard the words reverberate through my skull with the voice of every man who had ever underestimated me.

This isn't right. I shouldn't be going in to do this job with my head like this. Some echo of reason rose in my mind to counter the emotional spiral, but I shook my head to clear the thought. This was my mess. I owed it to the Boyles, the Academy, and myself to clean it up.

CHAPTER 36

"We know where we're going," Jennings announced as we entered the briefing room. I glanced toward Welsch, noting that Bryant must already have returned to her post with the first lady, and I noticed that Katz was notably absent from our meeting. *Good thing too, so we can speak freely.* I glanced at Welsch again. *If he can be trusted,* I amended silently.

"Is it just the four of us?" Welsch asked, seeming startled. *I guess he doesn't know yet.*

"Yes." Jennings scrutinized Welsch's face closely.

"I knew Bryant was staying behind, but I thought that Katz…" Suspicion wrinkled between Welsch's broad brows. "Did something happen?"

"Yes," Jennings repeated mildly. Shock spasmed next across Welsch's face, and I watched curiously as he fought for composure. *No panic, no fear. Just surprise.* A faint sensation of relief trickled through me as I realized that Katz really had been the only villain. The feeling was squashed as Welsch started shaking his head violently.

"I don't want any part of this." Several heartbeats thundered in my ears as I exchanged a look with Luke. Jennings, for his part, remained stoically unexpressive.

"It's your job to be a part of it," he said darkly. Welsch shook his head again.

"No. I won't be part of this again. There has to be some sort of mistake, and I don't want any part of it." Jennings's eyes fairly snapped with annoyance, but before he could reply, Luke butted in.

"We don't have time for this." For my part, I was inclined to agree.

"For God's sake, Welsch. Go switch with Bryant. We'll discuss this later." Displeasure coated his voice. Welsch looked as though he might say more, but in the end, he departed with only a nod.

"Should we be worried?" I asked as the door thudded shut behind the retreating agent. Jennings closed his eyes, rubbing at his temples with one hand.

"About Welsch? No. He's always had a weak stomach for this sort of stuff. Thinks it goes beyond our job description." I wrinkled my nose in response. They had Sara. Our job was to protect the First Family. In my mind, that made this *exactly* our job description.

Luke muttered something under his breath that I didn't quite catch, but I got the sense that it wasn't something that would have flattered Welsch to hear. I occupied myself with flexing my knuckles; we'd wasted too much time already, and the waiting was making me antsy. Thankfully, I did not have to wait long, because in the next several minutes, Agent Bryant thundered through the door, breathless, bright-eyed, and looking as though she had run the entire way. Somehow, her hair had returned neatly to its bun. I made a mental note to ask her how she did it.

"I came as quickly as I could," she breathed, flicking a wayward curl back into place.

"Then let's be off. We'll finish coordinating on the ride over." Bryant glanced in my direction as Jennings stalked past her, but I simply shrugged, motioning that we should follow him. We had wasted enough time.

It was a silent walk to our waiting car. We moved in

purposeful formation, and I felt some of the nervous energy I felt dissipate with the movement. I did my best not to look at Luke, but I wondered to myself how he was handling all of this. Was he feeling as edgy as I was? The thoughts about what Luke was feeling—about many different situations—clouded my head for a moment, but then we made it to the car, and there was no room to do anything but strategize our approach with Jennings.

"It looks like Katz has her holed up near Dupont Circle," Jennings said without preamble. I blinked at him, surprised by the revelation.

"Dupont Circle?" I repeated without realizing that I had spoken aloud until Jennings's eyes snapped to my face.

"That's what I said." I grimaced at Jennings's tone.

"Why there, I wonder?" Luke mused. *At least I'm not the only one surprised.*

"Probably because neither of you would have expected it," Jennings said acidly. "Now, as I was saying, Katz has her holed up in Dupont Circle. The agents I had tailing him said it was a townhouse on a busy street. There's not really a way for us to clear out the other residents without tipping him off and putting Sara in more danger, so we're going to have to do this fast, and we're going to have to keep it clean." A chill ran through me, and I shuddered involuntarily. If we timed this wrong, the possibility of collateral damage could be catastrophic.

"And he has no idea he was followed? Where does he think we all are?" Bryant leaned forward, the same unease that I was feeling glittering in her large, dark eyes.

"He knows nothing. I sent him to investigate a *tip*," he air-quoted the word, "in Brentwood with some other agents. They'll arrest him once we retrieve Sara and I give them the word."

"And if we don't…?" I let my words trail off as they

slipped out.

"Then he's none the wiser that we know he's involved."

"Hopefully," Bryant added.

"Hopefully," Jennings confirmed.

"So what? We just bust in through the front door? If it's a true townhouse, there can't be many ways in," Luke pointed out.

"This one only seems to have an external door, which I'm sure they've secured. Based on blueprints I've reviewed, there should be window access points in the back, but you two," he nodded between Luke and me, "should know firsthand how easy it is to disguise a residence." I thought back to the facade-front of our own safe house and nodded.

"So, we're basically going in blind?" Luke asked sharply. I flashed a warning glance in his direction, but he did not notice it. He was too busy focusing blazing eyes on the older agent.

"I pulled blueprints from the city, but if they've had them altered somehow, then yes," Jennings said idly, flicking a piece of lint from his pants. I tore my eyes from Luke to see that Bryant was staring at her lap, looking equally unsettled.

"I'm assuming you think that any attempt to look more deeply into the location would tip them off?" I interjected. Jennings nodded, staring out his window as we entered the neighborhood.

"Yes. We need to work with what we've got. That's why we're a small team. We get in, get Sara, and get out before they realize we're there." I nodded, trying to keep my mind clear. If I thought too much about it all—the risks to myself, to Sara, to Luke—I would freeze, and that was the last thing that we needed. As the car swung into street parking, repressing those thoughts felt like trying to dam a river with a twig, but then Jennings was giving instructions, and there was no time for anything else.

"Bryant, you and Ryder will go in through the back. There's a window there. Richards, you and I will go in through the front." Jennings leveled his gaze at me. "Make as much noise as possible. We need to draw them to the front to give Bryant and Ryder a chance to find Sara." I glanced toward the foreboding brownstone face of the home.

"And when they rush us?" My lips moved without my consent.

"Neutralize them before they can hurt anyone else." The cool calm in Jennings's voice made a finger of ice shudder through my veins, but I steeled my spine against it. *In, out, protect.*

"Ready?" Bryant asked, her wide, dark eyes looking at me as she said it. I swallowed thickly and nodded, resisting the urge to glance at Luke one final—*no, don't say final*— one *more* time.

"Showtime," Jennings said, seizing the handle of the door. Bright light flooded into my face as I stepped out of the car behind him. It was time.

CHAPTER 37

"Follow my lead," Jennings ordered in a hiss, and I nodded grimly, feeling woefully unprepared. Out of the corner of my eye, I saw Luke and Bryant step casually away from the car; they might have been taking a stroll around the neighborhood. *Good luck, Ryder.* I swallowed the lump in my throat as I refocused my thoughts on the task at hand, staring up at the cookie cutter stairs that lead to a foreboding door that was stained a deep walnut. It was a bottleneck entry point, and I didn't like it in the slightest.

We climbed the steps with soft footsteps, and as they narrowed, I fell into step behind Jennings. The railings felt as though they were closing in on us as we rose, and the air suddenly felt thick and heavy. In my chest, my heart pounded with the effort to keep pumping oxygen through my veins, and my head started to spin. *Not now, Richards. Get your shit together.* I inhaled deeply through my nose, willing the panic away. Sara depended on me. Jennings and Bryant and *Luke* depended on me keeping it together. Still, I jumped at the explosive bang of Jennings's fist as he raised it and pounded on the door.

"Federal Agents. Come out, or we're coming in!" he

roared, punctuating each syllable with another bang of his fist. He waited a half-second before turning to usher for me to I stand aside, and I fell back two or three paces. With another thundering force of contact, Jennings kicked in the door, and then he was in. I moved to follow him before spotting an errant, decorative brick tucked into the side of the landing. Without thinking, I hefted it in my hand before sending it crashing through the window to the left of the door, smiling grimly as the glass shattered. If Jennings wanted us to make noise, then I was more than happy to do my part. I slipped my sidearm from its holster and followed the senior agent inside, my previous thoughts of panic vanishing into the mists as cold, calculated efficiency settled in its place.

The house was disturbingly quiet outside of our footsteps and aggressively loud movements as we cleared the first floor of the house, and it wasn't until we made it to the back window that we saw Luke or Bryant. Bryant's eyes were narrowed suspiciously, her jaw uncharacteristically clenched with worry. Luke's face was shadowed, and I could tell that he was as unsettled by the silence as I was. The four of us froze as a thud echoed from upstairs, and Jennings put a finger to his lips as he made eye contact with me and pointed up. I nodded, heart pounding in my chest once more. Jennings locked eyes with Bryant next. *Make noise*, he mouthed soundlessly. She nodded her understanding, eyes bright, and slipped into the far end of the house. I jumped as a crash sounded from one of the front rooms where, presumably, Bryant was knocking over furniture.

Jennings turned and crept toward the stairs like a cat on the prowl, and I followed close behind him, conscious that Luke remained stationary behind me. One silent step at a time, we ascended to the second level like burglars in the night, and I kept every muscle in my body tensed at the ready for what was waiting for us overhead.

The top of the stair opened up to a surprisingly airy space; I had been expecting a hallway for some reason. This meant that it would be harder for someone to hide, but it also meant that it would be harder for us to figure out where the noises had come from. Three doors branched off from the main room; two were on one wall across from the stairs, and one was on the left side of the room. All were shut to conceal whatever was waiting on the other side. I glanced at Jennings for guidance, and he gestured toward the two doors across from us. I considered the plan for a heartbeat before realizing that if someone *was* behind the left door and they tried to flee, Luke would be waiting down below. I inhaled a fortifying breath before I nodded at him and crept across the floor to one of the doors, watching from the corner of my eye as Jennings did the same. *This is a bad idea. Really, really stupid.* Going in without backup went against every instinct I had, but we were out of options. I stretched a hand toward the knob grasping the cool metal in my hand and turning it until it made a soft click. As I cracked it open, I saw light seep through the opening, and gripping my weapon, I burst the rest of the way into the startlingly empty room. I lead with the muzzle of my gun as I scanned the room, looking for anywhere that someone might have hidden, but the room was as empty as it had appeared. *It hasn't been that way for long, though,* I reminded myself as I looked at the single, uncovered bulb that flooded the room with light. Still, the space was clear, and I needed to move on or risk becoming a sitting duck myself. With a last glance around the room, I returned to the main landing, glancing toward the doorway that had swallowed up Agent Jennings. He had left it ajar, and beyond the threshold was the hallway that I had been expecting. *I should probably go after him in case he finds something,* I reasoned, but before I could do more than raise my foot to take a step in that direction, I heard a whimpering sound coming from behind the door that we had passed over earlier.

"Sara?" I whispered, knowing that even if it was her, my voice was too soft for her to hear through a closed door. *This could be a trap.* I glanced back toward where Jennings was undoubtedly still doing his sweep before I heard the noise again. *This is no different than sweeping the first room without backup*, I told myself sharply. Decision made, I took purposeful steps toward the closed door, crossing the room in a matter of heartbeats. Much like I had with the first, I reached out my hand to grip the doorknob, and I twisted sharply against immediate resistance from the mechanism. *Locked.* This time, I heard a sniff from behind the door, followed by a soft plea.

"Help," the voice said faintly. *Sara.* Throwing caution to the wind, the door crashed open with a well-placed kick of my foot, and there, bound to a chair in the center of the room, looking exhausted and tearful but unharmed, was Sara Boyle. My eyes roved the rest of the room cautiously, looking for any sign of her captors, but except for Sara, the room looked as empty as the first.

"Where are they?" I asked, my voice cold and unrecognizable. Sara blinked back a renewed surge of tears.

"I don't know. We heard you come in and they left me in here and didn't come back," she sniffled, and after a final once-over of the room, I let my arm drop to holster my gun.

"Did they hurt you?" I asked, approaching Sara cautiously. There was no telling what her kidnappers had put her through, and I didn't want to traumatize her any more than she already had been. She shook her head, tears spilling over to trail down her cheeks.

"No. They didn't touch me other than tying me up. I just want to go home," she said in a breaking voice. I noted the knots in the ropes that bound her wrists behind the chair and her ankles to the legs, taking in the raw, angry skin where the rope had rubbed. I groped in my pocket for the knife I had packed on a whim and began sawing.

"I'll get you out of here," I said as I went to work on the ropes. I had just snapped through the one holding her wrist when Sara gasped.

"Artemis, look out!" she screamed, the last word muffled by the unmistakable bang of a gunshot. I dove on top of Sara, clenching my eyes shut as I knocked the chair on its side. I winced at the crunch of our landing as I waited for the burn of the wound to appear on my body. When it didn't, I opened my eyes a sliver, expecting to see blood blooming on Sara. Somehow, it never appeared. My eyes rose to the wall behind us, where a neat hole now marred the light blue wall. *They missed.* I scrambled up and spun to face our assailant, only to see that he was already engaged with someone else.

Luke had the man in a headlock, the offending gun currently resting at our attacker's feet. I froze in horror as the man turned his head and drove his elbow into Luke's ribs, and I was too far across the room to help as he freed himself from the hold and lunged for the gun. Without a conscious thought, I found my own weapon and took aim at the man. As his scrawny arm rose to point his gun in Luke's direction, my finger twitched, the gun kicked, and the man dropped. I froze meeting Luke's wide, green eyes in silence for a moment. Then the screaming began.

"Oh my God. Oh my *God*," Sara shrieked. I holstered my weapon numbly, staring down at the shell of the man who had just been thrashing against Luke's hold as blood pooled beneath him from the hole in his chest. *A chest that's still moving*, I noticed.

"He's still breathing." My voice, somehow still cool and collected, cut sharply through Sara's screams.

Luke knelt by his side, making ripples in the spreading pool of red.

"Is there anyone else here?" he growled at the man. The scrawny chest fought to rise again as the man shuddered, refusing to answer. My eyes fixed upon each of his ragged breaths as my body rooted itself in place.

"Luke, I—" I began, but he ignored me.

"Is there anyone else *here?*" he demanded again. An awful gurgling noise emanated from the man's throat, his Adam's apple bobbing up and down for a moment before he answered with an imperceptible shake of his head. In the next moment, he was still. *Dead*, my mind corrected. I was still silent, and Sara was still screaming, the sound muffled by the ringing in my ears. I should have said something to comfort her, to assure her that she was safe, but the words wouldn't come. All I could find it within me to do was to right her chair and free her ankles. She stood, brushing away the strands of hair that were stuck to the tears on her face before her knees wobbled. I caught her before she fell, staggering slightly under her sudden dead weight. When I looked back up, Jennings had appeared in the doorway, where he stood staring down at the dead man with disgust. Sara's screams faded into whimpers as Jennings surveyed the situation for several moments, and when I released her, her knees did not buckle again.

"Was he alone?" Jennings asked in a gravelly voice.

"Fortunately," Luke answered before I could, his face fixed into an eerie blankness. I felt a tremor in my hands, and I was thankful that I had put away my gun. *He almost killed Luke. Luke could have died.* The thoughts raced through my mind, and I felt as though I was about to jump out of my skin. I gritted my teeth against the onslaught of thoughts and emotions as rage and then terror thundered through my bones at the thought of what had almost happened.

"We need to get Sara out of here," I interjected curtly, finding my voice at last. Luke opened his mouth to say something else, but one look at my face seemed to stop the words in his throat.

"I agree," he said instead. Jennings simply inclined his head. I turned to face Sara, who had fallen silent, giving her a quick once-over with my eyes.

"Can you walk?" I asked robotically. Sara nodded, her eyes locked on the man—the body—on the ground, her blue eyes as round as saucers.

"Then let's not waste any more time," Jennings took back control of the situation and led the way down the stairs. The three of us were on our guard as we escorted Sara back down to where Bryant stood waiting, clearly also prepared for anything. A faraway part of me admired her discipline in following orders. If I had heard the sound of a struggle and then a gunshot, it would have taken an army to keep me from running upstairs to ensure my team's safety, whatever Jennings had instructed. *She has more self-control than I do,* I chanced a quick glance over at Luke before I dropped my eyes and refocused myself.

"All okay?" Bryant asked, eyeing us.

"All but the other guy," Jennings answered.

"Let's get Sara home. We can debrief later," I said. I was surprised by the take-charge tone of my voice; I was even more surprised that nobody argued with me.

"Wait." Jennings paused, holding up a hand, and my breath caught, wondering if we had missed another of Sara's kidnappers.

"What is it?" Bryant asked sharply. Instead of answering, Jennings pulled out his phone, pressed a couple of buttons and put it to his ear.

"Yes, this is Jennings," he said into the phone. "You can bring him in now. We're finished here." He clicked off of the call and then turned to look at the rest of us, all mirror images of anticipation.

"Well?" Bryant asked again, clearly annoyed.

"And that was their cue to arrest Agent Katz. It's all over," he said the last part with a glance at Sara, and we all let out a collective breath of relief. *She's the president's daughter. Will it ever really* be *over for her?* Somehow, I didn't think so.

CHAPTER 38

I knew for sure that the trouble wasn't over yet when one of the president's aides met our car outside. Her eyes were wide, her hair windblown, and she glanced nervously around her as though she was terrified that she had been followed. I'd seen her around the Oval a time or two, but in that moment, I couldn't for the life of me remember her name.

"Shit," Luke muttered under his breath. I was inclined to agree.

"Sandra, what's wrong?" Jennings asked as we leaped from the car—with the exception of Sara, who still looked as though she might faint. *Sandra. Sandra Green.* Now, I remembered; I'd read her file. She was young, but she was ambitious, and above all, she believed in President Boyle. We could trust whatever she had to tell us.

"He's got them holed up in her office. He won't let them leave, and he won't let anyone else in!" she exclaimed. "I think he might hurt them." Her voice broke as her eyes widened further in terror.

"Who?" Jennings demanded. Sandra shook slightly as she fought for composure. "Damn it, Sandra, we don't have time for this. *Who?*"

"Agent Welsch. He has the first lady and her son," she replied. Without missing a beat, Jennings turned and glanced wildly between me, Luke, and Bryant, before fixing the latter with a penetrating stare.

"Stay with Sara," he ordered in a voice that left no room for argument. "You two," he pointed at me and Luke, "you're coming with me," he finished, and then we were running. Somewhere in the back of my mind, I questioned our lack of knowledge of the situation. *Is Welsch working with Katz? Are we running into a trap? Where are all of the other agents?* None of it mattered, of course, because our job was to protect the first family at all costs, but the thoughts were still there.

"Wait," I gasped out as we approached the East Wing, a little breathless from the run. Apart from the pounding of our footsteps against the floor of the hallways—and of course, the thudding of my own pulse in my ears—our route had been strangely deserted. *Either he cleared out the staff, or this is about to get a whole lot darker.*

"We don't have time for this, Richards," said Jennings, narrowing his eyes at me before taking off again. Luke paused for a moment, glancing at me in concern.

"What's wrong?" he asked. I shook my head.

"Don't worry about it Ryder. Jennings is right," I said, and then I was off again. My blood ran cold when we approached the East Wing to raised voices and the undeniably thundering sounds of a scuffle. We picked up the pace, then, and I twitched a hand toward my holster to reassure myself that we weren't going in helplessly. As we approached the first lady's office, the door looming ahead, the sounds of the scuffle were punctuated by a shrill scream. A loud thud followed, and then there was silence. Luke and I skidded to a halt in front of the door, but Jennings plunged forward, slamming his shoulder into the wood as it burst open. Weapons drawn, Luke and I followed close behind, and I blinked as I took in the scene. Jesse was crouched in front of his mother's desk, staring mutinously down at the limp, gasping form of Agent Welsch, who was leeching blood from a nasty wound to the side. Allison Boyle stood over him menacingly, covered in blood that was not her own, a letter knife in her hand. She whirled around to face us, her eyes wild as she held her weapon aloft.

"It's over, Allison. You're safe now. Put down the knife," Jennings said in a soothing voice that I had never heard from him before.

"How do I know I can trust you? You're the one who sent the other agents away!" she cried, holding it further aloft as she backed up a step. She let out a sharp noise as her shoes slipped on Welsch's blood. Jesse's eyes looked too big in his pale face as they rose to look at Luke before they rested on me.

"Mrs. Boyle, Jennings didn't send them away. He's been with us the whole time," I said softly.

"*He* told me." She jerked her chin at Welsch's prone form. "Why would he lie? Where's Sara?" she demanded without taking her eyes from Jennings.

"She's with Sandra. Sandra stayed behind to let us know what Welsch had done. Agent Jennings never sent away the others. That was a lie that Agent Welsch told you," I reassured, taking a step toward her.

"Mom?" Jesse whispered in a small voice. She glanced down at her son for a moment before locking her eyes on Jennings once more.

"Then where are they? Why did they go? They were supposed to keep us safe," she said. I nodded, although in retrospect, she wouldn't have been able to see it, focused as she was on Jennings.

"Mom, Agent Welsch was the one that told them to leave on Jennings's orders. He knew we would overhear. Agent Ryder and Agent Richards wouldn't be working with him if he was going to betray us too," Jesse said, rising from his knelt position. He still looked shaky, but determination slowly slid down to replace the shock on his face.

"He tried to kill us," Mrs. Boyle whispered, half in disbelief as she finally dropped her eyes to look at the half-conscious form of Welsch.

"But they didn't. You can trust them," Jesse urged. I felt a surge of pride for his ability to keep his head in one hell of a situation, and after a moment more of contemplation, the first lady let her arm drop, the knife clattering to the floor beside her feet.

"He's still alive," she said. Allison Boyle turned her back on the man still clinging to life on her office floor, stepping delicately around the pooling blood as she made her way to her desk, where she sat in her desk chair and put her face in her hands.

"Is my dad here?" Jesse asked, sounding suddenly quite young. I glanced at Jennings, who was likely the only person who would know the answer to that. It was not encouraging when the older agent simply paled.

"His plane was supposed to land an hour ago. Let me make a call." He pulled out his phone again. "Richards, Ryder, see if you can keep Welsch alive long enough for us to figure out what to do with him," he ordered, tossing the words carelessly over his shoulder as he left the room. I heaved a sigh, placing my gun in its holster once more and glancing at Luke before moving toward Welsch's prone form.

Mrs. Boyle had done her work well. It was a solid jab, placed up under the ribs. Someone had clearly taught her where to strike… or she had just been very, very lucky. Blood was still coming from the opening in his torn flesh in bursts; she had hit her mark.

"We need to slow the bleeding," I said unnecessarily. Luke had already materialized at my side and was extending the shirt that he had been wearing in my direction. My cheeks burned as I took in the sculpted planes of his chest. *Why are you focusing on Ryder's bare chest when there is a man bleeding out in front of you?* My eyebrows lifted, but I forced myself to look away as I took the shirt from him and crouched by Welsch's side. I pressed the fabric to the wound, curling my lip at the squelching feeling of blood as it seeped between my fingers.

"This isn't going to work for long," I called to Jennings over my shoulder, readjusting the shirt. To my annoyance, he waved me off, still on the phone.

"I'm sorry. I—I…" Mrs. Boyle raised her head from her hands for a moment before dropping it again.

"You have nothing to apologize for," Luke said forcefully. "You were protecting your son."

"Stab and twist. That's what they told me I should do if I ever had to…" she trailed off again, the words muffled behind her hands. The sound of retching told me exactly why she had stopped speaking before a soft splattering noise joined it. I wrinkled my nose as the rancid smell of stomach acid joined the coppery scent of blood filling my nose.

"You did everything right, Mrs. Boyle," I said, pressing more firmly into Welsch's side.

"Call me Allison," she said weakly. "I think we're past formalities today."

"Do you want me to take over?" Luke asked in a soft voice. I shook my head without looking up at him.

"I'm good here. If you want to go tell Jennings to stop dragging his feet out there, though, I won't argue." I readjusted again, but the shirt was coated with red now.

"What do you need from me?" Jesse asked, and a glance up at him showed that while he was still pale, he was still strong-stomached.

"Do you know if there's a First Aid kit anywhere in here? Gauze would be a little more absorbent here than Ryder's shirt." My mouth set into a grim line. Welsch had grown eerily still. Either way, we were running out of time.

"I'll go look," he said, moving to step out of the room.

"No!" an otherworldly shriek emanated from Allison. My eyes shot up to stare at her wide-eyed figure, still looking green. "No," she said more softly. "I have one here." She bent to open a drawer in her desk. I heard the sound of ruffling papers before her head popped back up and she was extending a small kit my way. I shot a helpless glance at Luke, my hands still pressed to contain Welsch's bleeding. He reached out his hand to take it from her.

"Thanks," he said quietly, before snapping it open and rustling through it to find what we needed. Allison took a deep breath.

"I think… I think I would like to see Sara now. Now that it's all over," she said quietly. I paused to think for a moment, taking advantage of the opportunity when Luke passed me a wad of gauze.

"I think it would be better to wait," I said carefully. "She's safe with Sandra and Agent Bryant. She wasn't hurt, and she doesn't need to see this." I jerked my chin down at Welsch's body. *She's seen enough death today.* Allison opened her mouth, looking as though she might protest before she shut it again and settled for a dignified nod.

A thundering of footsteps near the door had me spinning wildly, hands still pressing the gauze against Welsch's body as Luke stepped protectively in front of the rest of us. I tensed, not sure what else the day could possibly throw at us, but as the tall figure stepped through the door, blue eyes dark with worry, I felt every muscle in my body sag.

"Allison, Jesse? Are you okay?" President Boyle crossed the room in a few strides, eyes roving over the figures of his wife and son before he turned to take in the rest of the scene.

"Mr. President," I greeted with a nod of my head. "Sorry, I can't stand right now, given…" I jerked my chin at Welsch, and his eyes darkened further.

"Bastard," he spat at the unconscious man.

"You're not wrong," I sighed, my joints beginning to grow stiff from holding the same position.

"Where's Sara?" he asked, eyes searching the room as though expecting to see her in a corner.

"She's safe. We didn't know what we would be walking into, and we didn't want to put her in any more danger." At President Boyle's raised eyebrow, Luke clarified, "she's with Agent Bryant and Sandra Green."

"Good," he said softly. "Good." I sucked in a breath as I caught sight of his hands. The normally manicured fingers were swollen and scraped, split on some of the knuckles, while his remaining knuckles were painted an angry, puffy red.

"Your hands. Do you need something for them… sir?" I added as an afterthought. He glanced down at them, seeming embarrassed.

"I—uh—no. I just… They wouldn't let me in here when Welsch was… I lost a fight with a door when they locked me in," he finally admitted. "I'll be fine."

"He's in here!" I broke my eyes away from the president to see that Jennings had returned, flanked by who I could only assume from the uniforms they wore were two EMTs, a tall, lanky man, and a small-framed woman. Their eyes flicked around the room to survey the situation before they approached, kneeling by my side. The woman's hands replaced mine on Welsch's gauze, and I met her eyes uncertainly.

"It's over now. We'll take it from here," she said reassuringly. I let go of the wound I had been holding together with my hands, and for the first time, I let someone else take the lead without questioning it.

CHAPTER 39

"Thank God that's over," Luke said on a sigh, flopping down onto the couch in our shared quarters. It had been a long day. Sara had been reunited with her parents, and we had sat through meeting after meeting of working out who had been involved in the conspiracy and ensuring that there were no further loose ends. Thankfully, most of the rot had taken root in Agents Welsch and Katz, but of course, as part of the inner circle of protection in the White House, they had held considerable influence. Stamping that out quickly had been necessary, which had made for an exhausting investigation, but it had been easy enough to unravel the trail of money once the first threads had been plucked.

"You can say that again," I said with a sigh of my own.

"Thank God that's over," Luke repeated, his eyes twinkling with amusement. I let out another long-suffering sigh as I rolled my eyes.

"Very mature, smart-ass," I snorted. He chuckled in response, but his stare turned serious as the laughter on his face faded.

"So, what now?" he asked in a low voice. I knew that he wasn't talking about future occupational hazards.

"We go to sleep, wake up, and do our jobs tomorrow, I guess," I deflected. Something disappointed flashed in those marvelous, green eyes.

"That's not what I meant," he said quietly, and I winced.

"I know."

"Then we should probably talk about it," he pushed again. I whirled around to stare him in the face, torn between the part of myself that knew what I wanted to do and the one that knew what needed to be done.

"What's to talk about, Ryder? We had a lapse in judgment. It almost cost us everything. Why go there again?" Even to myself, I sounded cruel.

"You think I don't know that?" his voice rose hoarsely. "You think I haven't thought about it every day since Sara was taken?"

"Then why bring it up?" I fired back, springing to my feet. "It was just a kiss. Why can't we just pretend it never happened?" As I spoke, images and sensations flashed through my mind: Luke's lips on mine, his hands pulling me close. I battled them back, forcing myself to return to the here and now. To my surprise, he did not rise to my challenge. Instead, he settled back on the couch, crossing his arms and evaluating me with a long cool look that made me feel about three inches tall.

"That's what you want?" he asked finally. I willed my lips to move, to form the words that would tell him yes, but they stubbornly refused against the force of his penetrating gaze. I turned away, unable to face him.

"It doesn't matter what I want," I mumbled, moving to step away. I should have expected the arm that caught my wrist and spun me to face him, but the movement was too quick, and I was too unbalanced, so instead, I stumbled into the hard planes of his chest.

"Why?" he asked. "Why wouldn't it matter." I closed my eyes, willing every bit of self-control I possessed to me in that moment before I looked up to meet his eyes, blisteringly green as I sank into their depths.

"Wants aren't practical in our line of work. Why does it matter so much to you?" I asked softly. His eyes flickered down to my lips, and my breath caught, knowing that I wouldn't have control enough to step away if he lowered his mouth to mine. He looked…. uncertain? More than anything else, that unsettled me, because Luke Ryder didn't look uncertain—at least, he hadn't before all of this mess had begun.

"It matters to me," he swallowed, "because you matter to me." I heard a rushing sound in my ears. It wasn't a declaration, and I wasn't some heroine in a cheesy novel, but the effect was the same. A million and a half responses leaped into my mind, laughing ones, scorning ones, words that would cut and bite and hurt. I thought back to how far we had come, from the tense rivalry we had shared to the different kind of tension that had developed, and in the end, I chose none of them.

"You matter to me too," I whispered, wondering how in the world we had come to a place where it could be true. His eyes sparked with some new emotion, and I realized that I had never seen it from him before; at least, I hadn't ever seen it when he was looking at me. It was happiness. Something in my face must have frozen it in its tracks, because in the next moment, caution had slammed down to replace it, like someone yanking down the blinds on a sunny day.

"So, what do we do now?" he asked. I knew what he meant. We couldn't work together, not like we had been, if we were both feeling something for each other. It would be too much of a liability, and we would just distract each other. Sara's kidnapping had proven exactly why two people with feelings for each other couldn't work together in that way. Feelings made things sloppy. Sloppy work led to dire consequences. I sank back down to my seat on the couch, suddenly drained.

"I don't know," I said softly, staring at the ground. I didn't flinch when I felt the sudden warmth of his hand taking mine, of his thumb rubbing over the back of my hand. His fingers paused to squeeze mine lightly, and I gave a quick squeeze back. *After all that we've been through in the past few days, this is what's going to be the hardest for me.* The thought made me feel for all the world like a preteen girl.

"Me neither," he said quietly. His thumb stopped tracing circles on my hand, and he let it go, the sudden cold shocking after the warmth of his touch. I only had time for a flash of disappointment before he lifted his arm and wrapped it around my shoulders, wordlessly pulling me to him so that I leaned against his body. I let my head rest against his shoulder as I sank into the embrace. We sat like that for what could have been only a few minutes or an eternity before reality sank in for me. All those years hating each other, and we would have to be just a missed connection. It was more than a little ironic.

"We need to go tell someone," I said quietly. "Make sure we're not a liability to anyone again." I felt Luke flinch at the words, despite the fact that I hadn't said them unkindly, before he nodded. We couldn't ignore what we were feeling; we needed to come clean.

"Just another minute," he said softly, picking up and twirling a lock of my hair. It was hard to believe that this was the same person I had once hated so deeply. *Proof that anything can change with time.* It was a simple thought, but it echoed through me like a gong. There was still more change to come, but right now, in this moment, I was content to soak it in and let the future, however soon to pass, stay ahead of me.

It felt as though someone should be playing an occupational death march as we made our way up the hallway. Luke had sent a message to Jennings asking for a meeting, and the affirmative response had come more quickly than I would have liked, but we could only delay for so long before we had to face the reality of our situation. We were a liability. We were two people working a high-stakes job, and we saw each other as more than just colleagues. We were a distraction to each other, and we had already proven that. One of us would have to go.

I knew in my bones that it would be me. *Committing career suicide over a boy. Add that to my list of things I said I'd never do but did anyway.* We rounded a corner and before I could blink, we had made it to our meeting room. I cast a sidelong glance at Luke, and the muscle in his jaw was twitching nervously. *He doesn't have anything to worry about. They'll keep* him. I fought to banish the flash of resentment; it was just another consequence of being a woman in a decidedly man's world, and if we wanted to explore—well—whatever this was, starting with resentment would make for a pretty shaky foundation. I didn't bother knocking as I pushed open the door, hoping that the motion would banish my tumultuous thoughts. It didn't.

"Ah, Richards, Ryder. That was quick." Jennings's greeting was curt, and I felt a sudden prickle of worry spark down my spine. *He knows*, the thought stabbed through me like a knife. Except he couldn't know, because Luke and I had barely acknowledged ourselves what had happened between us. *Unless Jesse told him what… no, he wouldn't do that. Not now. Not so soon after what had happened to all of them.* I shook away the self-centered thought; the Boyles had more to worry about than my love life. Maybe Jesse would confront it after the shock wore off, but I doubted that he was the reason for Jennings's current tone. I realized belatedly that Jennings was still looking at us expectantly; neither Luke nor I had replied.

"Well, you know…" I trailed off lamely, glancing helplessly at Luke and unsure of where to begin.

"I'm glad you called the meeting, Ryder. I was about to schedule one myself. We have some staffing problems that we need to address," Jennings said with a raised eyebrow, directing his entire statement at Luke. I sighed. After all that we had been through for the past few days, I had thought that maybe I would have earned some acknowledgement in not-so-casual conversation, but apparently that was still a pipe dream.

"Well, yes." Luke swallowed heavily. *Must really be eating him if he's showing his hand this early.* We had been trained to wear a mask. That the prospect of discussing our almost-liaison with Jennings had dropped his guard so thoroughly was the perfect evidence for why we shouldn't be working together like this anymore. *Come on, Ryder. Keep it together.*

"We thought that as well, and we wanted to bring it to your attention," I said smoothly, trying to cover for his obvious nerves. Jennings shot me a look of derision, and I met his stare evenly. *You're getting ahead of this. Don't act like you have anything to be ashamed of.*

"I'm well aware of the problem at hand, Miss Richards," he said.

"Agent," Luke and I said in unison. I shot Luke a startled look; it was the first time that he had ever corrected Jennings. The corners of Agent Jennings's mouth twitched, and he looked almost amused for a moment before his face settled into its familiar lines of well-worn condescension.

"In any case, we need to make some staffing adjustments," he continued, clearing his throat.

"We understand," Luke said impatiently. Jennings stared hard at him with an expression that told him not to interrupt before he continued once more.

"The defection of Katz and Welsch has left a hole in our core security team. Bryant can still serve as the primary agent on the first lady's detail, and I will still work closely with the president, but I also have other responsibilities. The last two…situations with our team have led me to believe that I need to focus more heavily on team management, which means that we need to pull someone we can trust to work more closely with the first couple. That will leave one of you managing Sara and Jesse by yourself until we can vet someone as a replacement, but we can't afford to have another fox in the henhouse," he justified. I blinked at him. He wasn't scolding us, and this wasn't about our lapse at all. *One of us is getting a promotion?*

"That makes sense," I managed, steeling myself for Luke's promotion as my mind whirled to make sense of it all. We would still have to disclose our relationship if it became more concrete, but even if our spheres of work crossed from time to time, we would be working at enough of a distance that it shouldn't be a conflict. *Which means we might actually be able to explore how we feel… If he wants to.* The thought sent a shiver down my spine.

"I think the best course of action right now would be for *Agent* Richards," he emphasized the title, "to assist with this." I stared at him, wide-eyed in disbelief.

"Me?" I asked. Luke snorted beside me, earning him a scowl.

"You. You and Agent Bryant seem to have a good working relationship. It makes sense," Jennings said mildly, raising an eyebrow. "If you feel up to it, of course." I fought for composure, but inwardly, I was reeling.

"I—uh. Of course," I managed, my eyes darting to Luke to see how he was taking the news. His face was, once again, an impenetrable mask.

"Excellent," Jennings said smoothly. I'll start the paperwork and fill Bryant in. Ryder, your new partner will be chosen just as soon as I can get through this mess. You'll have to run solo until then, but it shouldn't be too involved. We won't have any big events the kids need to attend for a while; the first lady wants to give them some time to recover." Out of the corner of my eye, I saw Luke nodded.

"Understandable. I'll manage," he replied, his tone giving no indication of how he was feeling.

"Perfect. For now, you two can keep living where you are. Katz and Welsch wanted private accommodations off-site. I guess now we know why," his mouth twisted, "but if you'd rather stay somewhere different once the change goes through, Richards, I'm sure that won't be a problem. Otherwise, I'm afraid that's our only open option." *And here I had thought we'd only been placed together because we had the same assignment.* I shook my head.

"I'm fine with it if Ryder still is," I said as blandly as possible, my heart pounding a staccato in my ears. Would Luke suddenly decide that I wasn't worth being around now that I had moved on to a new role? One that he might feel he should have been given? I fought through the roaring in my ears for long enough to hear Luke's response.

"I'm fine with it," he said, his voice still giving nothing away.

"Alright, then. It's settled. I'll pull you later to get you up to speed, Richards," Jennings replied with a finality that told me it was a dismissal. I nodded silently, and with a last glance at Luke, I turned to leave the room.

"You can go too, Ryder. I don't think we'll have anything else to discuss until all of this is finalized." I heard Jennings's voice behind me, but I couldn't make out Luke's low-voiced reply as I exited the room. After a second of internal debate, I decided to wait for him, trying to ignore the sense of foreboding that was building in my chest. When he emerged, I had collected myself and was leaning against the wall beside the door. He stopped short when he crossed the threshold, surveying me with an inscrutable expression, before he jerked his head in the direction of our rooms. I pushed myself off the wall, and we walked together in silence, each of our footsteps echoing through the quiet hall. With every step, my pulse thundered in my ears, and I repressed the tremor that threatened to overtake my hands.

"Congrats on your promotion," Luke said as we crossed the threshold to our shared quarters and the door snapped shut behind us. I glanced at him out of the corner of my eye, but his expression gave nothing away.

"Thanks. It was… unexpected," I searched awkwardly for the last word, feeling painfully conscious of every breath I took and every movement that I made.

"You deserve it. Plus, us working on top of each other like we have been…" Luke paused in a silence that seemed to stretch an eon. Despite the seriousness of the exchange, I lurched slightly as I repressed the urge to crack a joke at his word choice. "It'll be easier this way," he said finally. I swallowed; my mouth was suddenly dry. I had grown accustomed to working alongside Luke, and while I knew that working apart from each other would be less complicated, I wouldn't have ever dreamed of calling it easier.

"Ah," I said blandly.

"Mmph," came the vague response. I waited a beat, but he didn't say more. When we arrived at the door to our suite, Ryder held open the door and motioned me inside. When it closed behind us, I turned to him again to break the silence.

"So, you're not mad, then?" I asked tentatively. Luke wrinkled his nose at me in such an animated expression that I almost laughed aloud.

"Why would I be mad?" he asked, startled. I stared at him for a moment, conscious of my mouth hanging open before I shut it and regained my composure. I narrowed my eyes as a slow smile spread across my face.

"Well, I never thought that I would see the day when Luke Ryder would be content being beaten by a girl," I teased. He snorted.

"You wish! Your charges will have the biggest targets on their backs. Think of the incident reports; you just got me out of doing extra paperwork." I rolled my eyes.

"Yeah, right."

"Besides, this is my chance to be paired up with someone who *isn't* the world's biggest smartass at every opportunity," he said smugly.

"Impossible," I cleared my throat, "since you've worn that crown for as long as I've known you." He laughed then, a clear sound that made me smile in spite of myself, and before I knew it, my own laughter bubbled out to join his.

"You're ridiculous, you know that?" he said as his laughter started to fade. I dropped into a theatrical curtsy.

"If you say so, your highness," I said in mock-reverence. He snorted again, his lips curling into a lopsided grin as the light changed in his eyes, brightening them somehow.

"Do you know what the best part about this arrangement will be?" he asked. I felt my heart resume its sprinting pace again at the expression on his face.

"What's that?" I asked innocently, trying to keep the breathlessness out of my voice as something in his spring-green eyes turned searing.

"I can do this without worrying about it now." He stepped to close the gap between us, and before I could do more than squeak out a response, his mouth was on mine.

Warmth tingled from the thundering of my heart to the tips of my fingers as his hand rose to cup my face and then moved behind my head. He kept it there for a moment before his hands slid down my back to pull my waist toward him. There was triumph in the kiss this time, and as cliche as it sounds, time absolutely stood still. We broke a part for a moment, and I was taken aback at the staggering breaths he took as his chest rose and fell.

"Don't expect this to be easy, Ryder. I still plan to give you hell," I said with a smirk of my own. He ran a hand through his hair and shook his head.

"I would expect nothing else, Artemis," he answered, laughing breathlessly before he pulled me to him again.

ACKNOWLEDGMENTS

To those readers who have stumbled across this novel and taken a chance on it, I want to say thank you for choosing to spend time with my book. I hope that you enjoyed reading it as much as I enjoyed writing it.

To my sister, Reid, thanks for listening to me ramble about this story until I was blue in the face and for providing your honest opinions throughout my process. Your candor was incredible beneficial in helping me to produce this work, and I cannot thank you enough!

To my husband, Colten, who has been with me through the high highs and low lows that come with crafting a creative work, I offer my sincerest thanks. Your willingness to believe in me, even in the times when I didn't believe in myself, humbled me too many times to count.

To my mother, thanks for always offering a listening ear whenever I need a sounding board throughout the process—even when my rambling doesn't always make sense. Thank you also for allowing me to hijack your printer when I felt I needed a hard copy to edit this piece. And to your printer, I'm sorry for overworking you (more than once).

Special thanks to the team at GetCovers for the beautiful cover. The finished product came at a time when I was feeling discouraged, and I still can't believe that such a wonderful cover belongs to one of my books!

To Cassandra Lawler, thank you for helping to tighten this story so that Artemis and Luke could shine to the fullest. Your fresh eyes and feedback meant the world! Thank you for your continued support and insights.

Finally, to my daughter, who has made me smile on the days when it felt impossible. This story, and all my stories, are for you.

Customer reviews allow independent authors to continue sharing their stories. If you enjoyed this book, please leave a review on your chosen platform.

For updates about Sage's current and upcoming projects, you can connect with her on the following platforms:

Facebook: facebook.com/SageKafskyWrites

Instagram: @sagekafskywrites

TikTok: @sageofthewoods

Goodreads: Sage Kafsky

ABOUT THE AUTHOR

Sage Kafsky began writing at a young age. She is passionate about puns and the great outdoors. When she's not writing, Sage enjoys spending time out in nature, reading fantasy novels, and going on adventures. She currently lives in Tennessee with her husband, their daughter, and their furry and feathery family members.